PRAISE FOR
WE CAN ONLY SAVE OURSELVES

"Captivating."

—Publishers Weekly

"Beautiful and wry, *We Can Only Save Ourselves* is the story of a teenager who breaks free from the confines of her suburban home to try to find a more authentic way of living. I wanted to look away as the novel spun toward an ominous conclusion, but I couldn't stop reading. A haunting and immersive debut with echoes of Tom Perrotta's *Little Children* and Jeffrey Eugenides's *The Virgin Suicides*."

—Kate Hope Day, author of *If, Then* and *In the Quick*

"This is a melancholy, dreamlike book about group dynamics, power, growing up, and the choices people can't take back. Alison Wisdom gives her haunting story a quiet but inexorable forward momentum—like that of adolescence itself."

—Lydia Kiesling, author of *Golden State*

"Alison Wisdom's clear-eyed debut lulls you into a tenuous comfort, only to jump out when least expected. The collective narration flawlessly juggles youthful idealism and hardened maturity, marking the decisions women make—both deliberate and coerced—and their struggle to break free from societies determined to stifle their freedom to choose. Insidiously haunting, subtly clever, and impossible to put down."

—Julia Fine, author of *What Should Be Wild*

"A haunting, beautifully written story of a girl falling into darkness. Alison Wisdom renders a fascinating portrayal of the subtle shifts in tension, power, and affection among the young women who follow a Mansonesque cult leader. With the propulsion of a page-turner and the detail of a psychological study, *We Can Only Save Ourselves* is a stark and captivating novel. "

—Jennie Melamed, author of *Gather the Daughters*

"In this tense, complicated novel, the loss of a daughter is observed through the singular, haunting voice of the town's mothers as they wage a daily battle for safety under the guise of conformity and belonging. What is the cost of leaving, and what is the cost of staying? There are no easy answers in this thrilling debut novel by Texas writer Alison Wisdom, whose taut, steely prose reveals new complexities, questions, and dangers with each turn of the page."

—Elizabeth Wetmore, *New York Times* bestselling author of *Valentine*

"Alison Wisdom's addictive, down-the-rabbit-hole debut reads like *The Girls* by way of *The Virgin Suicides*, with an extra dash of Cheever's unsettling suburbia. The result is sinister and surprising: a novel I couldn't put down, and one that I kept thinking about long after I'd reached its unexpected, chilling end."

—Emily Temple, author of *The Lightness*

"In her beguiling debut, Alison Wisdom exposes the menace concealed just beneath the surface of the ordinary. When Alice Lange falls off the map, abandoning her status as a beloved it-girl in her suburban enclave to pursue a mysterious stranger, I fell right with her. A story of mothers and daughters, the competing allures of safety and danger, and the volatility of early adulthood, this is a spellbinding novel that followed me into my days."

—Alexis Schaitkin, author of *Saint X*

WE CAN ONLY SAVE OURSELVES

A Novel

ALISON WISDOM

HARPER

An Imprint of HarperCollins*Publishers*

WE CAN ONLY SAVE OURSELVES. Copyright © 2021 by Alison Wisdom. All rights reserved. Printed in the United States of America. No part of this book may be used or reproduced in any manner whatsoever without written permission except in the case of brief quotations embodied in critical articles and reviews. For information, address HarperCollins Publishers, 195 Broadway, New York, NY 10007.

HarperCollins books may be purchased for educational, business, or sales promotional use. For information, please email the Special Markets Department at SPsales@harpercollins.com.

FIRST EDITION

Designed by Jen Overstreet

Library of Congress Cataloging-in-Publication Data has been applied for.

ISBN 978-0-06-299614-5 (pbk.)
ISBN 978-0-06-304817-1 (library edition)

21 22 23 24 25 LSC 10 9 8 7 6 5 4 3 2 1

To my family

PROLOGUE

I N OUR NEIGHBORHOOD, the streets were dark for
many years. There weren't enough lamps to light the
streets properly, only a few per block, shining like small yellow planets in the dark. We had porch lights and glowing
windows illuminated by table lamps; we had the stars and
the moon.

Now the world is different: there are lampposts every few
houses. So much brightness. "Every time I look outside in
the evenings, it looks like an alien invasion came down to
earth," April Morris complains to Bev Ford one afternoon.
"I half expect to see a UFO floating over your house." The
new lights are tall and silver with odd fluorescent heads, the
wiring inside of them visible under the surface, like brains.
The women sit on lawn chairs in April's yard watching Billy
and Tim throw a football back and forth in the street. April
holds a drink in her right hand, and Bev holds the baby, a
tiny girl who chews on her hands and leaves a dark circle
of drool on her mother's shoulder. The baby is wearing her

brother's old clothes. People always think she's a boy; they congratulate Bev on the little gentleman. The rest of us would correct the stranger. "A girl, actually," we would say. "Isn't she beautiful?" Yes, they would say.

"It's safer," Bev says now, "with the lights."

"Is it, though?" April asks. Unconsciously, her eyes flit over to the Lange house.

"You don't have a daughter," Bev says. "You don't understand." They both look at the baby. She has her father's short eyelashes, a swirl in her fine hair at the back of her head. Bev reaches up and dabs at a glistening wet spot on the girl's chin and then sticks her fingers in the baby's mouth. Her gums bulge, and she bites down, trapping her mother's finger until she wiggles it free.

"She's getting more teeth," Bev says.

"So many so early," says April. "That's good."

"Yes," Bev agrees. "She'll need them."

April doesn't say anything, and they watch the boys tossing the ball—Billy is more athletic than Tim, catches it every time, and when he throws the ball, it spirals prettily, like the pattern inside a seashell—and they don't leave until the lights come on, filling the street with an otherworldly glow. We think of Alice Lange often in moments like these. Even if we don't want to, even if we shouldn't, we hope there is good light where she is, that the streets are safe and bright, that she isn't afraid.

CHAPTER ONE

WE ALL SAW the man in our neighborhood on the same day. But there are always men in our neighborhood, and they're relatives or fathers of playdates or old college roommates, still bachelors, their beards and clothes and cars out of place among our clean-shaven husbands and their practical automobiles, their sharply cut suits. We always notice the outsiders, but we are rarely alarmed. This is not the kind of neighborhood where we need to be.

Even as he drew nearer, passing in front of our houses, his presence registered, but that's all. Those of us inclined to take more careful note of outsiders did; those of us who are not did not. Mrs. McEntyre, for one, always notes the kind of shoes people wear. It's a cautionary measure, she says, in case, somewhere down the line, the police need as many details as possible.

This particular man wore boots. The color: brown, faded under a layer of dust or dirt. Toes: pointed. Rise: unknown; they were hidden beneath his jeans, the legs of which were stovepipe straight. Mrs. McEntyre almost forgot to notice the shoes entirely, though, because as he passed her on the sidewalk, her dog, Sweetie, did not bark. Sweetie has barked at all of us, even though we've known her since she was a young pup, turning herself in circles in the front yard and nipping at the calves of all who passed the McEntyres' threshold. But this man walked right past the pair of them, woman and dog, and Sweetie was still. "She always barks," Mrs. McEntyre found herself telling the man as he went by, then reminded herself to look at his shoes.

He didn't slow down, but he smiled at her, then said over his shoulder, "Animals always like me." His voice was deep and pleasant. Soft and somehow pliable, the way she imagined the leather of his boots would feel. Across his chest was a brown leather strap attached to a small bag, almost, Mrs. McEntyre thought, like a lady's purse, but it didn't seem out of place. He wore it the same way a person wears his arms, his legs, the hair on his head—naturally, organically. She didn't watch him as he moved down the sidewalk, but only a moment later Sweetie barked, and Mrs. McEntyre looked over her shoulder, and the street was empty.

On another street, a few turns away from where Mrs. McEntyre strolled with Sweetie, a group of children playing soccer saw the man, too, but barely noticed him. Those who did saw an adult, expecting him to tell them to get out of the street, to watch for cars, to go in and wash up for dinner. Billy Morris squinted up at the sky. It had been cloudy all day, and it had barely changed color from hour to hour, but the sun had begun to set, and the bearded man would have been right if he had told them it was time to go home. But he didn't. Christine

Pittman kicked the ball in his direction, hoping—what? That he would come play? That he would speak to her? But it hit the curb and rolled back to her. "Nice one," Billy Morris said. The man kept walking.

April Morris, Billy's mother, was on the phone with her neighbor across the street, watching the kids outside through the window above the kitchen sink. Her fingers wrapped up in the curls and loops of the phone cord, she leaned back to see the time on the stove. "I'm going to have to go in a sec," she said. "I've got to get Billy back inside and into fresh clothes before Eric gets home. Has Tim gotten horribly smelly lately, too?"

"It's too awful," Bev said on the other end of the line. "It's ungodly. I can't even talk about it. Why can't they all be girls?"

April laughed. She turned and leaned against the sink, her back to the window. "You know why," she said suggestively. Bev was seven months pregnant. April waited for her friend to respond (Bev has a quick wit, though sometimes too much so) but she didn't say anything. "Bev?" April said.

"Sorry," Bev said, "I got distracted. Some guy just walked past the kids, and it looked like Christine Pittman was going to kick a ball at his head."

April turned back around and looked out the window. The game was back on, Billy winding past the other boys, kicking the ball carefully, skillfully, as though it were an egg that might break if he was too forceful. She looked down the street and saw the broad back of the man Christine had nearly hit with the ball.

"Who was he?" April asked.

"Who?" There was a hissing sound that puzzled April until she remembered Bev's phone was anchored to the wall near where the ironing board unfolds.

"The man on the sidewalk," April said.

"I didn't know him," Bev said. "He was young and had a beard. Dark hair."

"Hmm," said April, and she was about to say she had to go, had to call sweet, stinky Billy inside, and she could tell Tim to go home, too, if Bev wanted, when Bev said, "He looked at me."

"The man?"

"Right into the window," Bev said. "It was odd."

"Was he handsome?" April said, teasing.

"Yes," said Bev, but her voice was funny when she said it, like maybe he actually wasn't, or like it wasn't a good thing to be that kind of handsome, to look the way this man did. April wished she had seen him, too, not just the back of him.

"I should go," April said.

"Me, too," said Bev, and the women hung up. Seconds later, they waved at each other from their doorsteps as they called their boys back in.

Later, Earl Phelps said he'd had the feeling he was being watched by someone he couldn't see himself, but when he looked around, there was nothing out of the ordinary. The strange thing was that it was only then, after he had cleared the area and judged no incoming danger, that he saw the man rounding the corner and coming up the street. He told us he noted the man's hair and beard but his jacket was what caught his eye. It was army green, canvas. These young people, Earl said, their military-style clothes, and they didn't even have respect for men like him, men who had served their country, who had fought and watched people die. "Howdy," the man said as he passed, and Earl gave him a begrudging nod. Beyond the military jacket, he was a man carrying a woman's purse, and Earl didn't care to speak to him.

The last person to see the man in the neighborhood before he got in his car and drove away was Alice Lange. Alice Lange, the beloved, the beautiful! She would be crowned homecoming queen in two days. This was an unofficial prediction—the ballots had only just been cast and now sat in a box in the principal's office—but everyone knew she would win, because who else could it be? It had always been her, from her first day of kindergarten, when she had two skinned knees and a red ribbon in her hair; to fifth grade, when she socked Randy Neely in the stomach because he insulted her friend (and she wasn't even punished for it); to junior high, when she hurried out of her volleyball uniform and into her cheerleading skirt and onto the sidelines to cheer on the football team, because she could do it all, our girl; to high school, where the girls loved her, the boys loved her, the teachers, the parents, the women who scooped macaroni and cheese in the lunch line loved her. Yes, it had to be Alice Lange.

And no one else for this man to see than Alice Lange. She was on her porch swing with a book when he passed by, and he stopped and stood still on the sidewalk in front of her. "What are you reading?" he called out to her.

"*Adventures of Huckleberry Finn*," she said. She wasn't surprised to see him or to hear his voice. It seemed to her a perfectly natural question. She was a girl reading a book, and the cover was obscured from his vision. Why wouldn't he ask?

"A classic," the man said. "Do you like to read?"

"I do," she said. "Do you?"

"Yes," he said. "Hey, can I take your picture? You don't even have to move."

Alice must have looked hesitant because he held up both hands, as though he were showing her he wasn't armed. "I'm a photographer," he said. He tapped at the bag on his hip. "My camera's right in here."

"Oh," said Alice, relieved. "Okay. Yes. Here? Or?"

The man grinned. His teeth were worth noticing, though so far only Mrs. McEntyre had seen them. He'd smiled only at her and now at Alice Lange. They were straight and white, though maybe it was only that his skin was so tan, like he was a man who worked outside, on a ranch, on a farm, in the hills, on a dock somewhere outside the city. His eyes were bright, too, a brilliant blue, like the lightest part of the sky on a spring day.

"There. Don't move," he said. He walked up the stone pathway to her house, and Alice watched him as he approached, as he got larger and larger until there he was in front of her. He was like the sheer face of a cliff or the ocean, something vast. She could see nothing else.

He opened the camera bag and lifted the camera out. "Smile," he said.

"I don't want to," said Alice, lifting her head regally. "I don't feel like it."

"Okay," he said. "That's cool. It's whatever you want, girl." It was always whatever Alice wanted; we had told her that all her life. We would give her anything, but when the man said this, she felt somehow more powerful than she ever had before. Now, she thought as he took her picture, she was the ocean. She was the vast, wild thing.

"Thank you," the man said. "What a gift."

"Could I see the picture?" asked Alice.

"Soon," he said. "I'll be seeing you again."

"I suppose you will," Alice said. Neither of them said good-bye, and the man walked away, but Alice felt like he hadn't really left at all, that part of him was still there.

Alice read a few more pages and realized that if she wanted to continue, she would have to turn on the porch light, so she went inside instead. The afternoon was sliding into evening anyway, and we all had things to check off our daily lists before we could finally go to bed. We ate dinner, we watched television, we sang to our children as they fell asleep. We washed the dishes, the clothes, our bodies. We lay down, we reached for our husbands. We did not discuss the man we saw. Why would we?

The next morning Alice didn't wake up wondering about the man, but she thought of him as she brushed her teeth and looked at herself in the mirror. There he was in a corner of her brain, popping up amid calculus problems and the chapters of *Huckleberry Finn* she would be quizzed on and her plans for the afternoon—swimming in her backyard with Susannah Jenkins, and she was going to ask Susannah to undo the back clasp of her suit so she could tan her back; she knew, like we all did, she would be the homecoming queen tomorrow, and she wanted to be brown as a nut—and in her mind, the man looked different from how he did the day before. In her memory, he was tall and movie-star handsome, with a brilliant smile and an appealing, feral sort of quality around the eyes, like his eyes had teeth as well; the look they gave her as he lifted the camera up was sharp and hungry, but it was a ravenousness she liked. He appreciated her, that much was obvious. And though we did not know it then—then she was still our girl, our pretty Alice—she was beginning to feel the allure of a similar rapaciousness, the pull of being so hungry, how good it feels to want so much.

(We all know what it is to want. Not materially, maybe. Here we are well fed and well housed, well dressed, well groomed, and our children are well taken care of. Alice Lange was, too, no matter the stories you might hear now. When she came down the stairs that morning, she came down to breakfast: eggs, toast, glistening berries like rubies in a small glass bowl. What did she have to want? Like the rest of us, she had the entire world to want, but we've always known enough to stop the chase when there is something too big to lose, known when to bite down and stop the hunger that threatens to consume us.)

Downstairs, in the kitchen with the triangles of toast and sunny eggs, her mother read the newspaper. She looked up when she heard the slap of Alice's feet on the stairs and smiled at her daughter, a marvel, the miracle of her person in the house they shared together. It was only the two of them, Alice's father having died when the girl was five. She barely remembered him; her mother remembered him every day. When she looked at Alice, she saw him there, too, resurrected in the deep blue of her eyes, in the foot she bounced while she read or studied, in the length of her legs. It was an exquisite sort of pain, to look at her girl.

"Hi, sweetheart," her mother said. She nudged the plate of food across the table to the place at the seat across from her. On her own plate was half a piece of toast, buttered. "Eat," she said.

Alice wore a satchel on her right shoulder, heavy with class books, and for a second it seemed she was going to shrug it off so she could sit and have breakfast with her mother, but just as the bag was slipping down her shoulder, she hitched it back in place. "I'm not hungry," she said, but grabbed a handful of raspberries from the little glass bowl and popped one, then two into her mouth.

"What do you have going on today?" her mother asked. "Any tests?"

"A quiz," said Alice. "Susannah is coming over after school. We're going swimming."

"That will be nice," her mother said. "Anything else exciting happening?"

"No," said Alice. She reached down and plucked the toast from the plate and nibbled it. "Well," she said, "actually, someone took a picture of me. I'm curious to see how it turned out." She laughed. "That's not very exciting, though, is it?"

"Oh?" said her mother. "Who was it? Is there a photography class at school?"

Suddenly Alice didn't know why she had told her mother in the first place. "Just someone at school," she said.

"If it's good," her mother said, "maybe your friend can make a copy of it for me."

Alice shoved the piece of toast in her mouth, pressed a stray crumb on her chin, scooted it to her lips. She swallowed the toast, said, "I better go." She came around the table and kissed her mother's cheek, her hand on her mother's shoulder, her mother's hand lightly on hers. Her mother's fingertips were cool and soft.

"Be good," her mother said. "I'll make sure there are clean pool towels for you and Susannah."

When Alice got outside, she thought she might see the man there on the sidewalk. He would have had the photo developed in a darkroom, and he would be holding it behind his back like a bouquet of flowers, a surprise. *Look at you,* he'd say when he held it out to her. And Alice would get to see herself the way the man saw her. It would be revelatory, profound, and Alice would let the man keep it, an image of her to last forever, or she would take it if he would let her, and it would be a private thing, a secret. She knew no matter how good it was, she would not show it to her mother.

But on the sidewalk, there was no man. It was only us out there, with our children, beginning the day. Life continued around her. Even now, after it all, there are book bags to check, hands to hold, shoes to tie. There are mirrors to look in, lipstick to apply. Dishes to wash, phone calls to make. That day, the man did not come for her. Ahead of her, Alice spotted a pack of girls her age walking in the same direction, hips swishing in bright skirts, their legs as long and perfect as her own, and she hurried to catch them.

In science class, she took notes, drew marginalia in her notebook—curlicues and roses with petals like concentric circles, repeating in a spiral until they ended in a dot in the center of the flower. In history, she watched a film about Pompeii while their teacher, the basketball coach, sat at his desk with his feet up and head down, whiskered chin to chest. The film showed a reenactment of Vesuvius's eruption, uncredited actors and actresses playing nameless civilians running and falling and silently screaming, while a deep-voiced narrator spoke of ash like rain, fire chasing after them like demons with a million feet and wings. The destruction made Alice shudder, imagining herself in a situation in which the world began to fall apart.

We take pains, always, to assure our children of their safety; we remind them we will protect them. But we cannot control the way the earth moves, and a reality of living here, one we exchange for a beautiful home: sometimes the earth revolts. The sea churns with anger, cliffs crumble. The ground shakes, it splits open. It isn't often—only enough to remind us everything has cracks, everything can break.

There was an earthquake when Alice was a very little girl. She slept through it, woke up in the morning to tell her mother how she dreamed she was a sailor on a ship. There were mermaids rocking the boat, she said, and her mother marveled at her clever, wild little girl.

"It's better to be the volcano," the teacher said when the film was over, "than anything else in Pompeii." Hundreds of years later people caught in the ash stayed frozen in the positions they were in when they died, casts of their bodies preserved forever and displayed in museums. One was a dog writhing on its back. Alice couldn't stand to think of that, so instead she thought of the volcano. She imagined it as a person, a woman, wondered what it would be like to feel the bubbling and the heat, if the volcano knew what was happening or if she was as surprised as everyone else at what she gave birth to, the power of it, if the volcano felt relieved when it was over. It was easier to think about that than the petrified, anguished dog.

There was a pep rally after school that day to mark the end of homecoming week, and the gym quivered with blue and gold streamers. At one end of the basketball court, the drum line stood in a tight row, arms rigid, wrists limber, each beat of their music like a pulse. Students packed themselves in the bleachers, jostling each other and laughing. They had nearly survived another week; it would be over in an hour, and then they would be free for two glorious days. Soon they would celebrate.

Below the bleachers, spanning the length of the gym, the cheerleaders, Alice among them, stood in an evenly spaced line and clapped and bounced. They raised their voices in a rallying cry. They would fight and prevail, Alice yelled and chanted with the other ponytailed girls, unable to hear her own voice over the roar they made together. The man hadn't been on the sidewalk that morning after all, and the wanting inside her had yawned and stretched, but now it was filled with applause and drums and girls standing beside her. They looked at each other and smiled. Look at the frenzy they could whip up with their bodies, their voices. Look at the wildness. What else was there to want when you had all this power?

CHAPTER TWO

THE PEP RALLY was at once the last breath of a school week and the first act of a long celebration. The second act would be the football game, and then, the denouement of it all, the dance. Every Friday in the fall was a football game, every Friday night spent with the same people who this Saturday would crowd together at the dance, the boys sweating in synthetic suits their mothers had picked out, touching waists, grazing breasts with errant hands. But despite that, those nights were still a bit like magic. We remember what it was like. The parking lot of the high school became a fairground. The gym they decorated with their beauty, their youth, their small world transformed into something different, familiar if you squinted at it, but better. A world that would elect Alice Lange its queen.

"You'll win," said Susannah. "You know you will."

"I don't," said Alice, lying. "You don't know either."

"I voted for you," said Ben Austin. There were five of

them at his house, in his backyard, Alice and Susannah and Ben, Millie, and Andrew. Their team had won the football game, and to celebrate, Ben had pilfered a bottle of whiskey from his father's study. He held up two different kinds of glasses, wondered aloud which kind you drank whiskey from. No one knew, and he shrugged and poured a few fingers from the bottle into small water glasses.

They sat around the backyard fire pit, a stone circle like a well—another thing Ben was not supposed to touch and did anyway—and the flames made their faces shadowy and strange. Alice watched Susannah laughing at something Andrew said; half her face was the color of charcoal, the other half orange and bright, and it was like she was wearing a mask or she was another person laughing with Susannah's stolen voice. Her laugh was deep, like a man's. Susannah hoped someday it would be described by someone as throaty, sexy, instead of simply mannish. With the glow of the firelight on her face, Alice thought she looked beautiful, transformed, and in that moment she was happy for Susannah to be someone entirely new. "What?" said Susannah suddenly, looking at Alice.

"What?" said Alice.

"You're looking at me," she said.

"I wasn't," Alice said.

"I saw it too," Ben said. "It was a very romantic look."

"Make out!" said Andrew.

"Stop it," said Alice. But they both felt it, Alice and Susannah: not a desire to kiss each other out of love, though they were best friends and did love each other. And they had seen each other naked, changing in and out of wet swimsuits on countless summer afternoons, had marveled together at the eruption of breasts and the growth of strange hair in strange places, slept cuddled up in each other's bed every other weekend like kittens.

But now here was a boy watching them, asking them to give him something, and it felt like they should. And Alice thought suddenly of the man outside her house asking her the name of the book she was reading, asking to take her picture. How easy it had been to answer, and he had liked it when she did. Now she could lean over and kiss Susannah, and Andrew would like it. Ben would probably like it too. They would cheer for them, and what was it to her? A moment, just a few seconds. Nothing, really. What about Millie, though? She'd be jealous, Alice realized. Poor Millie sitting there, bare legs crossed and goose bumped, wishing she had been asked to kiss another girl.

"I'm not nearly drunk enough yet," Susannah said. But she turned, whole face in the gray shadows now, and blew a kiss at Alice.

"Boo," said Andrew, and they all laughed. Ben passed the bottle of whiskey around the circle again. "There's still hope," Andrew said when Susannah poured more in her glass. "Pucker up."

"Anyway, Alice," said Susannah, "less than twenty-four hours from now, you'll see I'm right about the vote."

"I saw the ballot box sitting on Mrs. Turner's desk," Ben said. "I should have looked inside."

"How would that have helped anything?" Susannah asked, rolling her eyes. "Unless you have superhuman counting skills you've never told us about?"

"I don't know," said Ben. He felt his cheeks beginning to burn, and he hoped Alice didn't notice, but when he glanced at her, she wasn't looking at him or at anyone else. She seemed disconnected from Ben and the others, like her body was there but the rest of her, the part that made her Alice, wasn't.

The next thing that happened surprised us, when we later learned of it. It didn't fit with our understanding of Alice. Of course, that doesn't mean it isn't true. This is something we've learned.

Alice Lange, in the light of the fire, under the canopy of a birch tree, its white bark stark as bone in the moonlight, said, "I know how we can find out who won."

"What?" asked Susannah. "How?"

"Let's break in," she said. "If it's on Mrs. Turner's desk, that's only one—no, two doors to get through. Only one of them will be locked, I bet." She could see it in her head, could see how easy it would be, how fun, how funny. Kissing Susannah, that wouldn't have been right for the evening, but this would. She grinned thinking of it, that yawning inside of her as deep as a cavern. Susannah in the fire's glow—she wasn't the only one who could be a different person.

"You want to know that badly?" said Millie. "Can't wait to see that you're going to win?"

"No," Alice said. "It's not about that. I want—I don't know. I want to do something." She looked around at the others. "Don't you?"

"I can pick a lock," said Andrew.

"I'm shocked," Susannah said dryly.

"Come on," Alice said. "It will be fun! It'll be an adventure."

"I'm in," said Andrew.

Ben nodded. "Me, too," he said.

"Well, I can't leave you alone with these two clowns," Susannah said. "Let's do it."

Millie stood up, her scrawny legs nearly as white as the birches, and straightened her skirt. "I'm going home," she said. "This is a stupid idea."

"Millie," Andrew groaned.

"It's dangerous," Millie said. "There are people who want to hurt kids like us." Here was a girl who had listened.

"What are you even talking about?" asked Susannah.

"A girl," Millie said. "Don't you remember? Someone took her."

"I promise it will be fine, Millie. This is a very safe neighborhood," Alice said, though she knew who Millie was talking about, it had happened last year but not here. Millie, too, could feel herself being persuaded, could picture herself walking down a dark street and only being afraid in the most delicious way, the image of that other nameless girl fading away. But then Alice continued: "I understand, though. No big deal. We'll see you tomorrow."

This was the Alice we knew: understanding, magnanimous. The Alice who once spent an entire afternoon helping little Tim learn to ride a bike. This, of course, is a father's job, but he was away on a business trip, and Tim had insisted he needed to learn right then, right that very second, and Alice had said well, she could do it, couldn't she, and we watched her standing behind Tim, her hands on the seat of his bike, keeping him steady. We watched him wobble and crash and wobble and crash, and we watched Alice pick him up and hold the bike for him over and over. When Alice let go that final time and he sailed away, she ran after him, whooping and clapping, and we all clapped too. We couldn't help it.

"Fine," said Millie, who, of course, wanted them to stop her, to tell her they needed her. But instead there was Alice dismissing her kindly and gracefully, and to the others Millie was already gone. If she had stayed there, she knew they would have walked past her, so Millie stood a second longer, feet turned out in first position, watching her friends make plans in hushed voices.

"Well, bye then," she said. And they all said, "Bye, Millie," without looking up, except for Alice, who smiled gently and waved.

Millie made it home easily and safely; she lived around the corner from Ben Austin, and her parents were asleep when she got home because they trusted her. And that was a nice thing, to be so young and to be so trusted that they knew you'd come home, that you'd turn off the living room lamp they'd left on for you, navigate around the sofa and the chairs and coffee table in the dark, find the stairs and climb them, feeling your way until finally you tumbled safe into your bed.

One evening not long after we had the lampposts installed, April saw Mrs. Lange taking the trash out and looking up at the lights. "Well, Mrs. Lange, what do you think?" April asked, nodding at them.

"They're nice," she said. "It's like leaving ten lamps on for Alice when she finally comes home."

April wasn't sure what to respond, couldn't bear to say out loud to Mrs. Lange what she was certain the other woman already knew, that Alice wasn't coming home. "You're a good mother," April said.

All Mrs. Lange said was thank you, and she turned and walked back up her driveway to her house, where, April could see, a light was burning in the window.

CHAPTER THREE

B EFORE THEY LEFT, they stood in Ben's kitchen and passed the whiskey around, the water glasses now sitting in the sink. Alice shivered as she tipped the bottle back and swallowed. She had reached that pleasant level of drunkenness when the burn of the alcohol was appealing and no longer distasteful, and she felt warm and giggly and brave.

Ben found two flashlights and gave one to Alice, who was standing silently in front of the refrigerator, looking at the various things his mother had secured there with magnets. A receipt; a list written in his father's handwriting, only one item—fertilizer with a squiggly question mark beside it—legible; a photograph of Ben as a kid. He was smiling and blinking. It had been bright outside, but his mother had insisted on taking it. When they developed the picture, she had laughed at his closed eyes. "I love it," she had said. Alice touched its curling corner. "Baby Ben," she said.

"Yep," he said. "I was in first grade." She thought she

saw his cheeks redden. She had done that, brought that color into the world, and she liked that she had.

"I remember when you looked like that," she said. "When we were little." He could remember her, too, when she was little, and Susannah and Andrew and all the others. We can, too, and it seems like we might peek out our front windows now and see them riding their bicycles or chasing each other, still in bathing suits, their mothers blocking the doors until they dried off. But when we look now, they're gone. It's only Tim and Billy and Christine Pittman, a whole new group of children.

"You were cute," Alice said.

"Were?" asked Ben. He raised an eyebrow, and Alice laughed.

"Let's go," she said and pointed the flashlight, still dark, toward the front door.

Ben saw the matchbook he'd used for the backyard fire lying on the counter and grabbed it, slipped it into his pocket. Later, his mother would ask him why. "I don't know," he said. He couldn't look at her when he answered, and she thought of him as that blinking little boy in the photograph, how she worried he was too sensitive, that he felt the weight of others' gestures and words and movements too strongly. "I thought it might come in handy," he said finally. "That's all."

Audrey Austin watched her son respond, and in the way that only we have, a superpower we gained as we transformed from women into mothers, she saw what Ben saw when he took the matchbox: himself in the dark school, no lights anywhere, a dead flashlight battery, perhaps. A pretty girl clutching his arm, the burning match between his fingertips the only light, and him hoping the girl would press herself closer. "Okay," his mother told him. "It's okay."

* * *

The walk to the school that night felt longer than in the mornings when there were clusters of kids ahead and behind them, all going in the same direction, when there were tests to agonize over, gossip to exchange, so many things to worry about, so many to hope for too. (We wouldn't go back to being seventeen or eighteen if you paid us.)

"This looks different," Susannah said. "It feels like we've been walking too long."

"Because it's nighttime," said Andrew. "And because you're drunk."

"I'm not!" Susannah said, but it came out in a squeal, and they all laughed.

"It isn't taking longer," Ben said. "I promise."

Sidewalks pale and smooth in the moonlight, like ribbons stretched out straight and tight, dark trees rising, their leaves black and spreading overhead, stop signs, fire hydrants, mailboxes: all these things washed in gray. Houses just like their own sat like rocks in a row. The lights inside them were mostly off. Susannah passed them and imagined herself inside her house, in her bed, and she hated herself for resisting the adventure they were on. Look at them! She could be wild and young and free. Uncontainable. She walked faster, like she could catch up to that version of herself.

Alice imagined herself inside, too, not in her own house, like Susannah, but these particular houses, alien houses. She saw herself walking through the dark rooms, the houses lifeless until she let herself into them and woke them up. Now, in the night, the people inside them didn't exist. In the morning they would again, when the front doors opened and cars turned out of the driveway and kids played in the yard, but now she looked at the houses and thought of tombs. She thought of the silence of Pompeii in the days after the ash fell and fire ravaged, when the life of people had drained out and they all lay curled up and still, and it scared her, so she turned and looked straight ahead.

(Even we catch ourselves lost in alarming thoughts. The things we only think in the dark. We surprise ourselves. Sometimes Bev thinks of intruders breaking into her house, imagines herself killing them with a knife from the wooden block in the kitchen, saving her child, emerging bloodied and triumphant, Tim clutching her leg. The pulsing adrenaline of bravery. "Do you ever feel that way?" she asked April once.

"What?" April asked. "Protective? Paranoid?"

"Angry," said Bev.)

They didn't speak until they reached the school parking lot, the building's limestone exterior bright against the night, the windows all dark. No lights on inside.

"Check it out," said Andrew, pointing at an entire small castle, complete with a knight and sword. "The freshmen's is actually pretty good."

"Where's your loyalty?" asked Susannah.

Four homecoming floats, flatbed trucks decorated by each of the classes, sat parked in the circular drive. In the dark they looked eerie, the papier-mâché flowers, the chicken-wire figures, all grotesque and strange. The seniors, who had picked "Anchors Away" as their theme and planned to dress as sailors, in nautical white and navy, had finished theirs just the day before; Alice and Susannah and their classmates had painstakingly attached thousands of paper pompoms to the outside of the truck, all different shades of blue to look like the ocean. Alice had set up a specific pattern, alternating the blues just so. Susannah had thought that wouldn't look right; the ocean wasn't so predictable; the color changed depending on the light of the day, but she let Alice do it her way. Rippling in yesterday's afternoon wind, the pompoms had in fact looked like waves, aqua and indigo, and Alice had been proud, but now they looked cheap and fake. Not like water at all.

They walked around the floats and stood still, side by side, each focusing on a different spot on the building before them, but Alice tried to see something past the walls, something more intimate. She wanted to look into the beating heart of the school and realized suddenly there probably wasn't one. It had no heart until she shared hers with it.

"Here we go," she said and strode up to the doors, pale hair flying behind her like a comet tail, and yanked on one of the handles.

"Alice!" Susannah said. The four froze, waiting to see if an alarm would sound, if a pit might open up beneath Alice and suck her into the earth.

But though nothing happened to her, neither did the doors open. "Oh, Andrew," Alice called, "your services are required, please." Cracking his knuckles behind her, Andrew trotted over and knelt down in front of the lock while Alice hovered over him, nibbling at a cuticle, telling him not like that, that can't be right.

"Alice," said Andrew, "I can't even see what I'm doing with you standing over me." She held up her hands and took a step back. Ben kept his back to the other three, his hands in his pockets, pretending he wasn't keeping a lookout.

"I can't get it," Andrew said loudly. Alice slumped against the side of the building, and her flashlight tilted down, creating a yellow oblong on the pavement. She turned her head to the side to see the rows of dark windows lining the side of the building. There was the window she had stared out during her freshman-year English class, and three more down, the one always covered by blinds in her sophomore geometry class. And this one, the close one, belonged to her history classroom. She never paid attention in that class; it was a notoriously easy A. And just this week, Mr. Fielding, a portly, sweaty man, had opened that window. "Damned stuffy," he'd said. The air rushing in was sweet and cool.

"Wait," said Alice.

"Let's go home," said Susannah. "This is getting boring anyway."

"The windows!" Alice said. She kicked at the outturned sole of Andrew's sneaker as he still fiddled uselessly with the lock. He rose and followed her to Mr. Fielding's window and stood behind her while she reached up to open it. "I need a hand," she said. As she reached up, her shirt rose a little, too, exposing a band of skin, not just gleaming in the moonlight but the color of moonlight itself.

"Here," said Ben, coming up beside her. "I can reach it."

"No," said Alice, "I can do it. Lift me up a little."

"Just let me," said Ben. "It will be easier."

"No," she said. She turned to him, grabbed both his hands and put them on her hips. "Lift," she said, and he obeyed. But once in his arms and up in the air, struggling with the window, she felt heavier than he expected, and he almost had to put her down. Instead, he shifted his grip on her, so that two fingers of his right hand were on her bare skin. If she noticed or cared, she didn't say.

"Got it!" she said, and then she was out of his arms and

into the classroom. He, too, had Mr. Fielding, had noticed the open window the period after Alice's class. Last week he had watched through that window as Carl Miller leaned against his green Volkswagen Beetle in the parking lot, staring at the school like he was waiting for someone. And he must have been because when Ben looked back, Carl was in the car, next to a blond girl he couldn't identify—her head was tilted down, hair covering her face—and then they were off, rattling out of the parking lot.

Ben climbed in, and then Andrew hurtled himself athletically over the window ledge, and when he landed in the classroom, he turned and pulled Susannah up behind him. Alice was standing at the chalkboard, her back to her friends, her hand moving smoothly, the chalk in it like a fairy wand, conjuring letters onto the board. *Hello*, she wrote in cursive. Her handwriting was neat, all loops and lines. That was it.

(Now that we know what we know, it seems possible that she was telling the world she was here, seeing if anyone would answer. Did we not give her enough attention? We would have said hello right back, would have waved, would have taken her face in our hands, kissed each of her cheeks, if we had known.

Or was it a hello you give in passing, a polite acknowledgment that there's a space you share for a moment before leaving it? Is there not a good-bye implied in every greeting? I'm here, she might have been saying, but not for long. It's possible—it's likely—no message was intended, that we're looking for a meaning that's simply not there.)

She went to put the chalk back below the blackboard but missed and bent down to retrieve it, her hair falling like a curtain in front of her face. "Hey," said Ben when she looked up again. "Are you friends with Carl Miller?"

She put the chalk back into a narrow groove on the metal shelf, and shook her hair out of her eyes. "Sort of," she said. "Why?"

"He's an asshole," said Ben. "Let's go."

Alice almost laughed. Carl Miller *was* an asshole, but no one spent time with Carl Miller because of his manners, his gentility. There was something else a girl was looking for when she got into his car at 12:45 on a Friday afternoon. "I'm right behind you," Alice said. For a minute, Ben thought she might reach for his hand, and he slowed so she could find it in the dark, but she did not.

The four of them left the classroom, turned down the maze of halls. Their shoes squeaked and tapped on the linoleum floor.

The door to the office was unlocked—a miracle, a sign, they thought—but the truth is that it was never locked. They grinned at each other. On Mrs. Turner's desk sat the box, plain and brown. A diagram of a pencil sharpener was on the side of the box—all the teachers had gotten new sharpeners this year—and it was disappointing to think of the name of a queen languishing in there on hundreds of slips of paper, with "Homecoming" scrawled in ballpoint pen on its outside. The box didn't even have a lid, just cardboard flaps open and extended, like the arms of a worshipper in church, reaching up to receive some kind of gift.

"I'll count," said Ben, and he pulled out a slip. "Alice Lange," he read.

From there, he drew each one methodically, separating them into piles. Alice's pile was wide at first, encroaching onto those of the other candidates, and then it stayed the same size;

it wasn't every slip or even every other, and then there were fourteen in a row that bore the name of another girl.

"Let's go," said Susannah. "It'll be better if you're surprised."

Ben stopped counting and looked up at Alice, eyebrows raised, mouth slightly open, waiting.

"It's fine," said Alice. "I don't care if I win. It's not a big deal." Ben dropped a slip into a pile. Not Alice's.

After another minute, he assessed the two biggest stacks, swept the other ones back into the box, and then counted the slips in the remaining piles. Alice was leaning against the desk, her profile facing him, and she held the flashlight up so that it made a big, flat circle on the ceiling. He straightened up and cleared his throat. Alice didn't look at him. Her ankles were crossed, so dainty, and her head back, the silhouette of her throat a gentle curve.

"Well," said Ben. "I think I might have counted wrong."

Alice's chin dropped. The circle of light on the ceiling shifted as she hoisted herself off the desk. "It's okay," she said. "It's a silly thing anyway."

"Very silly," agreed Susannah.

"Are you okay?" Ben asked.

"She said she's fine," said Andrew. "Let's get out of here."

"Of course," she said, turning to Ben and giving him a bright smile full of pretty teeth. "There are more important things, you know?" she said. "Like college or art or philosophy or anything else. Those are things to really care about, I think. Right?"

"Right," said Ben.

"See?" Alice said. "Some adventure, though, huh?"

And they all agreed yes, it was, they'd never forget it, the walk in the dark, crawling in through the window. But as they made their way back out of the building, Alice was thinking about the votes in their stupid box, so many pieces of paper that didn't say her name, how foolish she'd been, and then she thought of the man with the camera.

I'll see you again, he'd promised.

And she had stupidly spent her whole day expecting she would. Like a child, a little girl, not a queen at all.

They crossed into Fielding's classroom and one by one they slipped out the window, landing like cats on the grass. Ben pulled the window down behind them. Like they had never been there.

The floats loomed in front of them. An ocean, a rose garden blooming pink and red and green (THE JUNIOR CLASS: A ROSE AMONG THORNS), a farm with misshapen animals and a giant farmer (HOMECOMING HOEDOWN), the papier-mâché Camelot the freshmen had made (A KNIGHT TO REMEMBER). When they reached the senior float, Susannah and Andrew kept on going, but Alice stopped and touched the blue paper waves, and Ben joined her, touched her lightly on the elbow.

"Hey," he said, "are you sure you're okay?"

"I was thinking about things," Alice said. The man, the fire, the night. The game, the box. An ocean that wasn't really an ocean at all. She looked at Ben, then toward Susannah and Andrew. "Don't you ever feel like doing something?" she asked. "Something surprising?"

"No," said Andrew.

"I'm leaving," Susannah announced, but she didn't move. She thought of her friend's fist flying into the soft gut of a little boy, years ago. *He deserved it*, Alice had said. She'd laughed when Randy Neely cried.

"I get it," said Ben. He stuck his hands inside his pockets like he was cold, although there was only a slight chill in the air. But he felt something in his pocket, a tiny rectangle. "Here," he said to Alice. He took her hand and pressed the matchbook into it. She looked up at him with wide eyes, and then she nodded and took it from him.

"What is that?" asked Susannah, taking a step closer. Andrew grabbed her arm because he wasn't going to stop whatever was happening, and they watched Alice hold the matchbook up and examine it, like she was looking for flaws in a diamond. She pulled out a match. She struck it.

The flame looked tiny, only big enough to light a cigarette or a birthday candle. She held it to a blue pompom, then to a white. (The white had been Alice's suggestion. "Like the crest of waves," she had said.) Now they burned orange and bright.

"Holy shit," said Andrew. Flames devoured the ocean, each lick of fire a hungry mouth.

"Run," said Ben, and they did: Susannah, stepping on an untied lace; Andrew, fast, arms pumping; Ben, first two steps backward, staggering before turning around to catch the other two, calling to Alice; Alice last, worried she would burn it all down, the floats, the school, the books and ungraded tests and essays inside, worried also that she wouldn't, but oh. What a beautiful thing it was to burn.

CHAPTER FOUR

W<small>E KNOW BAD</small> things happen in the world, that they always have, that they'll continue to do so. We also know that we can't stop them, and this knowledge is almost worse than the bad things themselves. That's what we've learned from Alice Lange. Sometimes the darkness wins. It creeps in like a thick, gray fog, covering everything as we stumble around, and when it finally lifts, we see what it has done, what it has taken from us and what it has left behind.

Before Alice, there was another girl. Rachel Granger. This was whom Millie was thinking of that night, when she said it wasn't safe to be out wandering alone in the dark. Her mother had only talked about Rachel to her husband, changing the subject when Millie walked into the room, but she'd picked up on the story, had known there was something, someone out there, to be afraid of, and the idea of it lodged itself in her brain.

Rachel wasn't from our neighborhood, but she lived only a few miles away. Like Alice, she was here and then gone. As far as anyone knows, this is what happened: on a Friday, she went to watch the football game at the high school, and left early for some reason. Her friends say the strap on her shoe had broken and she didn't want to walk home, and she said she would catch a ride from someone. Unlike Alice, she was found. Here and then gone and then here, in one sense, again. Strangled, left near a park we never visit, but one Rachel probably did, only a few streets over from her house.

We didn't know her, but we felt we knew her face almost as intimately as our own children's because it came to us in our homes, every night on the news for a week, bright and large and blurry. Rachel Granger had big eyes and a blond bob, and she held a few strands back with a barrette so that her face was open and clear.

What we couldn't see of Rachel, we filled in with our own children's features, their preferences, their mannerisms. It hurt to imagine her as our children, our children as her, but we couldn't stop ourselves. We couldn't see her hands in her picture, but Christine Pittman's mother knew Rachel had short, strong fingers like her daughter's, hands meant for catching and throwing. We couldn't hear her voice, but Millie's mother thought she looked like a girl who would be in choir, probably a soprano, like Millie was. Susannah's mother pictured Rachel in a soccer uniform and that short blond hair pulled back into a stubby ponytail, with the same wispy flyaway pieces of hair that sprang from Susannah's head after a long game.

Worse, though, was what we could see and hear: her mother's hair, also blond but darker, coarser, her voice gravelly with grief, her hands empty. When Rachel Granger's image came on TV, we watched. When her mother came on, first begging for her daughter to be returned, then begging for something no one could give her, we turned off the TV. It's time for dinner, we told everyone. For homework, for a bath, for bed.

Alice Lange left us in broad daylight. She was not frightened when she left. She did not think of Rachel Granger. Because she was getting into the car of someone she knew, because her shoes were not broken, because she was Alice Lange, and we've always told her she could do anything.

We thought we would see Alice Lange's face on the news one day. We haven't yet, but who knows? Maybe one day we'll turn on the TV, and there she'll be, an imperfect, blurry-edged picture of her lovely face smiling at us, and we'll grieve her again, what the darkness took from us.

CHAPTER FIVE

T HE MORNING AFTER Alice struck that match and began to burn her world down, Bev hosted a Tupperware party. At this party we would hear about the fire, how Millie and a few others went down to the school first thing in the morning to put a few last-minute touches on the float and discovered the corpse of a brittle, black beast in its place. How they circled around it in shock. "It's ruined!" Stephanie Masters wailed. "Who would do this?"

"The stupid freshmen," said Matthew Flanagan.

What we didn't hear then: how Millie glared at the remains of the float, remembering the night before in Ben Austin's backyard, the adventure she had turned down, Alice Lange's smile, Good night, Millie, she'd said, like Millie was a baby who needed tucking in. What we heard only later: how Millie looked at Stephanie and said, "It wasn't the freshmen."

But on our way to Bev's house, we didn't know any of that yet.

We hadn't planned to walk over to the party together—we were all just leaving our houses at about the same time—but we looked like a parade ourselves, heading in happy twos or threes down the street. We were empty-handed except for our purses, all of us but Charlotte Price, who despite Bev's insistence that she had everything under control, carried a golden pie in a white ceramic dish. She and Mags Rollins walked together and speculated about Bev's sudden desire to sell Tupperware. "You know her husband makes beaucoups," Charlotte said to her. "More than Gary even! She doesn't need the money. And she's got the baby on the way. She should be busy enough."

"It's just a reason to throw a party," Mags said. "She probably won't even make any money. Not real money, anyway."

"Oh please," said Charlotte, lowering her voice. They were very near to the house now, and to their right Mrs. McEntyre was pulling her front door shut behind her, Sweetie barking from inside. "We'll all buy something from her because that's the nice thing to do," she said.

Of course we would. We take care of each other here. We support each other. If one of us wants to sell plastic containers, then we'll each take two. That's what makes this a special place. That's what makes us—we hesitate to say "better" because that kind of arrogance is unappealing—special, too, more so than other people living in other places. We bring pies even when we aren't asked because we know each other's weaknesses as well as strengths; we know, for example, when a certain hostess might forget to provide something sweet for her guests.

Inside Bev's home, all evidence of Timmy and Todd's existence had been erased. No stinky shoes by the door, no sound of roughhousing coming from the backyard. Instead, a crystal bowl filled with punch beside a tall vase of flowers on the dining table, where a tray of fruit and cheese had been set out. Plastic containers and bowls and lids were arranged artfully on the coffee table next to a low arrangement of flowers. Already, a few of us were picking up the Tupperware, unsealing the lids, listening to that satisfying burp of air and then securing the tops again.

"I burned the cookies," Bev said when Charlotte walked in. She immediately took the pie from her guest and handed it to April, who scurried off to serve it to the rest of us. "You're a lifesaver," Bev said. "As well as a mind reader. Thank you. Anyway, make yourselves at home!"

We remember this party so well because of what came after. Imagine Alice as she looked then, sitting with her mother on the sofa, Mrs. Lange's hands absentmindedly feeling the tips of her daughter's hair, twisting them around her fingers; picture the way the ends curled lightly in different directions, like a road sign pointing to all the ways a person could go.

Susannah sat across from Alice with the coffee table between them, and though they didn't speak, they looked at each other and crossed their eyes when one of the mothers said something they found silly. They didn't act strangely, at least not at first. We chatted about the game, congratulated Alice on cheering the boys to victory.

Alice only shrugged. "I didn't do anything."

"Sure you did. A team can't win with low morale," said Charlotte Price.

"Alice, Susannah," interrupted Mags, "let us old ladies"—laughter here; none of us are old, not really—"live vicariously through you. Tell us about your dresses for homecoming." Soon Bev would shush us all and expound on the merits of

Tupperware, but until then we were happy to hear the girls talk about their homecoming plans. "Mine was green," Mags told them.

"Lavender," said Charlotte, sighing at the memory.

"Pink," said Karen Prescott. Alice looked around, thought of us as plucked flowers, soft and limp and briefly beautiful.

"Mine is pink too," said Susannah. "But not a gaudy pink, it's a nice pink, kind of soft."

"Baby pink," said Mags.

"Blush," offered April.

"Exactly," said Susannah in that low voice of hers. "And strapless." She shivered a little when she said it; she'd never worn a strapless dress before, but now she imagined the touch of someone's hands on those bare shoulders, on her collarbone, and shivered again. Next to her, her mother noticed the tremor and draped an arm across her shoulders, covered now by a light-green sweater. She had thought about the bare shoulders too.

"Mine's about the same," said Alice when we all looked at her, waiting for her to speak. "Only red."

"I'm sure it's not exactly the same," April said. "I'm sure it's special in its own way."

But Alice shook her head, gaze soft and sweet and a little resigned. "No," she said. "It's about the same as everyone else's."

We looked at each other. This should have been a clue that something wasn't right with Alice; normally, she would have said yes, it's got this kind of hem, this kind of neckline, it's red as a rose, but instead there she was saying no. Not rudely. Just vacantly, as if she weren't thinking of us at all, of what we wanted.

"Well, you should at least make sure you style your hair so that the crown will fit on top of it," joked Mags.

But Alice shook her head again. "I'm not going to win, actually," she said, and Susannah looked at her, eyes wide. "But it's okay."

"I hadn't realized you could see the future, Alice," said Charlotte, who had been homecoming queen in the small town where she grew up, smack dab in the middle of the country. It was a dusty place, wretched in the summer and bitter in the winter, but still, she had been its queen.

"I don't need to," said Alice. But suddenly she could see the future, and it wasn't here.

Mrs. Lange had taken her hands away from Alice's hair and now squeezed her leg. "It really is okay either way," she said.

"It's actually kind of stupid," Alice said, "in the grand scheme of things. It's all kind of stupid."

Around the room we stiffened. Backs straightened, legs uncrossed and crossed again; we tucked our hair behind our ears. Alice took a sip of punch and put her glass down neatly on a coaster. She looked around, and she was pleased at the reaction, how we all tensed up, how we were all trying to translate what she had said. What was stupid, exactly? The dance? The dress? The desire to be queen? But we didn't ask. We felt embarrassed for her mother, who looked at her daughter with concern but also with amusement and pride, like Alice had suddenly begun speaking in tongues: it was alarming, but also, in its own way, impressive.

"It isn't stupid," Charlotte said. "It's tradition."

"What about dates?" asked April quickly.

"We're going in a group with other girls," said Susannah. "No boys allowed." She let out a laugh, but it wasn't a genuine one. It sounded like a cough. "It will be more fun that way, right, Alice? This way we can dance with whomever we want."

"Right," said Alice.

"No boys!" exclaimed Mags, glancing first at Susannah and then at Alice. "I can hardly believe you two couldn't find dates."

"We chose not to find dates," said Alice, who was suddenly feeling proud and defensive of this decision, though it had only come about because Susannah had wanted to go with Charles Wilbur, and he hadn't asked her, and she had been crushed. "Let's go together," Alice had said, stroking her friend's hair. "You and me and the other girls. Who needs boys anyway?" But now, in her mind, it became something else, a crucial and inextricable part of herself that she couldn't deny.

Charlotte raised her eyebrows, two thin dark arches. "Now, that's what seems stupid," she said. "People will think no one wanted to take you." Susannah blushed. She thought of Charles Wilbur, the way his legs looked in his basketball shorts. He was taking a younger girl, an elegant sophomore with long red hair. But Alice Lange was taking *her*. "Or," Charlotte went on, her eyebrows inching even higher, "they'll think you aren't interested in—"

"That's okay," Alice said politely, hands in her lap loosely holding again her cup of punch. "I don't mind if they think either of those things." She didn't look at Susannah, who she knew did mind a little bit.

"Martha, are you going to let her talk like this?" Charlotte asked Mrs. Lange. "She sounds like an insane person." Now Alice laughed. When she tilted her head back, her white throat glowed like mother of pearl.

"She's going to have a wonderful time," her mother said,

looking sharply at Charlotte, who stared right back, her eyes small and round and hard, like dark marbles. Mrs. Lange could see each swipe of mascara Charlotte had applied before coming, hoping to widen them. "Bev," Mrs. Lange finally said, searching the room for her hostess, "I'm very interested in this container." She held up an olive-colored one. "Are there more sizes in this shape?"

Bev, who had been hovering at the edge of the room and marveling at the conversation, thought Alice Lange seemed possessed. She rubbed her stomach, which was round now when it had seemed flat only last week. "That one," she said, moving toward Mrs. Lange, "that one does come in three sizes, and they're all stackable so they'll take up less room in your cabinets. They're like those Russian dolls."

"Excellent!" said Mrs. Lange. "That's exactly what I need."

"I won't say it's revolutionary," Bev said, "but I'll say it's always nice to have extra space." We all agreed with that. We listened as she modeled the containers, prying off the lids and then resealing them, and passed them around the room. They held in smells, they kept things fresh, if you dropped them and the lid was on correctly nothing would leak. What you'd worked hard to prepare could be saved: a small miracle. We each bought two.

Toward the end of the party, Nancy Wright, Millie's mother, blustered in. She was sorry she was late, but Millie had been upset and hadn't wanted to come. (Is it only in our imagination that she glanced at Alice when she said that?) There had been some fire, she said, an accident or maybe sabotage by another class, and the senior float had been destroyed. Terrible! we all murmured. Who would do such a thing?

"Me," said Alice, and we laughed. Her mother rolled her

eyes. "Oh, Alice," she said. "Silly girl." From her chair across from Alice, Susannah said nothing.

When we left, we thanked Bev. We offered to help clean up, but she told us no. She would return Charlotte Price's pie dish later. We had done enough, she said, we had been so generous. "Have fun tonight," she said to Alice. "Girls always have more fun with other girls anyway."

The Langes were the only ones left by that point, besides April, who Bev did let tidy up the kitchen.

"Thanks," said Alice. She looked at Bev. "My dress has a little line of tiny pearls along the neckline," Alice said finally. "That's what makes it different."

"It sounds pretty," Bev said, and she seemed like the Alice she had known since she was a little girl with skinned knees, whipping past on her bicycle. She must have been having a bad day, or—she thought of Alice and Susannah going together to the dance—maybe there was boy trouble or something else shameful she didn't want to talk about. "Thanks again," said Mrs. Lange, and the pair left, walking down the driveway.

Bev was about to go back inside when she noticed that Mrs. Lange had taken her daughter's hand in her own, like Alice was a little girl, the way Bev held Timmy's hand on the occasions he let her, and that Alice didn't shake her off. They walked together across the street and down the sidewalk, and Bev kept watching until they got to their house. They must have left the door unlocked because neither of them reached for a key. But Mrs. Lange let go of Alice's hand to open the door, and for some reason Bev felt a foreboding sense of sadness watching them disconnect, the mother's hand turning the knob, reaching to her daughter to sweep her in. The girl's hands empty and aimless, rudderless. Hold on to her! Bev wanted to cry out. Hurry!

But then they were inside and out of her sight, and later, when Alice was gone for good, Bev wondered if she had really felt that worry in the first place or if she had simply remembered it wrong or, now that she had a tiny new daughter of her own, if she was catching a glimpse of her future self, wanting to hold her daughter's hand but, for some reason, letting go.

CHAPTER SIX

B Y THE TIME we knew for sure Alice had anything to do with the vandalism, she had vanished. Weeks later, the school suspended Ben for his involvement because, weighed down by guilt and grief, he had come forward and confessed. "They were my matches," he said. "Alice didn't do anything." His mother felt both proud and disappointed—proud of his integrity, disappointed in his last gesture of devotion to a girl who, she knew, would never love him back. How ordinary, she thought, to love a girl like Alice Lange.

Lucky Andrew escaped punishment. Susannah did too. For her own complicated reasons, Millie, who had tattled on Alice, never named anyone else.

When Ben returned to school after his suspension, he had become a kind of folk hero. He caught whispered snatches of his name when he passed, his and Andrew's and sometimes Susannah's, though the world, for some reason, had mostly forgotten she was ever there at all. He heard Alice Lange's name as well, but in a different sort of tone: she had become a legend, too, a darker one that no one understood.

Just a few hours after the Tupperware party, Alice poked her head into the laundry room where her mother was putting a load into the washing machine. "Bye!" she said, and her mother jumped.

"Alice, you scared me," she said, turning to look at her daughter. She smiled when she saw the brown bag Alice carried—it had been her own years ago. "Off to Susannah's?"

Alice nodded. Mrs. Lange was sad not to see her daughter off to the dance, but she knew it was important for Alice to go. She and Susannah always got ready for dances and outings together, alternating houses each time; this time it was Susannah's, but spring prom, the last dance of Alice's high school years, would be hers and wasn't that the more important one? There would always be more time with Alice, and, after all, this was only one of the many goodbyes she would have to wish her daughter in her lifetime. "Have fun, sweetie," she said.

Alice remained in the doorway, watching her mother feed piece after piece of her clothing into the mouth of the washing machine, and her stomach clenched with guilt. How many dresses of hers had her mother washed over the years? How many pairs of socks? But she knew she couldn't stay; her time here—with her mother, with us—was over. Placing her hand on her mother's shoulder, Alice leaned in and kissed her cheek.

(From that night on, Mrs. Lange never slept soundly again, tortured by dreams in which Alice was tantalizingly nearby, just on the horizon, near enough to hear her mother calling and wave at her from far away, but never close enough to touch. She replayed Alice's good-bye kiss in the laundry room over and over in her thoughts, searching her memory of it for any clue of when her daughter would be home. The dry, quick feeling of her lips on her cheek. Alice's fingertips on her shoulder. Was any of it a promise? The way she slung that purse, Mrs. Lange's old bag, over her shoulder. How happy she had been to see Alice using something of hers. It was so hard with teenagers; you never knew if they loved you or hated you, and maybe Alice choosing that bag of hers was a secret signal to her mother that there was a part of Alice that still wanted to become her when she grew up, the way she had when she was a little, little girl, and her mother was the total embodiment of her joy and comfort, back when she hadn't even begun to conceive of herself as a different being with a body, a brain, and a heart all her own.)

"Good-bye, honey," Mrs. Lange said, and then Alice was gone.

Several of us saw Alice leave her house, a small bag in one hand. She didn't slam the door behind her, and no one came after her. She wasn't running, but she walked quickly, kept her head down as though she were being careful not to trip in the day's dimming light. The trees here, in the fall, drop leaves and little seeds like small nuts, and Alice crunched her way through them as she hurried down the sidewalk. She was wearing tennis shoes and could feel the snap of the leaves and seeds under her thin soles. An airplane flew overhead, and for a moment she stopped and looked up, and we saw her face, and this was the odd thing: she wasn't sad. She had always thought her real life would begin in college, almost a year from now, but she was wrong. It was beginning now, with a hundred slips of paper in a cardboard box, with the strike of a match, a red dress she would leave hanging in her closet, the pearls like a line of bright, unblinking eyes.

She wore a sweater and jeans, and her long hair was down, hanging past her shoulders. She had the hair color so many girls would kill for, so brilliant and shiny that in the light it seemed to glow, and that's what we watched turn the corner—that bright head bobbing along past the houses of her neighbors—before she was gone. That's how long it took her to disappear: practically no time at all.

CHAPTER SEVEN

CARL MILLER DROPPED Alice off at the beach, the same one she and Susannah had grown up going to, whose sand probably still hid Coke bottle tops they had buried there, had used as decorations on the castles their little hands had built. It was where she had gotten her first kiss on the lips; it was where she had ducked under waves, headfirst; where she smoked her first cigarette, drank her first beer, coughing, sputtering on all three occasions, and now it was the only place she could think of going.

She had slept at Carl's, with Carl, the night before; he was the youngest child in a large family, the only one still living at home, and his parents never seemed to care what he did or where he went or who he had over to the house, something that always struck Alice as both sad and desirable. When she turned the corner of our street, it was Carl's green car, cheery and round, that waited to take her away to a different life. Or perhaps the life would be the same, and it would be she who was different. Or maybe she would go home tomorrow, back to her mother. She wasn't sure yet.

It was late afternoon, and the day was gray, though not rainy. (It never rained here.) The only moisture in the air was from the ocean, a feeling that made you think the ocean wasn't just ahead of you but behind and above you too. Gulls wheeled and dove, and in the distance she saw wet-suited surfers, shiny and sleek as otters. She rolled the window down. The air was briny. It was quiet.

"I'm just supposed to let you out?" asked Carl. He was looking at the thin clouds rolling in, as though they were a kind of threat to the girl in his passenger seat.

"Yep," said Alice. "Thanks again. I appreciate your help." Her hand was already on the door handle, the small overnight bag on her lap. "Good-bye," she said. But then she reached over and kissed him. His mouth tasted like orange juice, and she thought of him standing in the kitchen that morning before they left his house, tipping the carton right into his mouth, a bright and sunny orange box. He had offered it to her next; no, thank you, she had said.

She shut the car door and walked toward the water, slipping her shoes off as she went. She held them by the laces, let them dangle against her leg. When she looked back over her shoulder, the little green car was gone.

Alice picked a place to stop and sat there for a while, looking out at the ocean, but for all the times she had been at the beach, all the life it represented for her, it wasn't a place that calmed her. It did not inspire her to think deeply or poetically. Until this moment, from the time she felt Ben press the matchbook in her hand to the kiss she gave her mother on her way out the door, everything had been clear and easy, each decision unrolling before her like a ribbon.

But now the roar of the ocean was a sound she couldn't tune out, like the breath of an enormous creature, slow and full. When Carl Miller had left, it had surprised her a bit, even though she told him to. She was too close to home not to feel a sudden urge to go back. Her mother would wrap her arms around her.

Alice sat there for a while, but soon she stood up, brushed the sand from the seat of her pants, and walked back up the beach to the line of shops and restaurants that overlooked it. Coffee. That was something she could do. Her mother kept cash hidden in various places all over the house—behind a picture frame on her bedside table, in between pages of *Great Expectations*, in other strange places—and Alice had taken the bills that were under a bag of rice in the pantry.

She unzipped her bag and dug around for the money, but her fingers kept finding clothes, underwear, toiletries thrown loose among them. She'd been able to fit a lot into the bag, and it was now fat and round, like some kind of featureless head. She dropped to her knees on the sidewalk outside a diner, pushed her hands deeper into the bag. The beach was beginning to wake up. People strolled around her, like she was a rock in the middle of a stream.

"Hey," she heard someone say, and she scooted to the side without looking up, trying to get out of the way.

"Hey," said the voice again.

It was one she knew. She looked up. That ribbon that had begun unrolling last night—red, she pictured it, and glossy—unfurled farther, because standing in front of her was the man.

"Hi," she said. Surprised but not surprised.

"I have something for you," the man said.

She was still on the sidewalk, knees bent like she was praying, and he stood over her. The first time she looked at him, outside her mother's house, she'd taken in each piece of him separately: the bag that held the camera, those same brown boots, long denim legs, tight in the thighs; and she thought she could see the shelf of his quadriceps; hair the color of the armoire in her mother's bedroom and as thick and dark and heavy as it, too, like she could wander into it and pull the doors shut behind her. Thumbs hidden, tucked away into his pockets, surprisingly delicate fingers on display: she wondered if he played the piano.

The second time she looked at him, she drank him in all at once.

"How'd you find me?" she said. He didn't put out a hand to help her up, and so she stood up by herself, like a gangly foal, shoving the items she'd removed back into the bag. When she straightened up, she realized he was shorter than she remembered, only a few inches taller than her. She slouched a little, not wanting him to feel embarrassed.

(When we imagine him striding down our street, he's tall in our memories too. "It could have been a different guy," Bev's husband, Todd, says one morning over coffee. Bev shakes her head, remembering how she saw him through the window months ago, the sensation of seeing him seeing her. Dark hair, the beard of a prophet, but his eyes were a light and icy blue, the color of winter in places that knew real cold. "No," she says. "It was the same one. Has to be." She's struck by an urge to move, to act. She stands up. "Hold the baby for a second," she says to her husband, and he obeys, but the little girl looks unnatural there in his arms, even though he loves her, rubbing his nose against her tiny one. "Never mind," she says. She takes the baby back.)

On the sidewalk outside the diner, someone bumped into Alice, and she took a stutter step closer. "Sorry!" the person called.

"It's fine," said Alice quietly. She could have been saying it to anyone.

"I didn't have to find you," the man said. His voice was friendly, confident, but Alice noticed that he didn't blink. In novels she read, people's eyes were always flashing, but she'd never been able to picture it until now. "Finding means I was looking, and looking means something is lost," he continued. "And you weren't lost, were you?"

"No," she said.

"Right," said the man. "So I knew you'd turn up if you were meant to, and here you are." He spread out his arms to show her where she was, and she looked too. A place teeming with life in every corner, deep in the sand, in the layers of ocean, animals she couldn't name, couldn't imagine, in the sky and carried on the wind, and passing her on the side-walk, passing them on the sidewalk, because they were now a sudden world of two. How giant it all was, and she'd never known.

"I've been coming here since I was a little girl," she said. "Did you know that too?"

"What do you think?" he said and laughed, a happy mod-esty to his tone. The easiness of it made her laugh too.

"I don't believe in magic," she said, "or mind reading or fortune-telling, if that's what you're implying." Her voice was low, teasing, the kind of alto that Susannah had hoped hers would be, Susannah who the night before had gone to the Lange home, knocked on the door, and asked, "Is Alice home?" Mrs. Lange paused, looked past Susannah, and said, "I thought she was with you."

"But you'd believe the truth when you saw it," he said. "When you came face-to-face with it. I can tell. Whatever that truth might be."

"I think so," she said.

"I'm never wrong about people," the man said. A smile full of well-shaped teeth. Alice imagined herself reaching out, a finger running down the line of them, up and over the peaks of their sharp points.

"Let's go," he said, already taking a step backward, his shoulders threatening to turn and steer his body away from her.

"Is the thing you have for me the picture of me?" Alice asked.

He grinned. "I've got so much more than that for you."

Another step backward, another hint of a turn, the prom- ise he would disappear again. He would go with her, without her, but he would go. "It's in my truck," he said. "I didn't want it to get bent. Come on. Let's get out of here."

"Okay," said Alice.

"Okay," he said. But she didn't follow right behind him when he finally turned, and we know how close she was to staying behind and letting him walk away.

(We taught Alice Lange, all of the children, to be careful. Don't talk to bad people, don't go anywhere with bad men. This was the mistake Rachel Granger must have made.)

"Are you good?" Alice asked the man. "A good person."

"It's hard to say for sure," he called over his shoulder, "but I'm going to go with yes."

"Fair enough," said Alice.

"It's the truth," he said, turning to look back at her, "and that's all I've got. But what else does a person need, really?"

"Nothing," said Alice. And so she followed him past the diner where she never got her coffee, past couples and families, past surfers and seagulls, under palm trees, under a sky that turned so blue it hurt her eyes, and instead she looked at the man's back as he led her away. But, we wish we could have told her, there are really so many other things a person needs too.

CHAPTER EIGHT

HIS FIRST NAME was Wesley. He didn't give her a last name. "Names are important," he told her. "You learn someone's name or you give someone a name—that's power. You're connected. And when you know someone's name, you can't ever unknow it."

"I forget people's names all the time," Alice said.

"Then you didn't really know their names in the first place," the man said. Wesley. "Not their true ones."

They were in his car, a truck that rattled each time he accelerated, but he hadn't said where they were going. Alice didn't mind.

"What's your true name?" she asked. "Is it Wesley?"

He glanced over at her and grinned. He was wearing sunglasses, and she couldn't see his eyes, so the action of smiling looked like it took up only half his face; the rest of it seemed untouched. "I guess you'll have to wait and see," he said, looking back to the road.

Alice held the photograph of herself in her lap. She kept

looking at it. "Fucking beautiful," Wesley said when he noticed her peeking down at it.

And it was. She was. She knew she was a pretty girl, and photographs had shown that all her life, but in this one, with her solemn face, serious eyes, she looked like something lovely and strong and ancient, like she had existed for a million years and would exist a million more, untroubled by the ways of mortals. Unknown to them, unknown by them, recognized only by this man with the camera. Wesley.

They were on the freeway, heading in the general direction of her town, and Alice suddenly wondered then if he was taking her home, if he would pull up to her house, the guts of the seedlings she had crushed underfoot still spattered on the sidewalk, her mother in the kitchen. The green sign advertising the exit for the neighborhood was in the distance, and everything around her, the billboards, the ridge of mountains, the restaurants and stores, was familiar. Here they came, now, closer and closer, and he changed lanes. One lane further to the right.

"Some people drive like assholes," he said, and the truck rattled again as he passed a car and moved back to the middle lane.

The exit was behind them, and Alice felt relief blooming inside her, taking up her insides until she felt full, happy. "Do I have a true name?" she asked.

"Of course," he said. "I don't know what it is yet. I have to see it on you, in you. I'm not sure, I'll just know it when I see it."

"I like that," said Alice. "My mom's name is Martha. My father is Edward. Was Edward. He died." She looked at him to see if she had volunteered too much. "What do you think?" she said quickly. "True names, yes or no?"

"Can't say," he said. "I don't know them."

"What about your parents?" she asked.

"What about them?"

His voice sounded casual, but Alice, the perceptive girl, could hear the effort in it.

"What are their true names?" she said.

Wesley didn't look at her. He watched the road, moved his right hand off the steering wheel, kept the left loosely on the top, so lightly that if they had to swerve suddenly, Alice thought there would be no way he could save them. The fingers of his right hand picked blindly at a seam on the bench seat of the truck. "My mother didn't have one," he said. "Because she wasn't a true person. She didn't deserve to have any name at all."

"Oh," said Alice. "I'm sorry. We don't have to talk about it."

"No," said Wesley. "It's okay." He took a deep breath. "I don't know my father's name," he said, "because I don't know who my father is. He could be anyone." He looked out his window at a blue car pacing them in the left-hand lane. "It could be that guy, for all I know." Alice leaned forward to see the driver of the other car, a black man. He wore a hat and had both hands on the steering wheel. He was singing along to the radio.

"I don't think it's him," said Alice.

Wesley laughed. "Probably not," he said. "But I know that guy as well as I know my real father."

"Maybe it's better not to know," Alice said. "You know?"

"Yeah," Wesley said. "Maybe."

He held the steering wheel with the pads of his fingers, his other hand still picking, picking, picking at a loose thread. Alice reached over, put her hand on top of his, settled those moving fingers.

Look, she thought, look at what I'm doing.

They exited the freeway half an hour later, turning right at a stoplight onto a road Alice had never traveled before, and drove up into the hills, green brush and brown stone out the windows, spiny cacti potted in terra-cotta planters, and houses that looked small until Alice saw them from the side, and noticed how languidly they sprawled. On one street they turned onto, parked cars lined both sides, and only here Wesley began to slow down. "Do you live here?" she asked him. By now the afternoon had grown late and golden, and with each passing minute, Alice was getting farther and farther away from us.

(On Saturday night, Mrs. Lange had called the police. We urged her to when she and Susannah, who had come looking for Alice, arrived on our doorsteps, knocking and asking first if Alice happened to be there by any chance, then asking when we had last seen Alice, asking if we had any idea of where she could be. We told her we would ask our children, Alice's peers but also our little ones, our girls who studied Alice like a blueprint for the kind of woman they would someday be, our boys who studied Alice for reasons they couldn't quite articulate. But they said they hadn't seen her. I dreamed about her, Billy said and blushed. That doesn't count, said his mother.

Report her missing, we told Mrs. Lange. But when the police arrived at the Lange home, and Mrs. Lange and Susannah showed them Alice's room, they saw it was clear Alice had left of her own volition. Her schoolbooks were stacked neatly on her desk. Her closet was missing clothes; the bathroom was missing her toothbrush, her deodorant, a hairbrush.

The policemen asked Mrs. Lange if Alice had any of her own money, or if perhaps she might have taken some from her mother to purchase bus fare, gas money, a plane ticket? "Alice would never," said Mrs. Lange. But she would, thought Susannah, and I would, too, and I would have if I had known Alice was going. Susannah felt her initial fear melt away as anger began to burn inside her. Alice had left. She hadn't been kidnapped. She was living. It was just that she was doing that living somewhere else, not here, not with her mother, not with Susannah.

"Mrs. Lange," Susannah said, her voice tight. "I have to get ready for the homecoming dance. I have to figure out a new plan."

But Mrs. Lange didn't answer. She was shaking her head at the policemen, even though they had asked no additional questions, as if she were anticipating the answer she would continue to give. No. Not Alice. Not Alice. No. So Susannah excused herself and went home. "Alice ran away," she told her mother.

"She'll be back," her mother said, and when Susannah started to cry, she took her in her arms and pressed her cheek to the top of her daughter's head. "She'll be back. Don't be sad," she said, though it wasn't often she got to hold her child like this anymore, and yes, she didn't want her to be sad, but she did want to luxuriate in the feeling of being needed. And Susannah, in an act of grace, let her mother think the tears she cried were the sad kind instead of the angry, jealous kind.

"Can you check any places where you might have cash lying around, please, Mrs. Lange?" one of the men asked. "Your purse? A safe?"

"Oh," said Alice's mother, and she took them around to her hiding places—the book, the picture, the bag of rice in the pantry. The money was gone.

"I'm sorry," the policeman said. "This is both good news and bad news. The good news is it's unlikely she's been kidnapped."

"Rachel Granger," said Mrs. Lange.

"Alice isn't Rachel," the policeman said. "This is a different case."

Mrs. Lange closed her eyes, wishing for a moment of oblivion, but when she did, all she could see was her daughter. "What's the bad news?" she asked. "You said there was good news and bad news."

"Oh," said the officer, looking uncomfortable. "She must have wanted to leave, and she did."

A difference, then: Rachel was trying only to get home, and Alice was trying to leave it.)

"We're just stopping by," Wesley told Alice as he parked behind a white convertible. "There's a party." He got out of the truck and closed the door, and Alice followed behind him as he walked up to a white house that glowed in the day's last hours of sunlight. She glanced back at her mother's bag on the passenger seat and felt a sudden sadness and worry at leaving it behind, like the purse had feelings she would hurt by abandoning it, but Wesley, of course, had nothing, and she wanted to match his every move. "Am I dressed okay for this?" she asked Wesley, but he was opening the door—he didn't knock, here was a man who could cross any borders, any boundaries, confident in being welcomed—and he left it open for Alice without looking back. She shut it behind them.

Inside, people stood in little groups in the kitchen, leaning against counters, in the living room, near big windows that overlooked a pool and two strings of paper lanterns already glowing as the day waned. By the windows, a man was playing a guitar and singing, badly, Alice thought, but no one else seemed to care. Some of them had their eyes closed. Some danced. There was music coming from somewhere else, too, out of sight, and the combination of sounds disoriented her. The air smelled of smoke, cigarettes and weed and something unfamiliar, a thick sort of scent. The house was sparsely decorated, or, it occurred to her, maybe the owner had removed everything, anything breakable, before he opened his home to anyone else. To strangers! Because that's who Alice was now, a stranger, someone unknown. The idea of it was thrilling.

Here Wesley, a stranger to her, was not a stranger at all. Here people came up to him, smiling, shaking his hand, clapping him on the back, sidling up to him, touching his camera case with eager fingers. Men in jeans, in breezy shirts, women in dresses or bathing suits despite the fading daylight—and one woman wearing nothing at all, draped over a couch in an open, airy living room, a hand over her eyes. Two men, the only ones in suits, like businessmen, stood behind her. They held drinks and talked, as if this were a perfectly ordinary scene. Wesley saw Alice looking at this woman. "I took her photo once. And guess what?" he said. "She took her clothes off then too."

"Oh," said Alice. She looked at the woman more closely. Her body was fine, ordinary, but she was curious how Wesley saw it. "What did you do?"

Wesley laughed. "Took her picture," he said. "Are you asking if I fucked her?"

"I guess I am," said Alice.

"I did," said Wesley. "Does that make you uncomfortable?"

Alice considered this. "But you aren't anymore?" she asked. "Fucking her." (Already she sounds different. Already she has taken a piece of Wesley, eaten that piece like a little slice of cake, absorbed it into her body.)

"God, no," said Wesley. "Stay right there. The light. Look up."

Alice looked up, and a spear of light steeling in through the window shocked her eyes, but she lifted her chin until her eyes were in the shadow. This time, she let herself smile.

"A new muse?" asked a girl.

"Sadie," Wesley said. Alice's face burned; he had forgotten her name. Or maybe he had given her a new one already. Sadie Sadie Sadie. She imagined herself answering to it.

"I don't go by that anymore," the girl said.

"Too bad," said Wesley. "It suited you. This is Alice."

The girl turned to look at her. She looked to be a few years older than Alice, and wore her hair piled high on top of her head and heavy earrings that tugged and elongated her earlobes. Her lipstick was red, and when she smiled, Alice had the sensation of being bitten. "Hello," the girl said.

"Hello," said Alice, but Wesley put his arm around her waist and pulled her away.

"Let's go outside," Wesley said, then called over his shoulder, "Good-bye, Sadie."

"Everyone here wants you," Alice said as they stepped into the backyard. Wesley waved at people and said hello to the ones who approached him, but he didn't stop to talk. He led

Alice to the corner of the yard, a quiet place, away from the party. Someone jumped in the pool. Everyone cheered.

"They want me to take their picture," he said. "There's a difference. Everyone wants to see themselves how someone else sees them."

"Not me," said Alice. "I'm tired of seeing myself how other people see me."

"I know," said Wesley. "That's why I'm so attracted to you." He opened up his camera bag and pulled out a joint and a lighter. "Does this bother you?" he asked, holding it up between two pinched fingers.

"No," said Alice truthfully. (We aren't naïve. She was popular and friends with everyone. Besides, haven't we conducted various experiments at our parties, with our friends, in hotel rooms with our husbands? What's offensive is that the experience is wasted on the young, because really, what do they need to escape?)

"Good," he said. "I don't like prudes."

"Good thing I'm not one, then," Alice said, and they grinned at each other. He passed her the joint, and she took a hit, and they passed it back and forth and then to two others who came to join them, more strangers. But soon, Wesley said to them to just take it with them and go. "We want to be alone," he said. But as they walked away, he took their picture.

"I hate these fucking people," he said.

"Why?" asked Alice. It was night now, full fledged, dark blue, the paper lanterns like bright, glowing birds flying south for the winter. "Did you fuck that other girl too? Sadie."

He looked at Alice, blue eyes intense and hot. A man, not a boy like sweet Ben Austin or even like Carl Miller, and she wanted to reach out and touch him, reach beneath his shirt and feel the skin there. She tried to see him the way other people saw him, the man who could make their ordinary faces and bodies into art, into something eternal. But looking at him, she thought oh, how wrong they were. He himself was the eternal thing they sought. She scooted herself closer to him.

"I will never lie to you," he said.

"So you did," Alice said.

He nodded. "But she wasn't right," he said. "She couldn't see. You can see, though. Can't you? I don't want to be wrong again."

"Yes," said Alice.

He leaned toward her, and she leaned toward him and closed her eyes, ready to be kissed. Instead, he simply pressed his forehead against hers. She listened to his breathing, slowing hers to match it. His shirt was untucked from his jeans, and she touched its hem before she let her hand creep up and under to touch his skin. He flinched for a moment, as if her hand were cold, and she began to draw back when he trapped her hand with his, his on top of his shirt, hers underneath it, the thin fabric between them. He crawled his hand up her shirt, and she let his hand explore that hidden part of her body, and she shivered. "You and me," he said softly. "We aren't like these people. We see things they don't."

"How do you know?" she asked.

"Come on," he said. "We're at this party. Let's have some fun." He jumped up to his feet and pulled Alice with him, and she followed him, eating and drinking whatever he gave her—thick-skinned black olives, an oyster raw and cold, slipping down her throat, a flute of champagne she dropped when someone bumped into her; everyone cheered, and no one cleaned up the glass, which sparkled on the ground like ice. She smoked whatever he passed to her, too, until the night became a dream. The bright clothes of the girls looked like sunbursts, birds of paradise, slices of tropical fruit. Someone spilled red wine on Wesley's shirt, and he peeled it off and disappeared inside the house. While he was gone, Alice felt the party outside began to sag, that the conversations happening in his absence were all focused on ways to say his name, as if mentioning him would cause him to materialize. The man with the camera, who is he? Wesley. I know him, he took my picture. He brought me here, Alice said proudly. Lucky girl. Eyebrows raised. This was a thing about Wesley, Alice could already see; people looked at her and wondered who she was, what was special about her. Alice had noticed herself wondering the same thing when she watched him talk to other party guests. If he would give a piece of himself to these people, they must be worth it. Though he was nowhere in sight, she felt him inside her, expanding and taking up room in her heart, lungs, stomach. He emerged a few minutes later in only a long white tunic that went past his knees, and Alice said his name, just to hear it. "You look like Jesus," she said, touching his beard. She touched the lines around his mouth when he smiled, too, parentheses that separated his cheeks from the rest of his face.

"Maybe I am," he said. He grabbed her hand and twirled her. She wished she were wearing a skirt that spun out like flower petals.

Later Wesley ended up with the guitar the man in the living room had been playing poorly, and he sat on the edge of a pool chair and played and sang, and Alice was delighted. Even his fingers and hands were lovely to her. "Is there anything you can't do?" she asked.

"Math," he said, and Alice laughed.

"It's okay," she said. "I've always been good with numbers, so if you ever need someone to calculate anything, I'm your girl."

"My girl, huh?" Wesley said, grinning. Alice almost felt embarrassed, but she pushed that feeling away, emboldened by the drugs pumping through her body and the night air and the beautiful people everywhere and the company of Wesley. Already he was changing her, making her better, braver.

Wesley picked up his camera. "Watch this," he said. "It's like magic." He stood up and pointed his camera at a couple sitting on the edge of the pool, their feet in the water and heads close together. "Hey," Wesley called, and they turned around, ready, Alice could see, to be annoyed, but when they saw it was Wesley, they smiled. The woman leaned into the man; the man put his arm around her, and she looked up at him in an admiring way, eyes wide under thick lashes, lips parted. But from where she stood, Alice could see what the man with his feet in the pool could not—maybe the woman with him truly did love him, but in this moment, she was role-playing a woman in love. I am in love, the woman was saying, and this is how I show it. This is how I want it to be reflected.

Around them people posed and blinked at the flash of the camera in the dark, turning their faces away. "It's good," he said. "To have them flinching, looking away in the photos." Alice loved to watch him turn his camera on them; it seemed to her that they gave him so little, and he took those paltry offerings and transformed them into something profound.

Wesley and Alice ended up in the pool, the Jesus tunic see-through and plastered to his body, Alice only in her bra and underwear. She shivered in the cool night air when they got out. Someone wrapped them in a towel and pushed them inside the house, Alice slipping a little on the tile floor, and in what she supposed was a guest room, Wesley found his original clothes, the shirt with the red wine stain. He had somehow remembered to grab her jeans and shirt from beside the pool, and she peeled off her wet undergarments, thinking of the nude woman on the couch. She had made her body a work of art for the public to consume, and Alice could do the same, but only for Wesley. He picked her up and dropped her, laughing, on the bed, and she expected that then they would make love, but instead he took her feet and slid them into the jeans. He shimmied them up her body. He buttoned them. He sat her up and pulled her shirt on over her head. He turned out the lights. He climbed into bed next to her. Alice waited, breathless.

"Let's get some sleep," he said. "Tomorrow everything begins."

Alice stared at the ceiling and felt grateful for the dark because her face grew hot. She told herself not to feel hurt that he didn't seem to want her because surely he did, she was the one we all wanted, and she needed to trust that he had a plan. "You didn't ever tell me why you hate those people," she said.

In the dark, he sighed. "They're not living in the now," he said. "Do you know what I mean? They're always thinking about the past or the future. When they let me take their picture, I can see them thinking about how one day in the future, they'll look back at this moment, taken in the past, saved for the future. But they're never really seeing anything. They're not here in the now. They won't let themselves feel anything. They're blind people."

Alice thought about this. She thought about the couple with their feet in the pool. The woman on the couch, Sadie with the red lips. She thought about herself, and then she thought about us, too, how we had shaped her. "Maybe it isn't their fault," she said. "Maybe it's the world's fault."

"Someday," said Wesley, "the world is going to burn, and I'm going to let it."

"Don't let me burn with it," Alice said flippantly. She was beginning to get sleepy.

"Never," Wesley said.

A sign, Alice thought, the fire, and then sleep pulled her under while outside the party burned on, its own kind of fire. (Miles away, we wondered what had become of Alice Lange, and her mother, alone in the house she had shared with her husband and then with her daughter and now with no one, wept until her insides felt empty, as though there were a fire within her, too, burning her from the inside out until everything was gone, an unquenchable flame her longing could never put out.)

When Alice awoke, disoriented and with an aching head, late morning light was streaming in through a window. Wesley was not in the room with her. Her bra and panties, which had been lying on the floor, were still damp, and she folded them both and tucked them into the crease of her underarm. She crossed her arms over her chest to hide her nipples, which she knew would be visible under her shirt, and stepped out of the room to look for Wesley.

She found him alone in the kitchen, eating a banana. "Where is everyone?" Alice asked.

"Oh, they're in the various parts of the house," he said. "And outside passed out on the grass. We were lucky we snagged a room. Do you want a banana?"

"Yes," said Alice, thinking, truly, for the first time of her mother, the glistening eggs, the berries in the crystal bowl. What was her mother eating? Was she worried about Alice? (Nothing. Yes.)

"What's under your arm?" asked Wesley.

"Oh," said Alice. She pulled out the small pink square of her panties and the folded-over bra and put them on the kitchen counter. Wesley laughed. "They're still wet," she said.

"That's the sign of a good night," he said. "Any night you end up swimming in your underwear is a good one."

Before this moment, as she'd wandered through the house looking for Wesley, Alice had prepared herself to find a diminished version of him, one that was not as handsome, not as clever, not as magical as the man whose image she was carrying in her head. She had told herself that maybe she would ask him for a ride to the bus station, and they would part ways. They had shared a perfect night, and that would be the end of it. What could be more sophisticated, more grown-up than that? But now, encountering him again, the man of him, the hunger in his light eyes and white teeth, Alice knew she would go anywhere with him. She walked over to him, took the half-eaten banana out of his hand, and kissed him. His hands tangled in her hair as he kissed her back. He smelled like chlorine, a scent she had always loved because it reminded her of sunshine, summertime, and then beneath that there was a heavier and warmer scent, like something that didn't exist in any physical form and only emanated from this one specific person. This, she thought, was the way Wesley smelled. It made her giddy. When he pulled back, he grinned. "Let's get the fuck out of here," he said. "You can bring your banana with you."

Outside, the air was cool. A man in running clothes jogged

by. A woman was parking her car in the driveway across the street. How could anyone be doing anything so ordinary, Alice thought, when a person like Wesley existed in the world? "Wait," Alice said, "shouldn't we thank the host? Or tell him good-bye?"

"The host?" Wesley asked, unlocking the door to his truck and swinging it open. "I don't even know whose house this is." He cranked the window down and slapped the side of the truck. "Let's go," he said.

Alice ran around to the other side and slid herself in. There sat her bag, safe and sound, and the photo where she'd left it on the dashboard, her eyes staring straight up at the roof of the truck.

"Let's go, then," she said.

CHAPTER NINE

THEY STOPPED FOR burgers and fries, and Wesley got a milkshake, and he took pictures of Alice drinking it. After lunch, he pulled up beside a park in a hamlet outside the city, and Alice thought maybe he would photograph her there, too, so she lingered beside beautiful things until Wesley grabbed her by the wrist—not too hard, just enough to make her pay attention—and said, "Don't." Alice's stomach turned, but she said nothing in response. She remembered the couple at the pool with their feet in the water, how the woman's true, natural self had become hidden behind the artifice Wesley's camera created. She vowed to herself she would not do that again. She would be authentic, the way Wesley liked her. Hadn't she enough of posturing and posing? Hadn't she left that behind with us?

So they walked in the park, down shadowy, lonely paths and talked—or Alice talked, and Wesley kept his eyes on her and listened, all about her life, what it had been and what she longed for it to be, about the fire she'd started. "A metaphor," said Wesley.

"No," she said. "A real one." He raised his eyebrows and laughed long and loud when Alice nodded.

"Tell me all about that," he said, so she did.

Finally, they drove long enough that Alice began to wonder if they were ever going home, to Wesley's home, but then he said, "We're not far from the house now. I just wanted to enjoy you and for you to enjoy me, and I felt like I needed to stop here, for a little while. But we're almost there."

They passed the university where Alice's mother had encouraged her to apply. The streets they turned down to get there were narrow, with cars parked tightly on each side so that the truck had to slow to a creep, as though it were sucking itself in, making itself smaller to squeeze through.

Alice never wanted to go to this school. It felt too expected, too predictable for a girl like her. The trees that grew up next to the buildings were too much like the ones that shaded our yards, our sidewalks; the smell of the air, the feel of it on her shoulders and her face—that, too, was familiar. "Do you go to school here?" she asked. She realized that she didn't know how old he was.

(Those of us who had seen him on our street in his boots, with his beard, the green canvas jacket, we would have told her that he was thirty, if he was a day.)

"Definitely not," Wesley said. "I'm not an institution kind of guy, if you know what I mean."

"Yeah," said Alice, "I do." But she had always pictured herself in one institution after another: school, more school. Marriage, too, she imagined Wesley pointing out. That was an institution, wasn't it? But those were prisons, weren't they?

Just ways to define people, borders to keep them locked in, trapped.

(Not trapped, we would tell her. Safe.)

"But we aren't going here," said Wesley. "Where we're going is close by."

They turned a corner, and Alice could see the campus now, unfolding like a page from a pop-up book, its buildings like fairy-tale castles with red roofs instead of turrets. Instead of stacked gray stones, their walls were smooth and white as pearls, as bones. "Pretty," Alice said. Wesley had told her to roll down her window, and she stuck out a hand now, like she could shrink the buildings down into dormitories and cafés and libraries and hold them in her palm, create a tiny world to rule. A sorcerer, a magic girl. "Is it your house we're going to later?" she asked Wesley.

"Sort of."

"Roommates?" Alice asked.

"Sort of," he said again.

(All kinds of gentlemen have brought us home in our day. Nice ones, bad ones, handsome ones, ugly ones. We've slept with them, we've slept beside them. We've left their houses early in the morning and called it nighttime so that we could tell our sisters and roommates of our own that we did not sleep over. But now when the gentlemen bring us home, they bring us home as wives. Their homes are our homes too. We sleep beneath our quilts, the ones our mothers bought us as wedding gifts. When we wake there now in the darkness of morning, we know where the bathroom is, where the switch is for the lamp on the bedside table. We do not hesitate to turn it on because we aren't worried about waking up our men, not anymore, because we know them. It is a navigable land. The

terrain is easy. Our bodies know it well. It is a wonderful thing
to know and to be known.)

Thinking of roommates, sort-of roommates even, Alice
began to feel nervous. She hadn't so far, strolling in the park
with Wesley, kissing Wesley, who was a good person, who
she had met, in fact, in her very own neighborhood. And as
long as they were in Wesley's truck, sitting on this bench seat,
Alice was in a liminal sort of place, a capsule shuttling them
from her world to his, and as such it belonged to no one. But
a house, a home: there was no question. That belonged to
someone.

Two trees, tall and straight with branches and leaves that
cascaded down and then flipped out at the end, like a series of
witches' hats stacked one on top of the other, stood in front of
the house where Wesley finally stopped. The house was small
and blue with trim in a shade of white Alice could tell was
meant to be creamy but appeared dingy, the matted color of
a sheep's wool. There was a porch that ran the short width
of the house, two wooden beams standing as columns, also
painted white, supporting the outcropping of roof. When Alice shifted in her seat, trying to get a better view, she saw a
small cactus in a terra-cotta pot by the front door. Because at
least when it came to manners (the rest, we'd now say, though
never to Mrs. Lange, is up for debate) Alice was raised right,
she said, "What a lovely home." She thought someone might
come to the door, the roommate, sort of, but no one did. "I
can carry my bag," Alice said, though Wesley had not offered
to take it for her. He stepped out of the truck and slammed
the door. Alice slid out and closed hers quietly, followed him
up the steps (also painted dreary white, cracked and chipping)
to the house, behind him as he opened the door, which was

unlocked. A dog barked from next door, and Wesley rolled his eyes. "I'd kill that animal if I could," he said. Alice laughed.

The lights were off inside, with the only brightness coming in from the windows, but then he flipped a switch, and a light came on overhead. There were plants everywhere, and she was surprised because Wesley didn't seem like the kind of man to be overly tender with living things. But there was ivy creeping out of a pot and down a bookcase, a plant with sharp leaves like razor tongues, a cluster of small, fat-leafed succulents sitting on a table beneath a window in a puddle of sun. A red rug on the floor, and even that had vines, green and snaking across the tapestry. When Wesley walked across it, Alice imagined him crushing a serpent beneath the heel of his boot.

"Janie?" he called. He sounded weary, the way her mother sounded when she came from the grocery store, arms bent and weighed down with shopping bags. She felt concerned he was weary because of her for some reason. He sank into a leather armchair. There was only the one chair and a sofa perpendicular beside it, the color of a tangerine, and Alice thought of Carl Miller yesterday morning, his wide hand covering the bright orange on the carton. The same wide hand touching her body, her face. How far away she was now from him, from all of them, from us.

Stretched out across the sofa was a guitar. Alice didn't want to move it, so she looked around. On the walls were photographs, taken by Wesley, she presumed, pinned up with thumbtacks. Most of them were of different women. Or was it the same woman over and over? Alice couldn't tell. On the floor, lined along the baseboards and leaning against each other, were paintings, but none of them depicted people, instead lightning bolts and storms of swirling color. Some of the canvases were completely covered, while others had only a few brushstrokes across the white. One was black, only black. She wondered if they were good and guessed they were.

"Janie?" Wesley said again, this time tilting his head back so that his voice carried. "Apple?"

"Is that a dog?" Alice asked.

"Is what a dog?" he said.

"Apple," Alice said, but he didn't answer. He stood up and crossed the small living room to a hallway, and Alice, unsure what to do—she still hadn't sat down anywhere—followed him to a closed door. He didn't knock but opened the door quietly and went inside the room. Alice took another step forward, but stayed just inside the doorway.

There was a bed in the middle of the room with a mismatched end table on each side, and a quilt patterned in a jumble of colors at its foot. On the bed she saw two girls sleeping, one on her back, her forearm thrown over her eyes and her hand on her stomach. The second girl slept on her side, curled up and small, like the shell of a snail, her forehead touching the first girl's shoulder. They both wore dresses, but on the second girl the dress was askew, and hiked up high enough that Alice could see a smirking curve of cheek. Dark hair on both girls, pink skin on both. They looked, to Alice, like the same person.

"Hey," said Wesley softly. He walked closer to the bed and nudged the corner of the mattress with his knee. "Wake up," he said. "I brought someone."

The girls stirred, and even this seemed choreographed, that they moved together or in response to each other, sitting up and scooting over and pulling at clothes. Hands in hair, hands rubbing at eyes. Mouths opening and almost forming words, almost smiling. Eyes: they saw Wesley, they saw Alice. They didn't seem surprised by either.

"Hi, Wesley," one of the girls finally said.

"I was so tired," the other girl said. "I couldn't stay awake."

Roused from their sleep, they didn't look exactly alike. Sisters, cousins. An actress in a film and the real-life girl she was cast to play. More similar than different. And young, Alice thought. Her age or close to it.

(We say, her age or close to it, meaning far away from this man's. Pay attention, we would tell her. Look around you!)

"Alice," Wesley said, "this is Janie." The one Alice thought of as the second girl lifted her hand and waved. "And this," he said, "is Apple."

Apple was the prettier of the two, with thick, shiny hair and wide eyes that would make beady-eyed Charlotte Price jealous. She didn't wave or say hello when Wesley introduced her, and Alice felt like the girls were examining her, and she realized, again, how completely out of place she was. The three dark heads of Janie, Apple, and Wesley, the beautiful bodies they seemed to share. And then there was Alice, bright haired and alien and wholly apart. Apple seemed to be waiting for her to speak.

"I thought you might be a dog," Alice said finally.

"Why?" asked Apple, scrunching her nose.

"I've just never met someone named Apple," Alice said. "It was surprising."

"But you've met a dog named Apple?" she asked. Beside her, Janie laughed.

"No," said Alice. She tried to laugh, too, but it came out higher than her normal laugh, and she was horrified with herself. (We cringe here, to think of our girl like this, uncomfortable and awkward, practically kneeling before these strange young women.)

"I like it," she tried again. "It's different. Everyone I know has an aunt named Alice. It's very boring."

"I actually do have an aunt named Alice," Janie said. "She always smells like boiled eggs." Janie tucked her hair behind her ears, and Alice could see they stuck out a bit, and her chin was a sharp little point, like an arrowhead. Unable to stop herself, Alice began mentally creating the hierarchy of the girls in the house: Apple was at the top, Janie was below her. Alice was nowhere, at least for now.

"Well, I had nothing to do with the naming," Apple said, shrugging.

"You should compliment Wesley," Janie said. He had moved farther into the room and was standing beside her now, and she moved so she could throw her slender arm around his waist. Alice tried not to look. "He's the one who named her Apple," Janie said.

Alice looked now at Wesley, who shrugged, still ensnared by Janie's arm. "Oh, so it's a nickname," she said. Apple did have pretty cheeks, round and pink. Like apples.

"Not really," said Apple. "It's just who I am."

"It's her true name," Wesley said, disentangling himself from Janie and stepping back toward Alice. Alice turned to him, like the fat-leafed plants in the living room growing to the window, reaching for the light. She thought of the girl at the party, Sadie. *I don't go by that anymore*, she'd told Wesley.

"I could see it in her right away," he said. "When I met her, I knew her original name wasn't right, and so when I figured it out, I told her. When you know something is true, you share it."

"What's your real name?" Alice asked. "Your old name, I mean."

"Betsy," said Apple, giving a thumbs-down. "But good old Betsy's dead now."

"RIP Betsy," Janie said. She put her hands together in solemn prayer and rolled her eyes to the ceiling, but Alice noticed her look down again, quickly, over at Wesley, like she wanted him to approve of her joke and laugh. But he did not, and Alice felt strangely reassured. These girls weren't infallible. They could be embarrassed too. She wanted to go over and squeeze Janie's shoulder, but she knew she shouldn't, so she smiled at her instead. Janie smiled back.

"Okay," said Wesley, turning away from the other girls even as he addressed them. "Get up. Kathryn's going to be home soon, and you need to make dinner."

"There's no food. We couldn't go to the store," Janie said. She pulled her legs up and folded them underneath herself. "We didn't have any money."

"Find a way to get some," Wesley said, heading back again to Alice, as if to signal the conversation was over.

"You might not like the way we find it," said Apple. She was out of bed now, on the side opposite Wesley. She pulled up the quilt and smoothed it out, flicking its top edge against Janie's toes until she, too, got out of the bed.

"I'm not so small minded," Wesley said. "Do what you need to do."

"I have money," Alice offered. "Not very much, but a little." She had paid for the burgers and milkshake earlier because it seemed like the right thing to do—weren't artists always broke?—and sharing it with the girls seemed right too.

"We'll take it," said Janie. She leaned on a dresser pushed

up against the wall and held her hand out to Alice, who still lingered in the doorway.

"Honestly," said Apple, looking across the room at Wesley, "there's enough food for dinner. She's exaggerating. We'll get something together."

Wesley nodded. "Good," he said. "And Alice, there might be a time we ask you for money, but not now. Tonight you're our guest. You'll stay for dinner, right?"

"Of course," said Alice. "Thank you. But are you sure about the money? I don't mind contributing." Apple was squeezing past her now, arms up and turning to the side so she was as slight as a playing card, and Alice stepped out of her way, farther into the bedroom. Closer to Wesley. He turned so they were facing only each other.

"Yes," he said in a low voice. It sounded private, delicious. "I'm positive."

"She's just staying for dinner?" asked Apple. She was in the doorway now, one hand resting on the jamb. Her whole body was a pause.

"You're welcome as long as you like, of course," he said to Alice, without looking at Apple. "We have room for you."

"Thank you," said Alice. So close to him, this strange man who had chosen her, she felt electric. Beneath that she felt the sting of uncertainty, the warmth of relief. She had planned on staying with Wesley, had assumed that since he brought her here, he was taking care of her, but maybe it hadn't been as much of a guarantee as she thought. Maybe he had only just now decided. She would be good and kind and open minded. She wouldn't ask questions about their names. She would give them money if they needed it. She would sleep on the floor.

"Help us with dinner," Apple commanded, lingering still in the doorway. "Are you a good cook?"

"Apple," said Wesley, now looking past Alice to Apple, "she's a guest. I'm going to take her."

"Take her where?" asked Apple. "I bet I can guess."

"Somewhere else," Wesley said. His voice crackled, and Alice felt glad she hadn't been the one to annoy him. "You need to calm down," he told Apple.

"I'm very calm," she said. "Come on, Janie," she called over her shoulder as she headed down the hallway.

Janie touched each of them on her way out, fingertips light as cat feet on Alice's shoulder. "Come on," said Wesley after they left. "I want to show you something."

"An adventure," said Alice.

"Exactly right," he said. "It always is around here."

CHAPTER TEN

WE MISSED ALICE right away. There are some people in our lives whose absence might go unnoticed
for days: the freckled woman who bagged groceries at the
store, the crossing guard at the intersection by the elementary
school. But not noticing that Alice was gone—it would be
like walking outside and not noticing that all the trees had
disappeared, leaving our world without respite from the sun,
without clean air to breathe, without beauty. She was special,
yes, but she also made everyone around her special too. And
it wasn't simply that we felt special. We became special. We
were transformed.

But we did miss her in practical ways too. When April
needed a babysitter one evening, she got as far as picking up
the phone to call the Langes' before she remembered that Alice wasn't there. She had to call three other mothers before
she found the name of a sophomore girl she might use instead.
"Where's Alice?" asked Billy. "Why can't Alice watch me?"

"She's not home, honey," April told him. When he asked

her when she would be back, April felt overwhelmingly sad, not just because Alice was gone but because she didn't want to have to tell her child something that might frighten him—that people could leave and never come back—or worse, give him ideas.

But our lives rolled on without her, starting right away, mere hours after she left, though most of us only learned she was gone for good after Mrs. Lange talked to the police. But we assumed Alice would be back, that she would come to her senses quickly and return; she was always a rational girl, and she had no reason to leave, especially not on the night of the homecoming dance.

When the other girls got ready in their bedrooms, they dressed partly for themselves, partly for their dates, and partly to gain Alice's approval, and when she was missing from the dark, streamer-filled gym, they noticed. They looked for Susannah to give them an explanation, but she wasn't there either. They did, however, find Millie, wearing a blue dress that hid her knobby knees and a smug look on her face. "She probably got arrested," Millie said, "for burning down the float. Maybe they can find handcuffs to match her crown."

"We don't know for sure that's what happened," said a girl named Ruth, a friend of Alice's.

"Will she still win?" asked another friend.

"Probably," said Millie, though she hoped she wouldn't, that Alice would not only be expelled from our world but also denied the thing we'd all but given her.

In fact, when Camille Humphrey was crowned queen at the dance, everyone was still confused as to whether she'd actually won, or if she was the runner-up and named the winner by default. Camille, too, wore a pink dress, with silver shoes she picked because they reminded her of moonlight, and she felt self-conscious in their high heels, rhythmically stepping back and forth with Phillip Turner, the king, as everyone watched. She was cute, sweet, well liked, she knew that. But she was the kind of efficient, responsible girl who was elected student council secretary, not homecoming queen, and she felt like the weight of everyone's gaze would crush her. When the song was over, she parted quickly from Phillip and put the crown next to her clutch on an aluminum folding chair against the gym's wall. "It was giving me a headache," she said, rubbing her temples. "I didn't know it would be so tight."

CHAPTER ELEVEN

WHEN WESLEY TOOK her to the college, the sun was setting, and around them everything was glowing amber, honey, though in some pockets, the light was already gone. In those places, things were going gray. They walked side by side, but didn't hold hands or touch at all, and as they matched each other's stride, they blended in with the students around them.

But where the other men and women carried bags and books and briefcases, Wesley and Alice's arms were empty. She had left her bulging leather bag on the orange couch in the living room, beside the guitar. She wondered if she should have hidden it or at least left it somewhere inconspicuous, but maybe that would have seemed rude. And besides that, no one had touched the guitar. Maybe the guitar was a special thing only for Wesley, like his camera. Before they left, she'd seen Janie sitting next to it, but giving it a wide berth, like it was another person.

"Here," Wesley said. Before them, tall and long with

white columns across the front, rose a white building, its red-brown roof the color of clay. "Come on," he said and pulled her up the steps. Inside, it all seemed brown to Alice: the tables and chairs and dim lights, spines of books, students in sweaters, standing up and pushing in chairs, swinging bags over their shoulders, walking out as Alice and Wesley entered.

"The library," Alice said, remembering, suddenly, standing here two years ago with Susannah and their mothers, visiting the campus for a statewide high school debate competition. Here's where you'll study, girls, her mother had said. And Susannah's mother had said, laughing, Here? You won't meet your husband in the library, will you? The girls had looked. The boys sitting at the tables, books open in front of them, had seemed to them like men. Yes, they had thought, they could meet their husbands here.

"This isn't the place," Wesley said. "Come on." She followed him up a curving staircase, two flights, down a hall, past classrooms with their doors closed. They didn't see another person.

"Where is everyone?" she asked.

"Probably dinner," he said.

"Oh," said Alice. She had forgotten there were days and hours, that she had been gone and time existed even when she wasn't following its patterns and routines the way she always had. Underneath her feet there was carpet—institutional, she thought, and the color of oatmeal. She watched Wesley's feet move across it in his brown boots. "This is it," she heard him say, and she looked up. He took a key out of his jacket pocket—Was he a custodian, then? Or a thief?—and twisted it in the lock, turned the knob and gently pushed it open, then flicked on the lights.

This room had the same bland carpet, but it also had tall windows with arched tops, and below the arches hung thick, green-velvet curtains the color of emeralds. Dark wood bookshelves lined the walls on either side, and in the middle was a table with heavy legs, the kind that ended in the carved, curving claws of some creature with sharp teeth. The spines of the books were scarlet, navy, green, their titles written in gold, in white, and they were fat and thin, and when Alice walked over to a shelf, she saw familiar names, authors she had read in high school, novels she had assumed she would read in college.

"What is this room?" she asked.

"First editions library," Wesley said, walking up behind her. "When I met you, you were reading."

"*Huckleberry Finn*." She laughed. It was a million years ago already. This girl who was here with Wesley had never read *Huckleberry Finn*. She was a different girl entirely.

"But as soon as I saw you, I knew you were a girl who deserved more than one book," Wesley said. "Which is why I brought you here. I knew when I saw you the first time, I knew it when I took your picture, I knew it when I saw you again."

Alice looked at him over her shoulder and smiled. "I still don't know how you did that, by the way," she said, "how you knew I was at the beach and how you knew to bring the picture, since I don't believe in magic." She meant it as a joke, but when it came out, it didn't sound like one. "Or unicorns," she added lightly. "Or fairies."

"What do you believe in?" he asked. "If you don't believe in magic?" He leaned against the table in the middle of the room. His arms were crossed and his ankles, too, the picture of ease.

"God," she said. "Maybe."

"Okay," he said, and he lifted his hand and rotated it at the wrist: *Go on*.

"I don't know," Alice said. "I guess I'd say people. I believe in people."

"People are more interesting than God," Wesley said, nodding his approval. "But what does it mean to believe in them? Will people save you?"

"Is this a test?" Alice asked. "I'm usually very good at tests, but I feel like I'm not doing too well on this one." She wondered if she should approach him, but she remembered the feeling of the cool air on her naked body on the bed at the party, how Wesley had dressed her but hadn't touched her otherwise, and she stayed near the shelves on the far side of the room. Home base.

"I just want to know you," Wesley said. "I picked you. Did you know that?"

"Yes," she said.

"So that's something you believe in," he said. "You believe in me."

She tilted her head back and laughed at the absurdity, not of him saying it, but of the fact that it was true.

"I do," she said in wonder. "I might believe in God, I do believe in people, and I believe in you. How did you do that?"

He straightened up so that he was no longer leaning against the table. "Don't believe in people," he said. "They're mostly bad. Other people, I mean. Not us." He moved closer to her, and she felt herself shudder a little. "And they don't know much," he continued, "and they don't see things the way we do. They're stuck in the past or they're only focused on the future. Trapped by what they think they need. They don't live in the now. They move through the world like they're asleep."

Now he was so close she could touch his shirt, the buckle on his belt. She could push a lock of hair behind his ear, put her lips to his beard if she wanted. "You mentioned that," Alice said. "Before. About the people at the party."

He nodded. "But you're not like them," he said. "Those other people."

"I know," she said and took a step closer to him. (We regret now the things we said to her, how we spent her whole life reminding her of this very thing, how special she was. But now we know she wasn't who we thought. If she is special at all, it isn't in a good way.)

"So here we are," he said.

"With all the books," Alice said.

"With all the books," he said. And then his hands were undoing her pants and slipping them down, and he was dropping before her, and she felt like a queen, Wesley the stranger, now a knight pledging fealty to her. Wesley, on his knees worshipping her. She let him. She closed her eyes. His mouth singing her praises.

(She is a child, isn't she? Not to know that it means nothing. Every mouth sings praises if it has someone who will listen.)

After, he pulled her pants up, buttoned them himself. "I'm going to keep you," he said.

"What if it's me who's going to keep you?" she asked, smiling.

"It isn't," he said.

"Oh," she said. "I was only joking."

"We better go," Wesley said. "The girls will be expecting us back soon."

"Apple and Janie," said Alice.

"And Kathryn," said Wesley.

"Right," said Alice. "Kathryn." Everything about her felt weak—her brain, her body. Only the beating of her heart reminded her she was alive, she was living, this was happening, this was the now.

"And Hannah Fay," Wesley added. "Come on." A fourth girl. No, a fifth, including Alice. Behind her, Wesley flicked off the light and locked the door behind them.

CHAPTER TWELVE

BACK AT THE house, the porch light glowed and hummed. A fat June bug beat its wings around it, hovering and then landing on its yellow surface. "Do you think it thinks it's landing on the sun?" Alice asked, pointing her chin at it. Now another one joined it, and they buzzed around each other, one crawling on eyelash legs around the other.

Wesley squinted up at the light. "I fucking hate bugs," he said. A shadow fell across his face, and he looked unfamiliar in the light and dark, and she remembered this man was, essentially, a stranger.

But he wouldn't be a stranger for long. Already, they knew each other so much more than they had just twenty-four hours ago, and in another day's time, he would know her even more deeply, and she him. And yet it was still important to be winning, charming. So Alice laughed as though he'd said something witty. "They can't hurt you," she said. "They're June bugs."

"I don't care," Wesley said, pushing open the door. "I just hate them on principle."

No one was in the living room, but from around the corner and out of sight came the sounds of conversations and plates clinking as someone stacked them, the sound of water from a faucet.

On the orange couch the guitar was in the same spot, and beside it, her leather bag leaned against a throw pillow. She felt silly she had worried about it at all. Perhaps she could become the kind of woman who could leave the house empty-handed, tethered to nothing. She could always just go out into the world with nothing but herself.

Apple breezed into the room, going over to the table where the plump-leaved succulents sat and picking up a matchbook. "Oh hey," she said to Alice and Wesley. "You guys snuck in." Alice thought Apple might embrace Wesley, but she stayed next to the table, one hand on her hip, the other holding the matches. She was wearing a sweater that looked like one Alice herself had, and Alice considered telling her in the hopes it might endear her to Apple. Twins! she might say, but then decided against it and just smiled warmly at her instead. Apple didn't smile back.

"What's the status of dinner, Apple?" Wesley asked.

"Ready," she said. "I think you'll be impressed with it considering what we had to work with. Careful, though, Kathryn is grumpy again." She shrugged, rolled her eyes. "Tread lightly."

Wesley pointed a finger sternly at Apple as he walked past her. "Respect," he said. "She's been here longer than you." He disappeared around the corner and into the kitchen. Alice could hear his deep voice, warm and low, and the voices of the other girls too. They sounded happy, like a family catching up after a few days apart.

"Have fun?" Apple asked.

Alice looked at her. "Me?"

Apple didn't move, but her eyes cut to one side and then the other, like she was looking for someone, or something, hiding just outside her line of sight. Her eyes were green, the pale color of the Langes' front yard in winter. "Yes," she said. "I hope you did, because he won't do it again."

"Do what again?" Alice asked. Take her to the college? To the library? Touch her? Worship her?

"You know what I'm talking about," she said.

"I don't," Alice said, blushing. "I'm sorry."

"Fine," said Apple. She shrugged again. "Let's go eat. I'm going to light the fancy candles on the table for ambience." She waggled the matchbook and turned around. When she did, Alice noticed something on her sweater: a small snag, a thread hanging loose. She remembered when that happened; she had been leaning against a tree outside the school, waiting for Susannah, and when she stood up straight, she could feel the fabric clinging to the tree bark. She glanced over to her bag on the couch. The skin of it was smooth and slack, the bulges and lumps gone.

"Hey," said Alice. She reached out and grabbed the thread, pulled it. The knit puckered.

"What?" said Apple. Her eyebrows were long and dark, like they had been drawn on with a felt-tipped pen, and one arched as she looked over her shoulder at Alice.

There was a burst of laughter, and then she heard Wesley bellowing good-naturedly. "Apple!" he called. "Alice!"

"That color's nice on you," Alice said.

"Thanks," said Apple.

In the kitchen, a girl sitting at the table wore her red hair pushed back with Alice's tortoiseshell headband, and another girl, carrying a casserole dish to the table, was wearing a skirt Alice never wore at home but had packed for some reason anyway, with a long, gauzy tunic the color of springtime clouds.

"Hi, Alice," said Janie, who wore a thin gold bangle that Alice's mother had given her last Christmas. You have such delicate wrists, her mother had said. We should dress them up.

"Hi, everyone," said Alice. "Thanks for having me."

Apple breezed past her, her voice low in Alice's ear: "Welcome to Wonderland, Alice."

CHAPTER THIRTEEN

I T TURNED OUT that it was Kathryn's house, Kathryn who was wearing Alice's skirt. When she stood in front of a lamp, her tunic became sheer, and Alice could see the dark green knit of the skirt hugging her hips tightly, curving around her bottom so that it came up shorter in the back than the front. Somehow it didn't look like something Kathryn would normally wear, and Alice pictured Apple standing over the leather bag, rifling through it and tossing things out to the other girls, distributing them as she pleased. She imagined Kathryn dutifully stepping out of the skirt she had worn to her job at the university library that day, folding it into a neat square, and then pulling on Alice's skirt instead.

Kathryn gave Alice a tour of the house. "I was always my great-aunt's favorite, and she left me some money when she died. Then I bought this house," she said, opening a door. "Here's my room." It was small and tidy, with two big windows, and the floor was bare except for a large round rug at the foot of the bed. It made Alice imagine Kathryn as a nun.

"So this is where you stay by yourself?" Alice asked, looking out a window. Then, worried she sounded judgmental, she looked back over her shoulder and added, "Of course it makes sense you have your own room, since it's your house, obviously." She turned back around to face Kathryn.

Kathryn shook her head. "Wesley sleeps in here a lot."

"And then where do you sleep?" asked Alice.

Kathryn raised her eyebrows as though she were surprised by the question. "Here."

"I see," said Alice, who pointed to an ivory-backed hairbrush on the dresser. "That's pretty," she offered politely, trying to cover her surprise.

"My mother's," said Kathryn. (Somewhere, then, another bereft mother. We ask God to think of Kathryn's mother on our behalf because we cannot. We cannot worry about other people beyond our own. It hurts too much. It takes too much out of us.)

When Alice looked at the room on her way out, before Kathryn closed the door behind them, it no longer recalled a nunnery. It was, she thought, the room of a grown-up, a woman who made her own choices, who shared her bed with a man who shared the beds of others.

There wasn't much else to the house, really: one level with two bedrooms, the living room, a cramped study at the front of the house that was made even more claustrophobic by its deep crimson walls, lusty against the shabby white crown molding, and a kitchen with enough room for a table and five mismatched chairs.

"Sometimes Wesley sleeps outside," Kathryn said, taking Alice out the back door. Alice stood at the edge of the patio—a cement slab, really—and looked out at the overgrown and woodsy backyard. The trees were spindly and black in the night, like ink drawings on gray paper. She could sleep outside, too, she thought. "He likes the stars," Kathryn said, slipping on a fragile pair of eyeglasses. Alice assumed she was farsighted and was searching for something in the dark jungle before them. "Like a Boy Scout. Or a soldier."

"Those poor soldiers," said Alice, though the truth was she didn't really think of them very often. (It's easier for us, too, if we do not think too much about such things. We pray for them, but we do not dwell on it.)

"Yes," said Kathryn. "Poor boys. But you know, they aren't fighting for us. We didn't ask them to fight for us."

"What?" said Alice. She turned to face Kathryn. "What do you mean? Who else are they fighting for?"

"Oh," said Kathryn. "You really don't know much, do you?" Her lenses winked in the moonlight.

"I do," said Alice. "More than you think." Her brain was ticking off the classes she had taken, the books she had read, the grades she had earned.

"Of course you do," Kathryn said. "I didn't mean that you're dumb. I meant more like naïve. What we're doing here, Wesley and me and the others, we're our own country. Our own little nation. Or maybe even more than that. Like a whole private world. We don't answer to the rules of the other world. So those boys, they aren't fighting for us. But maybe they're fighting for *you*." She shrugged and crossed her arms over her chest, and when she did, it emphasized the fullness of her figure. Alice wondered if that was partly why Wesley went to Kathryn's bed, looking for something soft and safe, a place to rest. She felt jealous. The hierarchy: Apple or Kathryn, then Janie.

"So you just sit by," Alice said, "and let terrible things happen around you without doing anything about it?" She realized she would never say this to Apple, would certainly never say it to Wesley. But here was Kathryn, soft and plain in her wire-rimmed glasses and looking uncomfortable in Alice's skirt, older than her, not a girl, she could see now, but a woman, who went to work every day at an institution, the servant of men and women younger than her, helping them write meaningless term papers, and Alice let herself judge.

"Definitely not," said Kathryn. "We know the truth, that's all. And we do what the truth dictates. We have a plan we believe in."

"What kind of plan?" Alice asked.

"Can't tell you," Kathryn said and smiled. She had very small teeth but they were so white that even in the darkness it looked like she was holding two strands of pearls inside her mouth. "Not yet, anyway," she said. "You can still stay here for a while, no matter what you think. Wesley wants you here. He sees something in you he likes."

"I know," said Alice. The warmth of the first editions room at the university spread through her. The pressure of Wesley's hands on her hips, the cool spines of the books her fingertips grazed. How weak she had been after, her muscles spent, her bones loose as jelly. "I like him too," she added. She hadn't ever really liked Carl or any of the other boys. They were fine, but they had never made her weak. She hadn't believed in them, and now it was like they didn't exist.

"We all like him," Kathryn said. She took off her glasses and closed her hand around them. "He prefers me without these," she said, and they went inside to join the other girls. Alice saw Kathryn squint in the warm light of the kitchen. She imagined what Kathryn's world looked like now, everything fuzzy and strange. Or maybe it was that crisp, clear world she saw with her glasses that was the strange one, and the blurry world felt familiar to her.

"There you are," Wesley said when he saw them, as if they'd been gone for days.

"Here we are," said Kathryn, bright-eyed, taking both of Wesley's hands with her own. Alice wondered where she had put her glasses.

CHAPTER FOURTEEN

COMMUNITY IS IMPORTANT. We'll be the first ones to tell you that. That's why we live where we do. Almost all of us came here from somewhere else. Other cities farther inland, on other coasts, in the fingertips of the country, or other neighborhoods, ones that aren't as nice as this one. There are, of course, nearby fancier streets than ours, with bigger houses, more expensive cars in the garages. But this one is ours. This is what we chose.

We raise our families together. Our children play in the driveways, in our yards. We sit in lawn chairs and wear sunglasses and watch them. We throw parties where we buy Tupperware from each other, we retrieve errant baseballs in our flower beds for the street's sons. We trade recipes, we trade lovers when we need to, though we're discreet about this. What binds us together besides our mailing addresses, our shared zip code? This: we are committed to a way of life, to creating it for each other, to maintaining it for ourselves.

This is why Mrs. McEntyre studies the shoes of the people who come and go, out of their cars and into our houses, down the sidewalk. Take, for example, that man, Wesley. Brown boots. Dirt on the sole. Shoes of a man who works hard, who enjoys the beauty of the outdoors. But the toes were too pointed, the heel a bit too high. This may seem like nothing, like only the quirks of personal taste, but Mrs. McEntyre knows better. Those boots are not the shoes of a man who can be trusted.

"That's what she says now," Bev tells April. This is long after Alice has gone, after we know who has taken her away. "But at the time, do you remember how she went on and on?"

"'Sweetie always barks!'" says April, in a terrible, nasally impression of Mrs. McEntyre that makes Bev giggle. "'He's a good boy, but you know he's mouthy. Too mouthy for his own good.'"

"'But he didn't bark at the man,'" says Bev. "'He may be mouthy, but he's a good judge of character.'"

April laughs. "Eric wants to poison him," she says.

"The man?" asks Bev. "Is he back?"

"No," says April. "He wants to poison Sweetie." She cocks her head to the side, thinking. "Maybe he wants to poison the man too. I've never asked."

They are at Bev's house. When Bev called earlier in the evening to invite April over, Eric still wasn't home, and April was worried about leaving Billy, who was asleep in his room. "He won't think you left him," Bev had said. "Or he'll know you're over here, but he probably won't even wake up before you're home. Just come over now."

"It isn't right," said April. "It isn't safe for him to be alone."

She had paused then, and Bev had said her name, wondering if the line had gone out. Then came April again: "I hope you aren't leaving the children alone either, Bevvy."

Bev had laughed. "Where would I even be going?"

And now Eric is home and April is here, sitting and having a drink at Bev's kitchen table. All the children are being properly watched now, tended to and listened for.

April watches Bev, who's running rings around the bottom of the wineglass with her finger. "Do you want him to come back?" she asks. "The man."

"No," says Bev, looking back up to April. "Why would I?"

"I don't know," says April. "You just seemed interested. Overly interested."

"Of course I'm interested," she says. "It's like a television show or a movie."

"You're bored?" asks April. "But you have the baby."

"Exactly," says Bev.

When April gets home that night, she can't resist going upstairs to peek at Billy in his bed. His blanket has pictures of planets printed on it—there's Jupiter near his feet, Earth curving underneath his body, disappearing.

Before she goes to bed, she calls Bev. "Listen," she says when Bev answers. "I was only joking about Eric poisoning Sweetie. He would never really do it."

"I know," says Bev. "I can hardly even fathom the possibility."

"Good," says April. "I just didn't want anyone to get the wrong impression of me. Or of Eric. You know."

"I do," says Bev, laughing. "My impression of you is very positive. Don't worry."

"Thank you," says April in a serious voice, and Bev waits for April to laugh, too, to indicate that she's in on the joke. She's the one who raised the topic, after all! But then she only says, "Good night, Bevvy."

"Good night," says Bev, frowning at the phone as she hangs it up, and the lights of two lamps in two houses blink out.

CHAPTER FIFTEEN

KATHRYN HAD BEEN the first. She had met Wesley at an open mic night at, of all places, the university. "I thought you didn't do institutions," Alice joked to Wesley when Kathryn recounted the story. Alice had been here two full days, the longest she'd ever been away from her mother, except for the summer she went to camp for a week. There she had proved to be an excellent archer, and she wrote to her mother every day because she was worried if she didn't, her mother might forget who she was and begin a whole new life without the burden of a daughter. (She wouldn't, of course. We couldn't. Our hearts, our bones, the blood running through our bodies—we could never live without those things either.)

"It was for the sake of art," Wesley answered stiffly. "We make all kinds of sacrifices for our art."

"Oh," said Alice, looking at the other girls sitting around the living room. She wondered where their artistic talents lay, what they used their bodies to create. She knew they all modeled for Wesley. The photos were pinned to the walls with thumbtacks in every room: Kathryn at the library, behind a student asleep at one of the carrels; an earlier version of Janie, thinner, with something unclean about her, in a crowd of other dirty faces, dirty bodies. Hannah Fay outside somewhere, laughing, a piece of hair blown across her face and an orchard behind her. A picture of Apple, looking angry and sharply beautiful, holding a sleeping baby. Alice had asked Janie who the baby belonged to, and she said it was the baby of a woman Wesley knew; the girls, to bring in extra income for the household, sometimes babysat for her. "Apple hates babysitting, though," Janie said. "She said she'd rather give a stranger a blow job." Alice had laughed because Janie did, but she was (to our great relief) shocked to imagine performing that act for money, and beyond that, to prefer it to babysitting.

But the girls were never in the paintings. "Not that you can recognize, maybe," Wesley had said. "But if you know what to look for, you'll see them. You'll see yourself too. You'll see the truth."

"Everyone here's an artist?" Alice asked now. She considered herself. Perhaps Wesley looked at her and saw a latent ability in her, but Wesley said no, of course not.

"They appreciate art," he said. "They're not artists."

They were in the living room, and it seemed like there were girls everywhere, one curled up in a chair, another sitting on an oversized floor cushion and picking dry cereal out of a chipped bowl, a third opening the blinds so that they all could watch the last light of the day drain away.

The past two nights she'd spent outside with Wesley, and she was exhausted because she had never really slept—instead, in a dreamlike state, she found herself reaching for him in the night, finding parts of his body she wanted to touch. She thought she remembered that at one point last night, Wesley put a gentle hand on her hip bone, stilling her and saying, "I'll be here tomorrow. We both will. Now close your eyes." She remembered him laughing softly, in a kind way, like he was amused by her, pleased with her, and then there was nothing. She must have fallen asleep. She thought of what Kathryn had told her on the first night, about him staying in her room, in her bed. About all the girls who liked him. But Alice was special among the girls, she could tell. A favorite. And why wouldn't she be?

Now they all lounged in the living room, draped across the sofa and chairs and on the floor like silk shirts, like camisoles, like pantyhose and lingerie taken off by a lover and then left untouched. The front door was closed, but the back door was open, all that green like a secret the night was keeping, those vines and leaves and overgrown hedges growing unseen in the darkness. Keep the people out, the house seemed to say, the doors like mouths: let the wildness in.

So Kathryn had been first. They had started talking after Wesley's performance—"Everyone loved him," she said. "He sang and played his guitar. He was like some kind of ancient god, the music was so beautiful. Everyone wanted to talk to him." But it had been Kathryn, wearing a knit dress that came past her knees, bare faced and plain, who had asked Wesley back to her house.

"And I never left," said Wesley.

"Where did you live before?" Alice asked.

"Here and there," he said.

"All that matters is that we're here now. All of us," Hannah

Fay said, smiling at Alice. Alice had only been with Wesley and the girls for a couple of days, but she already knew Apple could be prickly, and Janie flighty, and Kathryn brusque, but Hannah Fay was always so warm and seemed genuinely glad that Alice had joined them. She and Alice were the same age, but Hannah Fay seemed wiser and older than Alice felt she herself was, and far older than Susannah and the other girls she'd known at school. Part of it was that Hannah Fay was here, on her own, living without parents, without an adult telling her what to do or where to go.

The other part of it was that Hannah Fay was pregnant, her hands nervously touching the bump of her belly, fluttering around like uncontrollable, pale little birds. That first night, when Hannah Fay had been sitting at the table, Alice hadn't noticed, and when Hannah Fay stood, and the curve of her stomach was revealed, Alice nearly gasped. Alice didn't ask who the father was, and no one felt the need to tell her. She was beginning to think they assumed it would be obvious, that she should just know.

Alice smiled back at Hannah Fay before turning again to Wesley. "What song did you play for the concert?" she asked.

"One of my own," Wesley said. He laughed. "There's so much you don't know about me."

"I'm learning!" said Alice. "But I feel like I know you already. Really."

"He's very talented," said Kathryn. "It's unbelievable. He's good at everything. Look at his photographs. And his paintings!"

"God, Kathryn," Apple said. She was lying across the orange couch, her head back on the armrest and her legs stretched so that her feet were in Janie's lap. Janie was pinching each toe and wiggling it, one by one. Apple didn't even turn her head to look at Kathryn, just kept her eyes on the ceiling. "You are the world's biggest suck-up. Did you know that?" she said. "And Janie, knock it off, please."

Janie pinched Apple's big toe even harder. "This little piggy," she said.

"I thought the same thing myself," Alice said quickly. "He played at the party we went to. Everyone loved him. I'd love to hear you play again," she said, turning to Wesley, who affirmed it had been the right thing to say by picking up his guitar. She was proud of herself.

He strummed one chord, two. "Apple," he said. His tone was warning, but he didn't say anything else.

"Have you ever thought of making a record?" Alice asked. "Like professionally?"

"He tried once," said Apple.

"He changed his mind," said Kathryn meaningfully. "It wasn't the right venue for his message. It needs to be visual, right, Wesley?" Wesley said nothing but frowned at his fingers plucking the chords, whether in displeasure or concentration, Alice couldn't tell.

"We know," Apple said.

Kathryn shot her a look. "I was telling Alice."

"I outgrew music," Wesley said. "But I have a lot to say, and I think a lot of it has to be said through art. I want to tell the world what it's really like. I want to wake everyone up." He turned to Kathryn. "I feel like taking a trip. I need to get out of my head a little bit."

"Great idea," said Apple, sitting up now. Kathryn left the room and came back holding a tin, which she handed to Wesley before taking a seat on the floor next to him.

"I'll just make sure everyone stays safe," said Hannah Fay from the oversized pillow on the floor where she reclined. "But I might go to bed early. My back hurts."

"Stay," said Wesley.

Hannah Fay pulled an elastic band off her wrist and twisted it around her red hair, like she was preparing for a battle, and yet her face looked rounder and younger than it had a moment ago. She rubbed her belly with one hand. Alice wanted to put her hand against that round curve too, feel how smooth it was. She imagined it would feel like a seashell.

All the girls were shifting now where they sat, pulling themselves up straighter, preparing, and when Wesley came to each girl, she would open her mouth and close her eyes, trusting and reflexive, and he'd place a tiny white tablet on her tongue before she would sink back to her original posture. His gait was slow and his face solemn as he went around the room, and Alice got the feeling they'd done this before.

"Open up," Wesley said to Alice, and she didn't hesitate. Mouth open, eyes closed, tongue relaxed. It reminded her of going to Mass as a little girl with her mother, not long after her father had died, how the priest would place that tasteless wafer on her tongue, and she would instinctively pull away. It had felt so intrusive: a strange hand reaching toward her mouth. But she was so receptive here, accepting what was offered to her. (Oh, Alice.) When she opened her eyes, she watched Wesley bite a tablet in half, swallowing one piece and placing the other back in the tin.

"That's all, Wesley?" Apple asked, frowning. "Come on."

"Worry about yourself, Apple," he told her.

"He always takes less than us," Apple said, looking only at Wesley, who met her gaze.

"Not all of us need our minds opened up the same amount," Kathryn said, glancing primly at Apple.

Apple rolled her eyes, and Alice laughed. Her eyes looked so big, rolling around in her head like that. They used to be green, like Alice's own, but they were suddenly dark now and getting darker. Like mud, she thought. Or the pits of cherries. Or the ink a squid shoots out.

"Why don't you play something, Wesley?" Hannah Fay asked.

He played for hours. At first, Alice couldn't move, even though she wanted to. She felt something inside her begin to stretch, and she realized it was her soul, it was reaching for Wesley, who played so well and looked so beautiful she nearly couldn't stand it, but her body was trapping her soul. So she tried to tell her soul what it was missing. Music like a waterfall, like the ocean so early in the morning that there is no one out to hear it, rain like a gift to the earth after a drought, and then alternately, Alice realized, like fire. Both. Everything. It wasn't only that Wesley was handsome. It was that he was handsome and talented and discerning, that he had looked around the whole world and he had picked her to be here. But handsome, yes. A strong and noble profile, like it was drawn by an artist with a gifted hand. Hands that could be gentle and strong, that could please her in multiple ways, a mouth that could do the same thing. Hands that held a camera, that held her, that painted, that played a guitar. Wesley stopped singing for a minute and grinned at her, a bright light in the darkness. "What?" she asked. "What's so funny?"

"Just you," said Wesley. "I'm so happy you're here."

"You're talking out loud," Kathryn said to Alice. Alice gasped, not because she learned she was narrating her private thoughts, but because she saw Wesley's beard was growing, like a dark brown storm cloud fattening up with rain, and she realized the hours he was playing had become days, then weeks. "It's almost time for Hannah Fay's baby to come," Alice said, ignoring Kathryn. "Isn't it? Does it feel like a seashell when you touch it?"

"The baby?" asked Hannah Fay.

"Your stomach," Alice said. "When the baby's inside."

Hannah Fay was still sitting on the floor, but around her the floor glowed and moved, and Alice remembered learning in biology about some kind of luminescent algae that made the water shimmer just like this, and she wondered how Hannah Fay had cast that algae around her. She pictured Hannah Fay holding out her pale index finger and pointing at the floor, a crackle of electricity zipping from the tip. Zap! Zap! Until she sat on a throne of light. Did the baby give Hannah Fay special powers? Would Alice have those powers someday when she had a baby? Did her mother have those powers too?

"I have so many questions," Alice said. Behind her, she could feel someone braiding her hair, their fingers like crabs, scuttling in and out. She reached behind her to still the hands, but they kept going. In the distance, somewhere outside the house, she could hear a low, deep rumble. She knew it was a volcano. She knew that Wesley could make it erupt if he wanted to, and Alice both wanted to see the lava take down everything, swallow every house they'd passed by, the school, the library with all its books—and was frightened by the idea of it, scared it might swallow her up too.

"You can come feel my belly if you want," Hannah Fay said, but she was suddenly far away, the luminescence around her now like the wink of a bright eye in the distance, and the plants had gotten so big and so green, so green that they were singing. And Wesley was singing, too, and she saw his guitar was really just an extension of his body, like a third arm, and that explained why he was so good. It was like wondering why your hand was so good at having fingers. It was made to have fingers! The music tasted salty when Alice opened her mouth, and she remembered how Wesley had found her so long ago on the beach. "I'm a seashell," Alice called to Hannah Fay, wherever she was. "Not you."

"Put her to bed, Hannah, please," Apple said. "She's being annoying." Apple and Janie were dancing in the middle of the room, having pushed the coffee table off to the side. They'd been laughing—hadn't they?—just a moment ago. Apple extended her arm, and Janie twirled away and then back to her. They didn't seem to hear the hungry rumble of the volcano. Alice knew she should stand up and go to the window, look for the plume of smoke, the tongues of fire, but she didn't want to. If she didn't look, she would be safe.

"She's fine," Wesley said. He had put the guitar down and picked up his camera instead. He walked to the window where the volcano was, and he took a picture of it, bravely, Alice thought.

"I guess you'll put her to bed yourself," Apple said.

"Maybe I will," Wesley said, heading back to the girls.

"Let's play a game," said Kathryn. "Let's play pretend."

"I'll be a wolf," said Alice, because a seashell couldn't really do much.

"Let's play Afraid," Apple said. "I like that one. I'll start."

"I'll start," said Wesley. "Kathryn, what are you afraid of?"

"Spiders," she said. "Poverty. That I'll lose the house somehow."

"To spiders?" asked Apple, but Kathryn ignored her.

"Good," said Wesley. "That was very honest. Hold on to that fear. Does the world seem more real now that you think about how much there is to lose?"

Kathryn nodded, and her head snapped off and rolled across the room, like a bowling ball, but also not because it was misshapen and lumpy. Alice gasped. With a zap of her finger, Hannah Fay sent it rolling unsteadily back to Kathryn, who positioned it back on her neck. Hannah Fay smiled. Alice wanted to have that power too. She would work on it. Her mind was opened, as promised, and she could see a baby for what it was: a cord that could keep her attached to Wesley, let her breathe, give her what she needed to live. But through the window the sky glowed red and orange and hot.

"Your turn," Wesley told Kathryn, and she pointed at Apple.

"Aliens," Apple said. "Invaders. Someone breaking in and taking what isn't theirs. You go now, Hannah Fay."

"Losing the baby," she said.

"You won't," Janie said. "Sweet Hannah Fay. The baby will be fine."

"It's not your turn, Janie," Wesley said. "She could lose the baby. We don't know."

"See?" said Hannah Fay. "It could happen." She had started crying in a soft, sweet way, and Alice wanted to crawl into her lap, lick the tears off her cheek like a kitten. Things were coming into focus now. The color green was only humming. Wesley wasn't playing the guitar anymore, and he wasn't taking pictures, either, but Alice wished he would. She noticed now the floor was covered in little white feathers. The corpse of a throw pillow on the couch, bleeding down. The volcano must be dormant now, she realized, noticing that the sky outside the window was black.

"Don't say that," said Janie. She walked over to Hannah Fay and put a hand on her head. She picked up a strand of her hair and let it fall. "It's cruel," Janie said. She went back to the couch where she had begun the night and lay down. With the white feathers surrounding her, she looked like a maiden on a bed of flowers.

"Fear is healthy," said Wesley. "We need it. It's the world's way of telling us to pay attention. Too many people aren't paying attention."

"I'm sorry," said Janie. "I just don't want her to be sad."

"You're stopping her from living in the now," Wesley said, moving closer to where Janie was lying on the couch. "Let her be afraid."

Alice saw that she herself had moved too. She was sitting in the corner of the room on the pillow Hannah Fay had been resting on. She looked at Hannah Fay, who was sitting in the same place, with only the wood floor beneath her.

"Sit up," Wesley said to Janie. Janie obliged, but kept her chin tilted back, so she was looking up at him, and folded her hands in her lap.

Then Wesley hit her across the face. A crack—her head turned, cheek red and streaked. She kept her hands together, and looked down at them, like she was checking to make sure they were still there, all the fingers intact.

Now he knelt in front of her, a hand on each of her knees. "Hannah Fay," he said, keeping his eyes on Janie. "Ask her."

"Janie," said Hannah Fay. Her voice was soothing and low, and in it Alice could hear the lullabies she would one day sing to her baby. "What are you afraid of?"

"The ocean," said Janie softly, eyes down, a girl who had misbehaved and been scolded. "It's so big."

"Good," said Wesley. He lifted a finger and touched her chin, then her lips. "Let's go to bed, everyone," he said. "But first, can someone hand me the camera?" Kathryn brought it to him. "Look at me, Janie," he said. She looked up, eyes wet and tired. He held the camera up to his eye, squinting through the viewfinder, and took her picture. "Thank you," he told her. "Thank you for sharing yourself with me." He pulled Janie up by the hand, and walked her out of the room, keeping his hand on her lower back.

"Looks like you're with me tonight," Apple said to Alice, sounding worn and tired. "You should have gone to bed hours ago." Wesley and Janie were gone. So was Hannah Fay, who had snuck into the study, which seemed to be her bedroom. Still in the living room, Kathryn cleaned up in silence. Efficient hands replacing pillows, arranging the chairs at pleasing angles from the coffee table. Then she picked up the small white feathers one by one.

"That's a game you like?" Alice asked Apple as she followed her down the hall.

Apple shrugged. "It's good to be a little bit afraid," she said over her shoulder. "Puts things in perspective."

"It's terrible," said Alice. "Poor Janie."

"She knows what it's like here," Apple said. She stopped outside the closed bedroom door and turned to Alice so they were face-to-face. Apple looked tired and bleary, like a girl in an impressionist painting. Everything about her seemed fuzzy and indistinct; even her sharp, dark eyebrows seemed out of focus somehow. "Janie's getting a reward now," Apple said. "You're the one who should feel bad. You have to sleep all alone."

"I thought I was sleeping with you," said Alice.

"I meant alone, as in not with Wesley."

"Fine," Alice said. "Let's go to bed, then." She went to open the door, but Apple didn't move, and Alice, her hand on the doorknob, didn't turn it.

"Look," said Apple finally. "He only hits Janie."

"Oh," said Alice. She remembered the hierarchy of girls she had imagined when she first arrived at the bungalow. This put Janie at the bottom. Or did it put her at the top?

"That makes it a little better, right?" asked Apple.

"Of course not," said Alice. But a few minutes later when she crawled into bed with Apple, who unexpectedly slept all curled up like a little snail in a shell, she fell asleep easily. She didn't have any bad dreams.

CHAPTER SIXTEEN

Now that Alice had been in the bungalow for a few days, she could feel the girls around her, even when they were out of sight. She would hear footsteps in the kitchen and think, that's Janie, and then Janie would be there, holding a handful of blueberries. She'd hear humming and know it was Hannah Fay leaning toward the mirror in the bathroom, plucking her fine red eyebrows. She hoped the other girls would hear the screen door shut and think, oh, it's Alice, coming inside, or hear her laugh in the other room and say to each other, that couldn't be anyone but Alice.

None of them worked regular jobs except Kathryn, and Wesley went out during the day, often to take pictures, but sometimes to do something none of them knew about. "He has his own life outside the house," Janie said when Alice asked. "It's his right to keep it private if he wants to. We don't tell him everything we do." (Though they didn't have to, because the girls did what Wesley wanted. He planted seeds in the wet earth of their brains every morning. He said, "I love a clean house at the end of the day. Don't you?" They cleaned the house. He said, "I think I'm getting scurvy. Not enough vitamin C," though he was always tan, and the girls went to the grocery store and came home with arms full of oranges they put in bowls all around the house, in the kitchen, on the dining-room table, the bedside table in Kathryn's room. He said, "No more cigarettes. Smoking is the sign of a weak will." The girls stopped that, too, at least when he was around, though we have to say, a weak will is exactly the kind Wesley preferred. He said, "The world outside is dangerous." And the girls stayed inside. We see the wisdom in this last one, we do, but the difference is that we decide for ourselves.)

But whenever Wesley found his way back to the bungalow of girls, it was clear to Alice that no matter what they'd done or where they went, they had been waiting. They spent the day in various stages of anticipation, everything building to the opening and closing of the front door, the sound of boots on the wood floors. Now, she waited too. Like the other girls, she listened for vibrations, felt the air for changes, a certain swing to signal that Wesley had come home again. They were like dogs and cats and birds, who sense the shifts in the earth so acutely that they could feel the rumbling of a latent earth-quake, could sense the pull of the ocean's tide before a giant wave came crashing in to eat the shore.

But instead of running from the wave and the cracks in the ground, Alice and the girls waited for it, hoped for it, went running toward it.

Wesley was mercurial, which made the days he was home exciting, unpredictable. Once he went to the store and came back with a crateful of exotic fruit, unfamiliar and robust, and they spent all day examining the various pieces, peeling the skin, picking the leaves off, cutting them open, and licking the juices off their hands as they laughed and tried to figure out how to eat each one. Another day he woke up and said he had a vision for the girls. "We're growing our hair out," he announced. "All of us. I want us to look like we all belong together." He took the scissors they used to give themselves haircuts at home and hid them until Kathryn demanded they be returned. But still, they never cut their hair.

On the days Wesley disappeared without leaving any directions, the girls spent the hours talking and smoking and then taking lazy, stoned walks around the neighborhood before coming home to read the old newspapers and magazines Wesley left around the house. There were no books anywhere, even in the little study where Hannah Fay slept.

Not a single one of the magazines or newspapers was recent. Their covers were black and white and showed crowds of people listening to a short man yelling behind a podium, straight lines of uniformed men beside him, behind him, or they showed soldiers or Russian tsars or people marching, holding signs, their mouths open, frozen and yelling.

"He loves history," Hannah Fay had told Alice, flipping through the pages. "They're actually pretty interesting. I never really went to class, so I'm learning a lot." Hannah Fay had dropped out of school early, she said. She, like Wesley, wasn't a person made for institutions.

But despite his disdain for traditional schooling, Wesley himself was undeniably a teacher. Whatever else he was, he said, first he was a teacher. He taught through language, he taught through music, he taught through his photography. He taught by walking into a room, by giving someone a certain look, by lingering in silence. In all of these things were lessons

for Alice and the girls to absorb if they paid close-enough attention. Sometimes Alice wanted to take notes the way she
had in school—which seemed so long ago and so silly, what
had she thought she would learn there?—but she imagined
Apple finding her notes and holding them up, laughing, and
so instead Alice tried to commit the lessons to memory. She
wanted to make them the bones of her body, the muscles that
let her run.

Wesley in the backyard, in a green plastic lawn chair, the
girls sitting like lotus flowers at his feet: "Of course the past
exists, and thankfully the future exists, because frankly this
world is shit, but it's the present that matters. It's what we do
in the present that determines what our future will be." (An
aphorism on a poster hanging in the office of a high school
guidance counselor. We see you, Wesley. We know your kind.)

Wesley in the kitchen, leaning against the counter, the girls
sautéing onions, setting the table, filling water glasses: "Our
future? A king and queens. Rulers of a new world."

Wesley examining a leak in the bathroom attached to
Kathryn's room: "Is it worth it to get this fixed? We're going
to be leaving here soon." When they got to the desert, that's
when everything would start, Wesley said. The grand awaken-
ing. "There will be violence," he warned. "It's hard for people
to acknowledge what they've been blind to their whole lives.
It's painful. They won't like it. And I can't say we won't be a
part of the violence, but I will say this: we won't be the victims
of it."

Wesley walking through the neighborhood, the girls beside
him and behind him: "The people who live in these houses are
blind and deaf and dumb. The world is going to burn down
around them, and they'll never know. They don't know why,

but they want to stop us. They see us and see we're different, and that scares them."

Wesley in bed with Alice, while Kathryn was at work, the other girls on a field trip to the post office to mail in the utility bill: "It's a bad world. But we can change it. I can save you."

Wesley to Kathryn, to Janie, to Apple, to who knows who else, what others there were: "I can save you. I can save you all."

But if Wesley was a teacher, he was also a storyteller, though he might not have called himself that. A story implies fiction, and he spoke the truth. Often, though, he referred to his photographs, the stories a picture could tell with no audible language, and Alice learned to look at the images and read them for what Wesley told her was there. "See the story unfolding here," he'd say, holding up a photo, pointing at the figure—because it was often people he photographed, in all their ugliness and weakness. The only frivolous pictures he took, he said, were of his girls, objects of pleasure, beauty, of all things good.

But truly, he could take anything—a car driving with its headlights off at night, an electrical fire in a restaurant near the school, a dead limb falling off a tree in their yard—and make it into a story. Sometimes Alice wondered if he was making it all up on the spot, and she listened the way a child listens to a teacher reading a fairy tale: for pleasure first, for wisdom second. The stories were often frightening, visceral, but sometimes funny, too, and everyone would laugh together.

She also knew that every story had a purpose for existing, and she began to listen for that. Silent, slow stalking in the dark; a pop, a flash, then flames; a crack and a crash of wood and leaves. All of it boiled down to this: the world outside is dangerous. Unpredictable, uncontrollable. The people in the world outside are dangerous too. Dangerous, blind, ignorant, asleep at the wheel and out of control.

One night Alice told them about Rachel Granger, how she had been picked up not far from Alice's neighborhood and murdered. "It wasn't as nice a neighborhood as the one I'm from," she said. "Mine is very safe."

But Wesley was shaking his head. "You disagree?" she asked.

"Nowhere is safe," he said. "And I know the man who killed her."

Alice felt her face moving itself into a look of incredulity, and she tried to hide her bewilderment—Wesley didn't like to be doubted—but he was already holding up his hand and saying, "Not personally. But this guy's been doing that for ages. I call him the driving man."

"So what does he do?" Alice asked.

"What does it sound like?" Apple said. "He drives."

"She's not wrong," Wesley said.

The driving man had never been caught. He would probably never be caught, Wesley said. Wesley wasn't even sure if he was only one man or if he had an army of driving men, all of them in their cars at night, prowling streets where young women might wave them down, ask for a ride. Then these girls were gone, like Rachel. They were gone for good or they were gone for a while, only to show back up in a ditch, in a Dumpster, even once in the front yard of her own house. It could be anyone. He could be anywhere. Any pair of yellow lights driving toward you, any man who slowed down, gliding beside you.

This was why the girls couldn't walk around outside after dark, couldn't go anywhere at night without Wesley. The truck was always fueled up, there were always quarters in the cup-holder for a phone call. "My main priority," Wesley told them now, "is to keep you safe."

Hannah Fay shivered. "Sorry, this conversation really creeps me out," she said. "It's so hard to think about what evil people there are out there."

Wesley nodded. "You know what, though? He's fucking waking people up." He stomped his foot for emphasis. "Everyone is scared, and they should be. We're the only ones who shouldn't."

"Should we toast him then?" asked Alice, holding up her wineglass. She was a little drunk. Both money and food seemed to be scarce around the house, and she was wondering if that was why the girls were so thin, but somehow there always seemed to be plenty to drink.

"That feels wrong somehow," said Janie.

"A toast," Wesley said, holding up his glass too, "to those who wake up the masses, through whatever means necessary."

Alice watched the other girls lift their glasses, the wine inside the pale color of moonlight. Cheers, they said, and clinked them together.

CHAPTER SEVENTEEN

ONE DAY WESLEY declared he needed new clothes, and moments later the girls were climbing into the truck bed, off to a secondhand store near the university. "Not you, Hannah Fay," Wesley said, gesturing instead to the passenger seat. Of course that made sense—it wouldn't be safe for Hannah Fay, blossoming with baby, to be bouncing in the truck bed as they navigated the roads, filled with potholes and careless drivers, but as Alice watched her ease into the front seat, she felt a twinge of jealousy.

"Alice, sit, please," said Kathryn, patting the truck bed, and Alice looked away from Hannah Fay and plopped herself down. As the girls settled and arranged themselves, Wesley took their picture.

"Well, isn't this a flattering angle," Apple said dryly, but Wesley shook his head.

"It's exactly the angle I want," he said. "Did you ever consider that?" When he got into the driver's seat, Kathryn turned to Apple.

"If you act like that, he won't take your picture," she said. "You have to let him do it just the way he wants to."

"I don't care if he takes my picture," Apple said.

"I don't really either," said Alice quickly, remembering Wesley's disdain for the people at the pool party, the ones desperate to feel the gaze of his camera on themselves.

"Oh, I do," said Janie. "I love it." She shivered, even though the day was warm. "Look, I'm getting chills just thinking about it." She held out her arm for the girls to see, but to Alice it simply looked like an arm. "He has a gift," she said. "And a mission. I feel privileged even to be a part of it."

"Right, but he doesn't want us to beg to have our picture taken," Alice said. "He wants us to be different from everyone else."

"We are," said Kathryn firmly.

The girls went quiet then. Through the window in the back of the truck, Alice could see Hannah Fay looking out the passenger-side window, angled away from Wesley, who was sitting straight and tight. There was room for a whole other girl between them.

Alice knew Wesley loved Hannah Fay. She was a sacred vessel, her body the first home for the child they made together, and because of this, he often treated her like she was breakable, like there was less of her now instead of more. But, Alice noticed, he did not treat her like he wanted to fuck her, though presumably at one point he had. Alice tried to imagine Wesley treating Hannah Fay the way he did Apple, grabbing her ass, pulling her hair, and couldn't. This, Alice told herself, would never happen to her if she ever got pregnant. She would do whatever it took to ensure Wesley would still want to reach his hand up her skirt, twist his fingers in her hair, growl into her ear.

(Once we, too, were unaware what our bodies could do besides tempt a man. We did not know the worlds our bodies could hold and grow, how powerful pregnancy made us. But power, too, is frightening, especially in people who haven't had it before, and some of our husbands turned away from us in bed, afraid to hurt the baby as they entered us, they said, afraid of their own strength and lust. But this wasn't true—they were really afraid of being, for once, the weaker ones. We didn't even know this until we'd pushed the babies from our bodies, and we weren't pregnant anymore, and it was too late. We only knew about the power we'd had when it had passed from our bodies, and in its absence, we felt ourselves sagging, wilting.)

They passed by the college campus, and because it was late afternoon, the lawns and pathways were covered in little herds of students. They looked fake to Alice, like paper dolls or figurines. "Inauthentic," Wesley called them on their way home after that first night in the library. "None of those people know what it means to truly live. They aren't free. They have a million masters they serve. Not us, though. We serve no one but ourselves." Even before she'd met the other girls and gotten to know Wesley, she knew what he said was true, and that she, too, had been one of those doll-house figurines, pretty and wooden.

"Are we shopping too?" Apple said when they arrived. "I mean, for ourselves." She slung a long leg over the side of the truck, even though Hannah Fay had come around and opened the gate of the truck bed so the girls could lower themselves down. Wesley stood with his hands in his back pockets squinting at the store, which was fronted by a wall of windows, and then began to approach it.

"Is there something you need?" Wesley asked the girls, calling back over his shoulder as they followed behind him.

"Excitement," Apple said. She carried an orange crocheted purse on a leather strap so long that the bag, round as a pumpkin, bounced against her leg. "The thrill of the hunt."

"New clothes," said Janie.

"You have Alice's clothes," said Kathryn. "She hasn't been here that long, so it's like you just got new ones." Apple was wearing a yellow dress that once belonged to Alice; she wasn't sure why she'd packed it, since she had only worn it once, to a Thanksgiving dinner the year before at her aunt's house. Apple had put it on, and when Alice saw how it suited her, pale and soft under her dark hair, she never wore it again. Now Apple had worn it many more times than Alice ever had. Here, the seasons changed—barely—but Apple in her yellow dress and her orange purse with the brown strap looked to Alice like fall, like the pictures she had seen in the brochures from the college campuses on the opposite coast, the drama and intensity of the changing leaves.

"I've been here awhile," Alice said, not to defend Apple's desire for new clothes; what she wanted to defend was her place there with the girls, her spot in the house, in the bed of the truck, beside Wesley at night.

"Don't worry," said Janie, coming up beside her and sliding her hand into the back pocket of Alice's jeans, the way a boyfriend might in the halls of a high school. "We know you're one of us," she said, then slipped her hand out. Alice wanted her to put it back.

"Not 'til Wesley names you," Apple trilled.

"Lay off, Apple," Wesley said. They were all in front of

the glass door, and Alice could see their reflections in the store windows and the clothes behind the glass. The six of them looked half ghostly, dressed in shadows of clothes that once belonged to other people. Wesley opened the door and ushered them in. "Look around, enjoy yourselves," Wesley said, "but don't embarrass me."

"Us?" Apple asked, eyes wide.

"You especially," Wesley said, but he was grinning, and Apple winked and turned away, but not before reaching up and dragging a fingernail across his cheek, like it was a sleek and silver knife cutting him open.

The clothes hung on plastic hangers and smelled like disinfectant, which made Alice's eyes sting and her head ache. "I think I'm allergic to whatever they spray on these clothes," she said to Apple, who was noisily pushing the hangers down the rack, evaluating each blouse with a quick eye.

"Poor little rich girl," Apple said without looking up. "Allergic to poverty."

"That's not what I said," Alice said, blushing. "I don't have any more money than you do." And she didn't. Whatever money she'd had, she'd given to Wesley. It had turned into food in the pantry, water in the faucets, power in the light switches.

"That doesn't change anything," Apple said. "Not really." She pulled a blue shirt off the rod and held it up to Alice. "This would look pretty on you," she said. "You should ask Wesley for it."

"I'm not the one who wanted new clothes," said Alice.

"Girls," said Kathryn, coming up behind them. "Don't let Wesley hear your bad attitudes."

Apple rolled her eyes. "Kathryn, God, I was trying to be

nice," she said, but she hung up the blue shirt and went to join Janie, who was looking at a rack of shoes.

"It would look good on you," Kathryn said, pushing the hangers apart so the blue shirt was visible again. "Sometimes Wesley likes to pick our clothes for us. You could call him over here and keep the shirt just like this and see if he picks it up," she went on. "Let him think he found it."

"I really don't need anything," Alice told her.

Kathryn shrugged. "Who really needs anything," she said. "New things are just fun. Everyone likes new things." She smiled, lips tight, no teeth showing. "That's how you got here, right?"

"How I got here?" Alice asked. "Wesley found me."

"Exactly," said Kathryn, but she didn't sound spiteful or jealous or cruel. She spoke the way a weatherman might report an oncoming heat wave. "You're his brand-new thing."

"I don't mind being new," Alice said, even though she had just been insisting that she wasn't new anymore, that she belonged. What she meant was that she didn't mind being special, chosen, untarnished, unsullied.

"Of course you don't. The new toy gets played with the most," Kathryn said, and Alice realized she had seen this before, had lived through it: first with Hannah Fay, then Apple, then Janie, and now Alice.

She imagined Kathryn the day Wesley brought home Hannah Fay, her stomach still flat, just a child, Kathryn taking off her glasses and folding them up, even though it meant feeling unsteady in every step because now more than ever it was important to keep Wesley happy. "But," Kathryn said, "then you aren't new anymore, and you know someone else will be eventually." Kathryn, moving with confidence around the kitchen, cooking a meal for this girl, this child, filling her wineglass at Wesley's insistence, showing her the bedroom she could sleep in. *I hope you'll feel at home*, Alice imagined Kathryn saying in a brisk voice, hand on the light switch as she pointed out the closet, the dresser she could use, and Hannah Fay responding gratefully. And Wesley saying, *This is home, your home. Our home*, and maybe Kathryn would look at him and know something she hadn't before, about the kind of man he was, about the kind of home her house had become.

"It must have been hard," Alice said, "to open your home up to strangers so many times." To be replaced. To become old.

"I would only do it for Wesley," Kathryn said.

But before Alice could answer, she heard Wesley call them, and they left the blue shirt on the rack and went to him. The girls gathered around him as he held up a long black garment. "Check this out," he said. "A priest outfit."

"A habit," said Janie.

"That's for a nun," Apple said.

"A cassock," said Kathryn. "I grew up Catholic."

"How funny that it's here," said Alice. "I wonder what happened to the priest."

"He probably just stopped being one," said Apple. "Because he probably realized it sucked. I doubt he was killed or anything interesting."

"It doesn't matter," said Wesley. He had moved in front of a floor-length mirror. When he held the frock up to himself, keeping the shoulder seam level with his shoulder, the hem grazed his boots. The black of the fabric made his eyes look even lighter, like the shallow edge of an alpine lake. "We were meant to find this," he said. "I'm getting it."

"A sign," said Alice, who had always been open to signs, and now believed in them in earnest. How could she not? There was the magic of Wesley finding her and finding her again at precisely the moment her life was changing. Then she had always liked the number five—it was a pleasing number, cheery and round, and when Alice joined, she made five. And she loved the other girls, and they loved her. If that wasn't a sign that she was in the right place doing the right thing, she didn't know what was.

"Who found it?" asked Kathryn.

"Me," said Hannah Fay. "I thought at first it might be wide enough to cover my belly, but then it felt wrong to try it on when I realized what it was."

"Why?" asked Janie.

"Because she's pregnant," Kathryn said. "Out of wedlock. That's a sin."

"Thanks, Kathryn," Hannah Fay said.

"Hey," said Wesley, throwing the robe over his shoulder. "Wrong. Anything that results in a beautiful baby couldn't be a sin. Besides, marriage is a trap. Being trapped by anyone or anything—now that should be a sin." (But, one might ask, what does he think a baby *is*?)

"And that's why we're all so free here," Apple said. She leaned her head back and spread her arms out wide, her dark hair tumbling down her back, her throat white and bare, like she was reveling in all the freedom. When she stood up straight again, she was grinning.

"You are," Wesley said. "No one is making you stay. Leave if you want to."

"Lucky for you," Apple said, "I don't."

"We are lucky," Hannah Fay said. "We need you." She

turned to Wesley. "Wesley, do you need anything else? Pants? I can grab some jeans if you'd like."

He shook his head. "Nah," he said. "Everything else can wait. I've got plans for this already."

"Something kinky?" asked Apple.

"You're going to hell," Kathryn said.

"Probably," said Apple, and everyone but Kathryn laughed, and Wesley took the gown to the cashier.

"This it for today?" the woman asked, giving him a strange look.

"I'm starting my own church," Wesley told her, pulling out his wallet. "Would you like to join?"

"It's free," said Janie.

"Except for your soul," said Apple.

"Yes, this is it for today," said Hannah Fay as the cashier looked in confusion from each one of them to the next. "Thank you."

They were piling back into the truck when Apple told them she forgot something and she would be right back. "Hurry," said Wesley. "I'm starving." Apple loped across the parking lot and darted inside the glass door of the store. A minute later, she was out again and jogging back toward the truck, stepping on the back tire to propel herself into the bed with the other girls.

"Here," she said, digging a blue bundle out of her bag and tossing it to Alice, who caught it and unfolded the shirt from the store. Alice held it up against herself.

"Thank you," she said.

"You're welcome," said Apple, and then they pulled out of the parking lot and picked up speed, and Alice's hair blew in front of her eyes so she couldn't see.

CHAPTER EIGHTEEN

I T I S V E R Y hard now to remember Mrs. Lange as anything other than two people: first, she was Alice's mother,
and then she was the mother of no one.

Or first she was like the stately mother of the sweet princess, untouchable and vaguely unknowable, and then she was
like the witch who lives on the outskirts of the village, untouchable still and even more unknowable now because, if
we're being honest, we are too frightened to really know her
at all. And if we are really committed to the truth, then we
can admit that she has always been something slightly alien
to us, this woman without a man in her home. When Mr.
Lange passed away, Mrs. Lange drifted further from us, like
a sailboat on the ocean; we could still see her, but she was
moving farther from shore, growing less distinct every day.

But now she has truly become someone we cannot relate
to; here, so far, the rest of us have been untouched by serious
loss. We know how lucky we are.

So Mrs. Lange, then, is no longer like us. Yes, her child

is still here, walking the same earth, but she isn't *here*. Her mother is a lost thing, too, a pinprick on the horizon. We simultaneously try to hold her in our hearts—we know she hurts, she is broken, she was much like us not long ago—and push her out of our thoughts, because if we think about her too much, the pain begins to burn like a tired muscle, and we can't carry her any longer.

At first, once we knew Alice Lange was still alive, that she had simply run away, Mrs. Lange tried to keep up. She attended the neighborhood civic committee meeting and sat in the back, a small beige purse on her lap. She came to a dinner party at the McEntyres'. She handed out Halloween candy to the tiny ghosts and princesses who knocked on her door, telling them they were scary or beautiful, even though her stomach turned hopefully with each chime of the doorbell, imagining, always, that it was Alice outside on the doorstep. She had forgotten her key. She was worried her mother would be mad at her. There were a million reasons why she didn't let herself right in. But then Mrs. Lange would open the door slowly, and instead of Alice, she'd be greeted by a group of children and an onslaught of memories of all the people Alice had once been. Ever since her daughter left, Mrs. Lange had a hard time sleeping, and that night, instead of counting sheep, she tried to think of every Halloween costume Alice had ever worn. Seventeen years, seventeen costumes, but she could only think of ten, and it made her so upset that she couldn't sleep after all.

When Alice was growing up, Mrs. Lange baked all the time. She said she liked having something to do with her hands. Before she became a mother, she used to paint. But, she said, what would she do with all those paintings she had living in her head and in her fingers, waiting to be birthed?

They would take up too much space. Whereas with a plate of cookies or a cake, you could see it, admire your craft, and then by the end of the night it was all gone, like a short and beautiful dream. Plus, she told us once, Alice by her side, her daughter was an excellent helper in the kitchen. "I can crack the eggs without getting any of the shell in," Alice said in a very serious voice. It was just after her father died, so she must have been five, the right size to sit on the counter beside her mother, one egg fitting perfectly in each hand.

In the fall, Alice and her mother made loaves of pumpkin bread, which they cut carefully in half, wrapped in tinfoil, and left on our front porches. At Christmastime, it was gingerbread men in brown-paper lunch bags. In the spring, soft sugar cookies with yellow sprinkles the color of duckling feathers. In the summer, it was too hot to bake, but come October, we would open the door and see the squat rectangles of tinfoil-wrapped bread shining on our welcome mats.

The first year that Bev was living here, she went out to get the mail one October day and almost squashed the half loaf of Mrs. Lange's pumpkin bread. She bent over uneasily, pregnant with Timmy, and picked up the loaf, then peeled back a corner of the foil and sniffed at it. At best, this bread was mistakenly left for her, or at worst, purposely left for her and poisoned. She walked over to April's house, bread in hand, and spotted an identical package on her doorstep.

"Oh!" said April in delight when she saw Bev. "It's pumpkin bread day!"

"I'm sorry," said Bev. "It's what?"

"Mrs. Lange," said April, pointing toward the Langes' house, "bakes these every October with her daughter, and they give them to everyone on the street. You never know what

day in October it's coming, so it's a wonderful little surprise."
April bent and grabbed her own loaf. Like Bev, she peeled
back the foil and smelled it, breathing in deeply. "It's like it's
not really fall until you get pumpkin bread," she went on. "I
can't believe it's already October."

"I can," said Bev, who was due the first week in November. "Okay, well, I just wanted to make sure no one had laced
the bread with arsenic in order to kill me and steal the baby
from my womb."

"That kind of thing doesn't actually happen," April said.
"Besides, if someone wanted a baby they could steal the one
from my house. Or the twins from down the street. Or the Pit-
tmans' baby. Why go to the bother of murdering someone and
then stealing her baby, when you could just commit the one,
easier crime?"

"Good point," said Bev, laughing, and this, she would
later say, was the moment when she made her first real friend
in the neighborhood.

Alice Lange left us for the first time in September, only
days before October would break through. Of course, we
didn't think about the pumpkin bread during that time. For
weeks, we were consumed with Alice's whereabouts, the theo-
ries and possibilities behind her disappearance, and it was our
own children who reminded us that time was moving on while
we sat and wondered about the past—Halloween was in less
than two weeks, and they needed costumes, we needed candy
for the trick-or-treaters, and once November hit, everything
would begin sliding fast into the holidays. So we snapped back,
living halfway in the present, a quarter in the future, and re-
serving the last quarter for Alice Lange, whom we could only
see behind us. On November first, exhausted from the night

before, we opened our front doors to see that silver-wrapped half loaf of bread waiting for us. April called Bev. "November first. Only a day late," she said. "I can't believe she still did it."

"You know," said Bev, "I bet she wasn't late at all. I bet she put them out last night after we went to bed. Just in the nick of time."

"Oh, that somehow seems sadder," April said. "I hope she put them out early this morning."

In fact, some of us had seen her walking down the street at night carrying a basket, like a very grown-up Little Red Riding Hood. When Sweetie had begun barking around eleven, and Mrs. McEntyre forced herself to peek out the window, she saw Mrs. Lange retreating down her path. Mrs. McEntyre had lost a sister when she was a teenager, and truthfully, Alice Lange had always reminded her of that other girl. Both blond, big-eyed, forever eighteen. She considered opening the door to call after Mrs. Lange—What? Thank you? Hello? I'm sorry?—but in the end, she waited until her neighbor was out of sight to retrieve the bread.

The other person to see Mrs. Lange was Billy, who typically went to his window to watch the dark street as soon as his mother tucked him in and closed the door behind her. That evening, he spotted a woman stopping briefly at each house and leaving an offering, but he couldn't see who it was, and thought she might be a ghost. Briefly, he considered being scared, but in the end decided not to be. He was safe in his room; here, he could observe her with the cool detachment of a scientist. He even made some notes about her in his journal. The next day after school, he told his mom about the ghost and showed her his written observations. That wasn't a ghost, April said, it was only their neighbor Mrs. Lange, and when

Billy walked into the other room to start on his homework, she got on the phone to tell Bev what she'd discovered.

Now it is October again, nearly a whole year since Alice left us forever. The air is a little cooler, and the leaves have dropped the same seeds Alice crushed beneath her thin sneakers as she hurried away from us. Some of the husbands sweep the sidewalks clear of them; some of our children gather the seeds in their open palms and carry them home, and we have to remind them not to bring them inside the house. Give them to the birds, the squirrels, we suggest, which pacifies the children. It makes them happy to think of feeding wild things who already know how to feed themselves. It feels like a gesture of kindness, even though we know it's an unnecessary one.

On the first of the month, as if she couldn't wait a day longer, Mrs. Lange brings us pumpkin bread. The bread is perfect. It is moist, soft, the right balance of dense and light, a perfect combination of nutmeg and ginger. Mrs. Lange, we say to her, you are an artist. What harm does it cause if we exaggerate, only a tad? Mrs. Lange is gracious and humble. She stops herself from saying, "It was always Alice who did the spices." Alice, excellent at chemistry, too, could eyeball a tablespoon, a teaspoon, even a half a teaspoon. She would line the spice jars up like little soldiers, rank and file, and she could anticipate what her mother would need and when, even if she was doing her algebra homework or reading *Pride and Prejudice* as her mother bustled around.

It had always been for Mrs. Lange a world of two; other people passed through, but they were only visitors. She and Alice were the sole true inhabitants, and the world was the size of whatever space they occupied at the moment—when they baked, it was the size of the kitchen; when they slept each in her own bedroom every night, the world's dimensions encompassed the house. Now, they are apart, and Mrs. Lange can't picture where her daughter is, and so the size of the world is infinite. And yet, for Mrs. Lange, regardless of the endless depth and breadth of the world, the population remains at two.

Instead of telling us about Alice and how it felt to share a warm kitchen with her, she simply thanks us and moves along to her next stop, to our immense relief.

Three days later, on a Sunday, we come home from church to find baggies of snickerdoodles at our front doors. "Who are these from?" asks Billy, already opening one.

"Stop right there," says April, thinking of all those years ago when she and Bev bonded over the poisoned pumpkin bread and the baby-stealing ring. "Just in case," she says.

"They're from Mrs. Lange," says Eric. "Who else leaves baked goods for us?"

"I'm just going to ask her," April says. "Don't let Billy have a cookie." She walks down the street to the Langes' house and knocks on the door. No one answers. The front porch swing glides a little on the breeze. A cool front, April knows, is blowing in later today, and she shivers in anticipation. Behind her, a dog barks. She turns around and sees Mrs. McEntyre and Sweetie watching her. "Sweetie's in everyone's business," Mrs. McEntyre says, even though now the dog has ducked her head and snuffles around the fallen seeds and leaves, and it is Mrs. McEntyre who looks at her. She takes note of April's shoes— beige, sensible heels. "Did you just finish at church?" she asks April.

"I did, but now I'm hoping to find Mrs. Lange."

"That sweet woman," Mrs. McEntyre says, already planning on telling the rest of us how she'd caught April snooping around. "First pumpkin bread and now cookies. Imagine."

April isn't sure what, exactly, she is supposed to imagine, so she nods and turns back to the door. After a moment, Mrs. McEntyre and Sweetie continue on, and April hears Sweetie bark in the distance.

She knocks again and considers trying to peek in the windows, but the blinds are closed up tight, and so she waits another minute and leaves.

Once home, she calls Bev. "Did you get cookies?" she asks.

"Yes," her friend says. "And we've all eaten one, and no one's died yet."

"That's all I needed to know," April says. She gives a thumbs-up to Billy, who is watching eagerly from the entryway to the kitchen, the plastic bag in his hand.

That night, April sits on the edge of the mattress as Eric gets ready for bed and tells him about the Lange house. "I hope she isn't, you know," says April.

"Dead?" asks Eric, dropping his pants to the floor.

"Fold those," says April. "Yes. I always worry she might, I don't know, you know what I mean."

"Kill herself?"

"Aren't you a little worried?" April asks. Eric folds his pants and sets them on a chair in the corner of the room. She sighs inwardly. How hard would it be to put them in a drawer?

"She's lucky to have such nice neighbors concerned about her," Eric says. "It really isn't my business, but it's nice to know other people are looking out for her." He climbs into bed, and April slips in beside him.

"The cookies were good," April says.

"They were," says Eric. He rolls toward her. "Turn off the light," he says, his voice low.

Two days later, muffins. A few days after that, loaves of heavy, beery bread. After that, there is nothing for a week, and then, unseasonably, sugar cookies with the duck fluff yellow sprinkles appear. We grow concerned. This is not normal behavior.

On the day the sugar cookies arrive, Bev, April, and Charlotte Price sit in front of April's house watching the children ride their bikes up and down the street. The baby sits on Bev's lap, the front of her gray dress wet with drool and her mother's bent knuckle in her mouth. A plate of cookies like small yellow suns rests on the lawn in front of them, blades of grass sticking up around its perimeter. "We should have an intervention," says Charlotte. "I love a cookie as much as anyone else, but honestly, this is too much."

"I don't mind it at all," says April, and laughs. Her midsection is thicker than it's ever been, and when she looks in the mirror, she sees the shape of her mother. But it worries her less than she would have thought it would; she likes, for example, the pleasant weight of her breasts, which have taken on a fullness they haven't had since she nursed Billy. She also knows, though, that Charlotte Price, thin as a reed, would never understand because here you should constantly be striving to be something better than what you are. We are lucky to be here, where so many of our problems are solved, allowing us the energy and time to devote to other areas of our lives that need improvement.

"I worry about what it means for Mrs. Lange," says Bev. "April, I know you feel the same way."

"Yes," she says. "All this baking. When does she sleep?"

Charlotte looks out to the street where her twins are racing side by side, the other boys behind them. When they ride, the boys stand up on their bikes, legs straight, and the wind pushes their hair off their foreheads. "I'll talk to her," she says, her eyes still on the boys.

Bev widens her eyes at April, who cringes. "We could," Bev says. "She's always liked me. I can bring the baby. She might like that." She props the baby up so she's standing unsteadily on her chubby feet. "Those feet are like pillows," Bev said last night to Todd. "How on earth can they be good for anything but nibbling?"

"I'll go," Charlotte says now, looking back to her. There is a glint in Charlotte's eyes and a note in her voice that both say this matter is resolved and will not be discussed further.

"Maybe she's right, Bev," says April. "You should let Charlotte do it."

Bev is surprised. She looks at her friend to see if there's a wink stirring at the corner of her eye, a sign that April is simply placating Charlotte, who is known for steamrolling anyone who disagrees with her, but April only looks concerned.

"All right," says Bev. "But I'm happy to go over there if you change your mind."

"I promise it'll be fine, Bev," says Charlotte, leaning over to pat Bev on the hand, but Bev moves it at the last moment to dry the baby's glistening chin.

A few houses down, a door slams, and the women all look up to see Christine Pittman bounding out of her house and waving at the boys.

"Christine!" Timmy calls, drawing out the last syllable of her name.

"I'm coming," she says. "Hang on!" Her bike lies on the lawn, and she grabs it, hops on, and starts down the driveway.

Charlotte stands up and waves at the girl. "Christine," she says. "Come here, say hello." Dutifully, Christine changes course and rides up the driveway of Bev's house. "Hi," she says.

"Sit," says Charlotte. "Join the girls."

Christine glances over at the boys, who watched her glide down her driveway and now are pumping up April's driveway and then speeding down, feet off the pedals. "Okay," she says, and gently lays the bike down, the front wheel still spinning. "Am I in trouble?"

"No!" says Bev. "You can go play! We just wanted to say hi."

"Sit," says Charlotte again. "Where's your mother?"

"Inside," she says. "She said it was fine if I came out since you were all out here. She has a headache."

"It won't kill you to watch for a while," Charlotte says. "The boys aren't going anywhere."

So Christine sits down with the women and together they watch the boys zoom by. At first, they yell for Christine each time they pass, but eventually they stop calling her name and start only hooting and waving, and the girls on the lawn wave back.

That night, Charlotte Price goes over and rings Mrs. Lange's doorbell. Surprised by the unexpected visitor, Mrs. Lange lets Charlotte inside and leads her into the kitchen, which is warm and smells like Christmas. Gingerbread, says Mrs. Lange.

We're worried about you, Charlotte says. All this baking. Please, Mrs. Lange, take a break.

Mrs. Lange says she doesn't mind.

Please, Charlotte says again. We all feel very uncomfortable.

She stands up and goes to the pantry, while Mrs. Lange takes a seat at the kitchen table, watches. Charlotte pulls out the bag of flour, a bag of sugar, a bottle of vanilla. She places them on the counter. A half-used bag of chocolate chips. A jar of molasses. Honey. This flour is old, Charlotte remarks.

It's fine, says Mrs. Lange.

You can bake us the gingerbread cookies at Christmas, Charlotte tells her. The sugar cookies in the spring. She holds up a hand. No more than that. Charlotte picks up the bag of flour, the top of which has been curled over to keep it closed, walks over to the trash can, and drops it in. Then she takes the bottle of vanilla, checks that the lid is sealed tightly, and puts it in her purse. I'm out, she says. Thank you. You'll feel better without all the extra work.

When Charlotte is gone, Mrs. Lange goes inside and takes the gingerbread from the oven. She places another batter-filled loaf pan inside. After it all cools, she slices it up and wraps it, making sure there's a half loaf for every neighbor, until every surface in her kitchen is covered in tinfoil-wrapped stacks.

In the morning, we wake up to the packages on our doorstep. We eat it with our coffee, break off pieces with our fingers, place them in our mouths. We think of Mrs. Lange, and, always, of Alice.

CHAPTER NINETEEN

THE NIGHT AFTER Wesley bought the priest's robes, he told them it was time for a game. Alice wondered if it would be the same one they had played the night he'd placed the little tablets on their tongues—when Hannah Fay had cried and Wesley had slapped Janie. But it turned out Wesley loved games, had an entire head full of games he carried around with him, complete with rules, and the fear game was only one of them. "A new one," he said to the girls as they rose to clear the plates after dinner. "I'm inspired." He sat at the table as Alice and the others flitted around him, grabbing dishes and cups, running a damp rag across the table. He leaned against the back of the chair, which was pushed slightly away from the table, with his legs out straight and his feet bare.

"So what's the game?" Hannah Fay asked him as she wiped down the stove, glancing over her shoulder. "Does it have anything to do with your new outfit?"

"Bingo," he said, pointing at her.

"Do we all get to dress up?" asked Janie. She took the dish towel she was holding and draped it over her head and held it together at her chin like a nun's habit.

"Sister Janie," teased Hannah Fay. Apple came up behind Janie and yanked it away, but Janie just shook back her hair and laughed.

"It's not a costume," Wesley said. "It's a sacred garment."

"Tell us how to play, Wesley," Alice said. "Are there rules?"

"Maybe game is the wrong word," Wesley said thoughtfully. "Play is the wrong word. I'm thinking this is more like a practice. Or a discipline."

"A sacrament," said Kathryn. She sat down at the table beside him, and Hannah Fay took the chair on his other side.

Wesley clapped his hands together. "Yes," he said. "Exactly. That's what it is exactly. You know, I wasn't entirely joking about starting my own religion."

"So you're saying eventually we'll all call you Father," Apple said. "Got it."

"Who's going first?" Alice asked quickly as she noticed Wesley's body tense. "I can if you want."

"I'm going to get dressed," he said. "And then I'll decide. Hannah Fay, we'll use your room if that's all right."

"Of course," she said. "It's not really my room anyway."

"It's everyone's room," Kathryn said.

"It's Hannah Fay's room," Apple said.

"I love you, Apple," Hannah Fay said.

"I love you too," said Apple.

"All right, calm down," Wesley said. "We've got a sacrament to perform."

* * *

Alice sat between Hannah Fay and Kathryn on the couch, and Apple and Janie took the floor. They all sat facing the study, whose French doors were closed, so they could see Wesley as soon as he emerged. During her first trimester, Hannah Fay had told Alice, she'd had terrible insomnia—any amount of light was enough to keep her awake—so Wesley had tacked blankets over the windowpanes on the doors. They were still in place, so no one could tell what he was doing, though Janie said he'd asked her where the extra candles were, the ones Kathryn insisted on keeping handy in case the power ever went out. Kathryn hadn't grown up here, with all our sunshine, and when she was a kid on the Gulf coast, she'd told Alice, summer storms had wracked her family's tiny house until the electricity went out and they were plunged into darkness. (And this is how we imagine Kathryn's mother, still in that rickety coastal cottage, the soil wet and shifting underneath, sitting, walking, sleeping in the dark.)

They were quiet as they waited for Wesley, and Alice remembered standing with Susannah and a line of other girls outside the locker room the summer before their freshman year, waiting to be called one by one into the room for the physical they needed in order to try out for the volleyball team. "I heard they give you a shot," one girl said. "In your butt."

"No way," Susannah had said. "But Mary Mueller said they ask you if you're a virgin."

"What does that have to do with volleyball?" asked Alice, not one to be easily taken in, and no one could give her a real answer. In the end, when the door shut behind Alice and she faced the school nurse and Coach Timmons, all she had to do was inhale, exhale, touch her toes, stand on the scale, and rotate her hips, her neck, her wrists. Alice made the A team and got to play in the big gym before the varsity team played. Susannah and whoever said they were getting shots in the rear (it was Millie, forgettable, dependable Millie) made the B team, whose games were relegated to the practice gym, the one with no bleachers. Jealous, Susannah didn't talk to Alice for a week, until eventually she couldn't keep it up anymore, couldn't stop herself from loving Alice Lange.

But this was the mood as the girls waited outside the study: excitement, tension, wonder. Who would they be required to be? Who would Wesley be? Father Wesley, Brother Wesley. Wesley in the cassock, Wesley in the shadows, Wesley in the light. The door opened, but he did not emerge. "Alice," he said, though it wasn't loud, maybe even a rung below the volume of his regular voice, and it seemed to her like the darkness of the study was calling her name. A disembodied voice, or maybe the voice came from the house, and the house was the body and the study its mouth, opening and summoning. Alice stood up. "When you come out, tell us what happens," Apple said.

"That will definitely be against the rules," Kathryn said.

"Whose side are you on?" Apple asked, but Kathryn—to her credit, Alice thought—ignored her.

Inside the study, Alice felt struck by a series of images, flashes of shapes she had to make sense of in the darkness— the glowing orbs of candlelight, the white square of collar at Wesley's throat, his hands folded on the desk like a fallen pair of doves. "Shut the door," he told her, but she was already doing it, closing herself in with him.

The study held a desk that Alice knew was made of some dark, heavy wood—it had been in the house when Kathryn bought it—and a chair. At night, Hannah Fay slept on a thin mattress in the center of the room, but now it was leaned up against the wall, the fitted sheet still wrapped around it and her blankets folded neatly beside it.

And Wesley sat at the desk, and he was both Wesley and not Wesley. It made Alice think of those pictures in which some people saw a vase, while others saw two people kissing, or they saw a crone or they saw a maiden. The picture was both a vase and not a vase, lovers and not lovers, an old woman and a young woman at the same time. This was Wesley in front of Alice. He was Wesley, and he was also a vessel, an act of love, youth, and age—he took everything in the room, in the house, in the universe, and held it all inside him, becoming both everything Alice knew intimately and everything she found alien.

"Sit," he said. Alice felt relieved he didn't call her "child," the way the priest at her grandparents' church did when she visited, or make her kneel or make the sign of the cross over her chest. She would've done either of those things, but she would've felt—wrong somehow.

Alice lowered herself into a dining chair, the desk a barrier between them, and crossed her ankles. She wasn't sure if she should keep her eyes down or meet his and finally settled on glancing up at him to see where he was looking: at her, his eyes bright, pinpricks of candlelight reflected in the black. She didn't know if she was supposed to be holding eye contact with him, or if this version of Wesley would find it disrespectful or presumptuous, so she looked instead at his right ear.

"Alice," he said, "what do you think we are going to do in here?"

"Ah," she said, thinking of everything she associated with Catholicism. "You said a sacrament. So maybe . . . Communion?"

"Do you see any wine?" Wesley asked. "Or bread?"

"No," she told him.

"And surely you don't think I would ask you to actually drink my blood and eat my body," he said congenially. He was smiling. White teeth above white collar.

"Of course not," Alice said, hoping he didn't hear the uncertainty in her voice. (A man like that, we would tell her, would never shed a drop of his blood for you, not even if you were dying and only he could save you.)

"Okay," he said. "So not that."

"Confession," Alice said.

"There we go," he said. "Nailed it." He paused. "Pun not intended."

"Pun?"

"Because Jesus," Wesley answered, lifting his hands and tapping each palm with a forefinger. "Nailed?"

"Oh," said Alice. "Right."

"Okay, so," Wesley said, "confession. What do you think is going to happen next?"

"I'm going to confess," Alice said. "To you. About . . . things. Bad things."

"Wrong again," he said. Around him the candles flickered, flames trembling. "I'm going to confess to you."

"Are you going to do the same thing to all the girls?" Alice asked. "Confess, I mean."

"Normally, I wouldn't answer that," Wesley said. "But since tonight is all about honesty, I'll tell you this: yes, I'm going to confess to all of you, and I'm going to be truthful, but each of you will get part of the story. My story. The part I choose to tell you." He pointed at Alice, his finger like a sword aimed at her chest. "You, specifically."

"Okay," said Alice. "Wow. Okay. I feel so powerful." She laughed. "I'm trying to decide what I should ask first."

"Sorry," said Wesley, "but your job isn't to ask questions. Maybe some other time, but not tonight. Tonight your job is only to listen. But if it's power you want, then think about it this way: there's power in listening too. You just wield it differently."

"All right," said Alice, nodding, though she wasn't sure she understood. "You've got my attention."

"All right," echoed Wesley. He took a deep breath. Alice watched his shoulders rise and fall. He bent his head so that he looked like a supplicant (or, we think, like an actor, trying to recall his lines), and Alice waited. A minute ticked by. Wesley lifted his head again. "When I was a little boy, I lived with many women. Not all at once. One by one. My mother first, and then when she left, my grandmother, and when she died, my aunt. It's my destiny to be surrounded, always, by women."

"Lucky you," Alice said.

Wesley held up a hand. "Don't interrupt, please," he said, and Alice's cheeks began to burn. "I want to tell you about them. First, there was my mother. She does not have a name. To the state, the country, yes, of course she does, but not to me." He said this like he was ashamed and divulging a secret vulnerability, sharing with Alice something he normally kept hidden, but she already knew this; it was one of the first things he'd told her, those weeks ago in his truck as they drove out here. (See, Alice? Every word of his monologue, the tone he has affected—all of it carefully chosen. An act. But he's sloppy too. Can't even keep his lines straight.) "She never earned a true name," Wesley went on. "She was a bad and unkind woman, and if I was older, I would have killed her. Does that scare you?" He paused here. "To hear that I could be a murderer? That I could kill my own mother?" He paused again, and Alice got the sense that he was waiting, and so she nodded.

"Yes," she said. She imagined it, Wesley as a boy or a young man with pricks of acne across his cheeks, lonely and angry. A woman with blue eyes like his, with the same cleft chin. This she could picture. A gun? Poison? This, she told herself, she could not (but another voice, one she could hear but told herself she couldn't—this voice whispered *knife*).

"It scares me too," he said. "But she left me. A little boy. Her son! What kind of woman can do that?"

"What about your father?" Alice asked.

"Alice," Wesley said. He rubbed his face with a weary hand. "Please. I'll never finish if you keep interrupting."

"But do you hate him?" she asked. Typically, she listened to Wesley and followed his orders, but not tonight. Maybe it was Wesley's vulnerability, maybe it was the cassock that gave the whole proceedings a kind of unreality, the way she always felt on Halloween, that nothing she did mattered, like the cool night two years ago when she had dressed as Cleopatra, heavy black liner rimming her eyelids, and she had let Carl Miller stick his hands inside her dress (Carl Miller, the first to chart the territory that was the golden Alice; we would have chosen someone different for her, someone who would not have felt her breasts and then pinched her nipples and asked her if she was cold), and it was only the next morning she realized that somehow something had truly been gained but lost as well, a real-life choice made for Alice by a long-dead Egyptian queen. "Do you?" she asked again when Wesley did not answer.

"No," he said. "He had no reason to be loyal to me, but my mother did."

"I see," said Alice.

"You don't," said Wesley. "You really don't. I've been working on opening your eyes, and I see it happening, but this is one place where I'm afraid they're still sealed fucking tight. You had a mother who loved you, but you're the one who left. That tells me you don't understand. If you did, you would never have left."

"I had to leave," said Alice. "You know that. You knew I couldn't stay there. I had to go."

"I knew you belonged here," Wesley said. "But you always have a choice. It's just sometimes it feels like you don't." He shrugged. "Maybe my mom felt the same way, that her only choice was to leave me. She didn't see herself as a mother, and she had to go. But even when you do what you think is right, what you absolutely have to do, there's some collateral damage along the way." He pointed to himself. "That's me," he said, then pointed toward the window that overlooked the front porch. "That's your mother."

"Stop it," said Alice, shaken. "This isn't about me."

"You're right," Wesley said. "I wanted to tell you about the women."

"Tell me, then," Alice said. "And I promise I won't interrupt."

"My mother left me, and I went to stay with my grandmother," he said. "She was kind and good. She taught me to read, made sure I went to school. When she died, I went to live with my aunt, my mother's sister, who blamed me, first, for driving my mother away, then sending her own mother into an early grave. Eventually, my aunt sent me away. I'd been getting into a lot of fights, nothing crazy, just boys being boys. But a few of the mothers complained to my aunt that I was a bully, I fought dirty, and my aunt got the excuse she'd been looking for to get rid of me. So she called an institution who dealt with 'children like me,' she said, children who were violent. 'I'm afraid I'm going to be next, Wesley,' she said. 'I can't have you here.' It's not like she woke up one night with me standing over her with a knife. Nothing like that." Wesley stopped here to look at Alice.

"So she sent you away," she said.

Wesley nodded. "From then on, I was the product of institutions," he said. "In and out, in and out until I was a grown man. This is what I need to confess to you. When I was a boy, I didn't know how to play the game, be who they wanted me to be, and Alice, Alice, I hate to tell you this, but when I was in there, those places, I did hurt people. I had to. You know how it is to have to do something, to feel you have no other choice. Well, that was the case. I had to do it to get by, until I realized that was what they wanted, they wanted me locked up because I was trash, just some bastard orphan, and I changed. I made myself change. I was good. I became good. And that's why I'm good now. Now I see the goodness in other people, like you and Apple and Janie. Like Kathryn. Hannah Fay. My good girls. And we'll keep being good until the world demands something else of us."

"Why would the world want us to be anything but good?" Alice asked.

"It won't," Wesley said. "It's more that the world might

not recognize our goodness for what it is. They'll want us to look like them and act like them, but we won't do it."

Alice, a girl who did know how to play the game, wasn't sure what to say. On the one hand, she knew the answer Wesley wanted her to give. On the other, she didn't think the world was so bad. But then again, he was right: she had been lucky, privileged to grow up in our community. The only institution she had ever known was school, and though she had grown tired of it eventually and seen it for what it was—a cage, a holding pen—it had been, for her, a warm and happy place. There, adults encouraged her, her classmates admired her. She grew strong, smart. When we told her she was exceptional, she heard us. She believed it. (And we would tell her, every institution would have cared for you, would have first held your hand and later kissed the ring on that same hand. Not everyone is so lucky, but you were.)

What must it have been like for Wesley, wherever he was? She imagined him again now, a boy with shaggy dark hair curling over his ears, standing in the doorway of a big, gray place, a duffel bag slung over one shoulder, a great room unfolding before him, one whose windows had bars, whose gray hallways branched off like flagella, whose gray floors were scuffed linoleum. Older boys watching. Adults out of earshot and unconcerned. His aunt's car pulling away from the curb. Of course he knew the world was a false place, that a person couldn't trust it to give a straight answer. Alice looked at Wesley, and he looked back at her. She saw he was true and strong, and his eyes were bright with tears. (But couldn't it have been the candlelight making his eyes shine?) She could believe him, he who knew the world so much more intimately than she did. If someday he said the time had come when what the world wanted and what was right and good had diverged so much that the two sides could never reconcile, that the world had closed its eyes forever, banishing itself into the darkness, she would trust him. "No," she said. "We won't do it."

"Good girl," said Wesley.

"Alice," Wesley said, "I sit here before you ready to confess: I have hated my mother. I have hurt other people, and I mean physically, not just emotionally, though I'm sure I've done that, too, without knowing it."

Alice wasn't sure what to say. "It's frightening," she finally managed. "And heartbreaking all at once."

"May I say one more thing?" he asked. Alice nodded. Wesley put both hands flat on the table, his fingers spread so wide his hands looked giant. "Anything you see in me is in you," he said. "Do you understand? If you look at me and see a—a—killer or I don't know, a criminal, that's what's in your heart. A darkness."

"What are you saying?" asked Alice. "That I'm a bad person?"

"No," he said. "You are good. And when you look at people, you project that goodness into them. You change them. You're changing me, and it's helping you too. I'm a mirror. What you see is what's in you."

And what did she see? A boy who had been broken and rebuilt into something stronger, into someone with a unique vision. Someone special, powerful. She had been rebuilt, too, she thought.

(We've always thought that part of what made Alice Lange so exceptional, so extraordinary, was a near supernatural capacity for empathy. Wesley must have known this about her too.)

Suddenly Alice heard the front door of the house opening and closing, and she involuntarily looked toward the window, which faced the front porch; Wesley did too. Two of the girls, laughing. "It's Apple and Janie," Alice said. She wondered if they could hear her inside the room. If they had gone outside to listen.

"Janie," Wesley said. "I've hurt her too. You've seen that."

"Yes," said Alice.

"Do you think I'll hurt you?" he asked.

He only hits Janie, Apple had said, *if that makes you feel any better.* It had made her feel better, and it also made her—strangely, she knew—a little jealous. Because it meant Janie possessed something extra, something that made her stand out to Wesley. She knew this was a horrible way to feel, but there it was sitting heavily inside her stomach, like a poisoned apple she had bit into only once before deciding to swallow it whole.

"You won't hurt me," Alice said. "Only Janie."

"Only people who need it," he said. "Sometimes Janie does. Sometimes she's far away from what she needs to be. She doesn't live in the now, and she needs someone to wake her up."

From outside she hears the girls again—Apple's laugh is rumbly, like springtime thunder, and Janie's is higher. She closes her eyes when she laughs, and Alice remembers Wesley's hand whipping across Janie's face, her eyes closed then, too, how she kept them closed a second after the crack.

"What is my penance?" Wesley asked. "How can I be forgiven?"

Alice considered this, the thrill of power she felt earlier rushing up inside her again. Love me, she thought, love all of us, but love me best of all. Bake us a cake every night, bring us breakfast in bed, take me on a trip. A road trip along the ocean, up and down the hills. Wear a sandwich board that says "Alice Lange is my queen," keep it on for a whole day. But everything she thought of was silly, childlike.

"What do I have to forgive you for?" Alice said instead. "You don't owe me anything."

Wesley bowed his head. "Bless you," he said. "The others won't be as forgiving, I'm afraid."

(But they will, even Apple.)

"What will you tell them?" Alice asked. "It will be something different, won't it?"

"I do the things I do based on what people need," Wesley said.

"I understand," Alice said.

"Will you send Kathryn in?" Wesley asked. From next door, the neighbor's dog barked. "God," said Wesley, "I hate that fucking dog."

(What did Wesley's confession say about Alice, about what she needed? Was it to be frightened? Because this would be what we ourselves would take away from this, that Wesley was a man formed by prisons, asylums, facilities, a person who heard no other voices but his own. Let nothing else dictate his behavior. She thought this: poor Wesley, strong Wesley, oh, how he had suffered, and he needed her to know this, she needed to know how his life had been defined by loss, how these women, his own family, left him. Alice could make it up to him. The girls could be his new family. She could be a wife to him, a mother to him, a sister, anything he needed her to be. Alice Lange loved redemption.)

The front door opened and closed again, and they could

hear that the girls were back inside. "And can you tell Apple and Janie to quit with the fucking door?" Wesley asked. He ran a finger between his collar and throat and rolled his shoulders back.

"Of course," Alice said. "Thank you, Wesley."

But he already had his eyes closed and his head bowed, preparing for Kathryn.

"How was it?" Janie asked when Alice plopped herself down in the armchair by the couch. Hannah Fay had gone to Apple and Janie's bedroom to sleep before it was her turn with Wesley, but Apple and Janie were still on the couch, Apple's head in her friend's lap. Janie held thin strands of Apple's hair, weaving them in and out and over and under until they were tiny braids.

"Fine," Alice said. "Enlightening."

"Oooh," said Janie. She didn't look up from Apple's hair, but she raised her eyebrows. "Enlighten us now."

"Jay," said Apple. "I don't know what the rules are, but you know that's got to be against them." Janie still held Apple's hair in her hands like reins, so Apple couldn't turn her head toward Alice, but she cut her eyes in her direction. "Am I right?"

"Yes, sorry," Alice said.

"Secrets don't make friends," said Janie. "That's what my mom always said."

"Your mom is dumb," Apple said. "Secrets make the best friends." Alice thought back to all the times she and Susannah had whispered to each other in the quiet places of their lives: dark bedrooms and living rooms in sleeping bags, the school library, the back of the bus on the way home from sporting events. Once when they were all on the school bus together, Millie had peeked over at the girls in the seat behind her and said, "What are you talking about?" And Susannah and Alice had erupted into giggles. "Nothing," said Susannah. Millie had looked at them suspiciously. "Really, Millie," Alice said. "Nothing." The subtext being *nothing we'll tell you.* (Of course in the moment when Millie decided to tell us about the floats, a slideshow of encounters with Alice Lange flashed through her memory, including this one of the bus ride, the shame she felt as she turned back around and slumped back onto her own bench.)

"Well," said Alice, torn between loyalty to Wesley and to the girls, "I'll just tell you one thing." She lowered her voice and leaned closer. Janie stopped braiding Apple's hair and looked up. "Did you know he grew up in institutions?" Alice asked. "Poor Wesley. Can you imagine?"

"Oh," said Apple. "I knew that." She shrugged. She sat up so that Janie's hands seemed to fall from her hair, and she crossed her legs underneath her.

"What kind of institutions?" Janie asked.

"Like orphanages, or reform schools," Alice said. Outside the neighbor's dog barked, paused, then barked again. Alice looked out the front window. The blinds were open but all she could see was darkness.

"Yeah, an orphanage," Apple said, "but also prison." And Alice's attention snapped back to her.

Janie's eyes went wide as she looked from Apple to Alice for confirmation. "No way," she said.

"Yes," said Apple. "Or maybe not prison because it wasn't for very long? So would that be jail? But yes, basically. That's the institution he was talking about, I'm sure."

"No," Alice said. She replayed the conversation in her head, Wesley sitting across from her, penitent and alone. "He didn't mention prison."

"Of course he wouldn't, to you," Apple said, emphasizing the last word.

"I'm sorry," Janie interjected, holding up a hand as Alice opened her mouth, "but let's get back to why Wesley was in jail."

"Shhh," Alice said. "Come on, we're not even supposed to be talking about it."

"You were fine talking about it earlier," Apple said, "until you realized you weren't the expert after all."

"I never said I was an expert," Alice replied.

"You didn't have to."

Janie leaned forward so her body separated Alice and Apple from each other's line of vision. "Hello," she said in a loud whisper. "Jail? Prison? Did he kill someone?"

Alice caught Apple looking sideways in the direction of the study. "He wouldn't say," Apple said. "So I don't know. But if I had to guess, I'd say no. Does he seem like someone who would kill somebody?"

"Of course not," Alice said. "If he did, none of us would be here."

Janie nodded.

"There you go," Apple said.

"Huh," Janie said, still nodding. The corners of her mouth turned downward in a pensive frown. "I wonder what else we don't know about Wesley." (There we go! The million-dollar question. But the girls let us down here, especially Alice, who we valued for her levelheadedness, her reason, who said only:)

"We know the important things." She spoke firmly, and

it sounded like something Kathryn would say, which troubled her briefly because none of them wanted to sound like Kathryn. But she meant it, and more than that, she wanted the conversation to end. It had felt good to sit across from Wesley at the big desk and listen as he told her about the world and what he knew of it. To re-create her vision of him and attempt to redraw him as a young deviant instead of a boy abandoned—that part had wrecked her head a little, made her stomach hurt, made the room around her sharp and blurry at the same time. All the colors of the room popped brightly—the orange couch, the fat green leaves of the succulents—but the edges of everything were dulled.

The dog from next door barked again, was always barking. Alice could picture him in his yard, nose pressed into the gaps of the wrought-iron fence that enclosed the neighbors' property, snuffling in the darkness and then reacting to every movement he saw but didn't understand.

"Can I braid your hair, Alice?" Janie asked. "I'm tired of Apple's."

"Hey," said Apple. "Rude." But she stood up and stretched, reached her long arms to the ceiling and pushed herself up on her toes so that the slender cut of her calves became elongated and defined, like the silhouette of a cliff above a canyon. Alice got up, too, taking Apple's place, and put her head down in Janie's lap, hair spread out in a fan. She closed her eyes at Janie's touch and fell asleep, waking only when Janie whispered, "It's my turn. I'm up," and Alice squinted her eyes to see Apple walking out of the study. Apple faced the living room as she pulled the door closed behind her, tenderly, like she was afraid its glass panes would shatter.

Alice sat up, groggy. "How was it?"

WE CAN ONLY SAVE OURSELVES | 163

"Enlightening," Apple said. "Like you said. Get up. You can share the bedroom with Hannah Fay. I'll take the couch."

"Are you sure?" Alice asked, but she had already gotten up, like the bed was pulling her to it, and she was powerless to move in any other direction.

"Good night, Alice," said Apple.

"Good night," said Alice, and she wove clumsily to the bedroom. She climbed into bed and pulled the quilt up as much as she could; Hannah Fay, always hot, was on top of the bedding. She closed her eyes and slept soundly, as if she were the one who'd had a burden lifted that night, not Wesley, as if she were free of a great and heavy weight.

CHAPTER TWENTY

A FTER THE SERIES of confessions, Wesley slept in the
study on Hannah Fay's twin mattress—was still sleeping, Alice guessed, since he hadn't emerged this morning.
"What did I miss?" Hannah Fay asked the other girls as she
joined them for breakfast, after waking to realize that Wesley
had apparently forgotten about her.

"Nothing really," Kathryn said, and took a sip of her coffee, shuddering a little as she did. They all had to drink their
coffee black because there was hardly ever any milk in the
house and certainly never any cream. Alice was used to it by
now, but Kathryn always had to choke it down. It amused
Alice that Kathryn, of all the girls, was the one who could
not tolerate the bitterness.

No one else said anything after Kathryn spoke. Apple was
leaning against the counter by the toaster, eating a piece of
plain toast, occasionally brushing crumbs off her shirt onto the
floor, and Alice sat at the table and ate from a plate of scram-

bled eggs. The plate was porcelain but had a hairline crack running through the center, and Alice always wondered if one day it would just break in two. She found herself thinking of her mother's crystal bowl, the berries glistening prettily in it, and her mother's slender fingers plucking them from the dish one by one. But then she thought of how the crystal bowl came to her mother and father as part of an entire set of crystal dishes, and with the crystal came settings of china, and from there, a person ended up with cabinets full of Tupperware, and Alice looked at her scrambled eggs, as yellow as sunshine, with gratitude.

"So nothing?" asked Hannah Fay again. "Really?"

"Wesley's giving each of us a million dollars," Apple said. "And we weren't going to tell you."

Kathryn rolled her eyes at Apple. "Apple," she said, "use a plate."

"Was it a religious thing?" Hannah Fay asked.

"Kind of," Kathryn said with a shrug.

"But Wesley hates the Church," Hannah Fay said.

"You know what he does love, though?" asked Apple, who had gotten a plate down from the cupboard but was still eating over the floor. "Wesley."

"He's his own church," said Janie.

"Is that what he told you?" Alice asked. A church, a mirror. What wasn't he?

"Wesley is the body and the blood," Janie said, dramatically casting her eyes heavenward and then laughing.

"I don't like the tone of this conversation," Kathryn said. "Get it all out of your system before Wesley wakes up."

"Well," said Hannah Fay, "I hope he does it again."

"A million dollars, Hannah Fay," Apple said, wiping the

last of her toast crumbs off her hands over the sink. She swept over to the girls at the table and rested her head on Hannah Fay's shoulder. "Think of everything we could do."

"Next time," Hannah Fay said. She reached up to pat Apple's cheek. "See if I tell you what happens when it's my turn."

But when Wesley emerged from the bedroom just before noon, he was already wearing his boots. "Where're you headed?" Janie asked. She and the other girls were sprawled around the living room.

"Outside," he said, without stopping. In his arms he carried the heap of black robes, and he walked straight out of the house, down the steps, and onto the driveway. He dropped the cassock on the pavement, where it sat like a black hole or some kind of dead animal. The girls followed him outside, and they all stood on the front porch, not knowing quite what to do. Alice leaned against the railing, the white paint cracking and scratchy under her arms. "Wesley," Kathryn called. "Do you need help?"

"Get my camera," he said. "It's in your room." Kathryn scurried inside and came back with it, but he ignored her outstretched hands. They watched as he instead reached into his pocket, struck a match from a matchbook, and dropped it onto the cloth. When the flames took hold, small creatures eating up the blackness, he grabbed the camera from Kathryn and took several photos of the robe, first standing on his toes and leaning over, a bird's-eye view, and then crouching until he was eye level with the mass. Then he turned and walked back up the driveway, up the steps, and through the front door. As he passed the girls, he said, "Kathryn, please take care of this when the garment is adequately burned."

"Sure," said Kathryn, though Wesley was already inside the house.

"Should I douse it?" she asked the others. "Or will it burn out on its own?"

"It'll burn out," Alice said, unable to shake the image of the match she'd struck, the one that burned down her old life, the one whose light woke her up.

"I'll keep an eye on it just in case," Kathryn said. She looked at the other girls for confirmation. "Shouldn't I?"

"I'll stay out here too," said Apple. She scooted past the other girls and sat down on the front steps, where Janie joined her.

"I guess I'll never get to play that game," Hannah Fay said. "I wonder why he wanted to burn it."

"The mysterious mind of Wesley," said Janie.

"You don't need to question him," Kathryn said. "If he wants to burn an old robe, let him. We don't need to understand why."

"It's probably for his art," Janie said, "somehow."

"Or maybe it's just fun to play with matches," Apple said.

"Maybe it made him feel weird," said Alice, "to tell us such vulnerable things."

Apple, her back toward Alice, glanced up and over her shoulder at her. "Wesley didn't tell us anything he didn't want us to know."

"That doesn't mean he wasn't being vulnerable," Alice said. She flicked a curving shard of old paint at Apple. It landed in her hair, and Apple combed her fingers through it, but it stayed put.

"Knock it off, both of you," Kathryn said. Apple and Janie leaned away from each other in unison to let her pass, and as she approached the driveway, she plucked a handful of grass from the yard and tossed it into the fire. Alice thought of a witch in a fairy tale, mixing a potion, casting a spell. A clutch of grass, a bundle of twigs, eye of newt, black cloth.

"See, everyone loves fire," Apple said.

Alice waited for someone to say they would go check on Wesley, but no one did, so she didn't either. The minute one of them walked into the house, she would've followed—to be alone with Wesley was to win, and she knew if she was the someone to go inside, another girl would trail her, a defensive move. The game would be over, a tie, a stalemate. The game was over this way, too, with all the girls arranged outside on the porch and Wesley inside, doing whatever he was doing. Now that she was here, it was hard for Alice to imagine Wesley before the house, to remember what he was like without the girls who surrounded him. Without them, who was he?

"No one," he sometimes told them, one perched on his knee, three at his feet, another somewhere else—running his errands, making him a snack, washing his clothes—but hurrying back to join him. "I'm no one without you." And it was a nice thing to believe that without Alice, without the others, he didn't exist, and he was only called into being when they conjured him up. There it was, that shock and tremble, again, of power.

In the end, Alice stayed on the porch. She picked the peeling paint off the rail, flicked it into the hedge below.

So it wasn't exactly a win, but it wasn't quite a loss either—to stand outside with all the girls, to blink in the afternoon sunlight, to watch the inexplicable little fire burn up the confessions of last night, to smile at the confused man who lived next door, as he walked past their house with his son, the little boy turning up the driveway toward the fire like he was drawn to it, until his father stopped him, steering him by the shoulders away from the fire, away from those strange girls, keeping him safe from the things he didn't understand.

CHAPTER TWENTY-ONE

IN THE MIDDLE of our neighborhood there is a square of woods that reminds us of what the land must have looked like before we tamed it. Wild. Dense. The city calls it a park, but we are mothers, and to us a park is a place with a slide, swings, a seesaw. This has none of those features. It contains only trees and dirt, and the things that live among them, and so we call it the woods. When we read stories to our children—Rapunzel expelled from her tower and into the woods, Hansel and Gretel left to wander in the woods, Little Red Riding Hood watched among the trees of the woods—this place is what they picture.

Now that we are mothers reading these stories to our children, we see that they are frightening. Mothers die and fathers replace them, children are taken or abandoned or eaten. But we remind ourselves we once heard these stories, too, and look at us. We are fine.

Once, Nancy Pittman and Christine took a cobbler over to Earl Phelps's house for Veterans Day—every year, one with raspberries and blueberries and a dollop of whipped cream on top, which we all know doesn't belong on a cobbler, but which Nancy adds anyway to be patriotic. Bev suggested once that Nancy bring over a Tupperware container of vanilla ice cream instead. "There's your Stars and Stripes," she said.

"I'll think about it," Nancy said, but she didn't.

Christine had just learned to read, and she was carrying a book of fairy tales. "Can you read that to me?" Earl asked her. He could remember how, when he was a little boy, the world seemed to open when he learned how to read and how it kept opening to him and opening as he got older, and he even left the country, left the continent, learned to read again, this time just a little of a new language, and the world grew, and then the war was over, and he didn't know it then, but that was the moment the world started closing back up again, and now it was just the size of the garage where he sat. So when he saw Christine with her book, he wanted to remember how the world had once seemed so big he could lose himself in it. "Sure," Christine said. "Do you want a story about a mermaid or one about a princess?"

"I'll go put the cobbler inside," Nancy said, lifting the pie plate a bit to remind him why they were there.

"A mermaid," Earl said.

"There are mermaids in our ocean," Christine told him. "Did you know that?"

"Everyone knows that," Earl said.

Christine sat on the driveway, cross-legged in shorts and her older brother's baseball T-shirt, and read to Earl as he listened and watched the street. It was a quiet afternoon. Nancy listened, too, admiring the cadence of her daughter's voice, the easy way her eyes flicked over the words and how each word was like a pearl on a necklace being pulled from her mouth, unspooling on the driveway like an offering to their neighbor. At the end, the mermaid stood on her new tiptoes and kissed the prince. "Kind of gross with the kissing," Christine said. "But it's a happy ending for her."

Earl Phelps frowned. "That's not the way the story goes," he said.

"Yes, it is," said Nancy quickly, though she, too, remembered a different ending, a sadder one. "It's right there in the book, just like Christine read it."

Christine frowned now, too, and flipped the page to see if he was right, and she had missed something. But on the next page, the tale of Snow White began. The mermaid's story was over. "How's it supposed to go?" she asked.

"Well, first of all, the prince doesn't fall in love with her," Earl said. "Because she can't talk, and no one loves someone who can't talk. And I can't remember exactly how, but I think she dies."

"Dies!" said Christine. "She can't die."

"She doesn't," said Nancy. "If she did, that's what your book would say." She pushed up her sleeve and pretended to check her watch. "Let's go," she said, reaching a hand down to her little girl. Christine put her hand in her mother's but didn't let herself be pulled off the ground.

"I'm sure that's right," said Earl. "She turns into mist."

"Like fog?" asked Christine. "Or clouds?" She looked up at the clouds, and suddenly they did look different to her. She thought she saw a mermaid's tail in one, a hair comb shimmering with pearls in another. "So she doesn't really die?"

"Are clouds alive?" asked Earl.

"Come on, honey," Nancy said, tugging gently on her

daughter's arm. "Thank you again for your service, Earl. Your country appreciates you."

"No," said Christine. Earl watched her tilt her head back and squint at the sky. "They move, though, so maybe. Probably. So even if she turns into a cloud, she might not be dead."

"Earl," said Nancy, but he was looking at Christine, noticing that her chin-length hair didn't quite frame her face; one side did, and the other side flipped out in the same direction, like two quotation marks closing a sentence. She was working so hard to make the story end happily, to make it so the mermaid lived happily ever after. Once, in that other country, in Earl's other, bigger life, there had been a village full of little girls and little boys, too, crying and raging and scared, but all the grown-ups were gone. "It's a trap," their CO said, and they burned the village down.

"In the other version," Nancy said, "she almost dies, but then the angels save her and turn her into one of them."

"But the prince doesn't love her?" asked Christine. "And she doesn't even get to be a mermaid again?"

"She does in the book you have," Nancy said.

"But there's another story," Christine said. "You just said so."

"They can both be true," her mother said. "But you're upsetting yourself thinking about it. Your story is right there in your book, you read it yourself. Put the other one out of your mind."

Christine looked at Earl, who shrugged. "Sure," he said.

"Come on," said Nancy.

"Bye," said Christine, and Earl gave her a brusque nod and watched them walk back down the sidewalk.

To get home, they walked past the square of woods, and it was a sunny day, and Christine was still feeling strange about the mermaid, so she told her mother she wanted to cut through the woods. Among the trees, no one could see her but her mother; she could be anyone, and the world could be anything she made it. If her mother was there, that was good, too, because any world she made would have her in it.

A couple of years later, when Christine could read anything, knew every word in every book, Alice Lange was gone. After she left, we searched the woods for a body, despite the police reassuring us that she left of her own accord. We couldn't imagine that she would leave willingly. Our husbands formed the search parties, and back at home we imagined them barreling down the paths and calling her name, and later picking gently through the undergrowth, poking at logs and piles of leaves. They came home somber and dirty. We took off their boots, we picked leaves out of their hair, we ran baths for them, and we didn't ask them anything about what they'd seen or what they'd been afraid they might see.

Anything could be in the woods. And with Alice gone, we thought about that more often.

One afternoon not long after the searches died down, we were all sitting on Charlotte Price's back patio, the door leading outside still open, and arriving one by one as we finished our responsibilities at home. Our husbands were at work, and the big kids were at school, and Charlotte had walked up and down the street, knocking on our doors and gathering us together for, she said, refreshments and community. We get together a lot even in the best of circumstances, but in those early days after Alice's disappearance, we were together even more, except, of course, Mrs. Lange.

Nancy had passed by the woods to get to Charlotte's, and she thought of the day Earl Phelps had told her daughter that the little mermaid had died and how Christine had begged to walk home through the woods. She started off telling it as a funny story but then said, "Actually, it was the strangest thing. I was so mad at Earl Phelps, and the woods are so creepy, but Christine was dying to take that route."

Go on, we told her.

"I guess I don't really have a point," she said, shrugging. "I was just thinking about it. That night I dreamed Christine was lost in the woods." This time we shuddered. A premonition, we thought.

"All the kids love the woods," said April. "For a while there, Bev and I thought the boys were going to move out and live in a tent there."

"I wouldn't have said no," Bev said.

"I love them too," said Mags. "I like to walk the dogs there. It helps them remember they're animals." Another thing we know about Mags and the woods: she had an affair once, or more of a tryst because it only happened once, right there under the trees, with Fred Austin, the father of Ben, who loved Alice Lange. She genuinely thought of the dogs at first but then on the last word thought of Fred, his fingers on the buttons of her dress. She was quiet the rest of the afternoon, memories blooming, and after, it was Bev who asked her if she was all right. Fine, she said, just feeling melancholy. Bev squeezed her hand. I know what you mean, she said.

"Well," said Charlotte Price, "I honestly don't know why they always want to go there. The woods are dirty."

Bev laughed, interrupting her. "You know it's nature, right?" she said. "It's not dirty. It's actual dirt."

"So Charlotte's right, then," Nancy said, and Bev laughed again.

"And it's dangerous," Charlotte added.

We all nodded, even Bev, who for a moment told herself she wasn't going to press the issue, but then said, "That's part of what makes it fun, though."

"In the woods, no one can hear you scream," April said, waving the fingers on one hand, like she was hexing us all.

"Exactly," said Bev.

"Exactly," said Charlotte.

But Charlotte remembered sitting in her stepfather's car late one night, a year before she could get a driver's license, her best friend, Lydia, in the passenger's seat, on their way home from a party they had snuck out to attend. She thought of how she'd driven fast down the dirt driveway to her house and then, at the last second, right before it seemed like they would hit the big tree out front, she'd veered left into the field and slammed on the brakes. Lydia had screamed, and Charlotte had laughed and laughed and pulled in under the carport on the side of the house. Her stepfather, she thought, had never found out, but now she realized he must have known as soon as he saw the ruts she had carved in the field.

Mags thought of Fred Austin again.

Sarah Jenkins, Susannah's mother, thought of a party she'd gone to with her husband, Robert, not long ago, where she had eaten everything offered to her, drank everything offered to her, ingested things she didn't recognize. "I didn't know what it was," she told Robert as he carried her home through the woods, taking that detour so they wouldn't encounter any of us, the flash of trees changing from dreamy to assailing. "How could I?" But she had known. She wasn't an idiot.

April thought of the woods. She had gone into them, too, but she wasn't meeting anyone there. It was at night, after the men had spent a long day searching, and she wanted to see for herself. If there was something out there, any fragment of Alice, she wanted to find it, but she came home with nothing but mud caked on the soles of her shoes, the ones she wore only for gardening. She hadn't told her husband she went. She hadn't even told Bev.

We thought of how we watched the news every night, how we dissected it the next day. We couldn't stop talking about Alice. We thought of Rachel Granger, the picture of her we had memorized. It was different seeing the picture of Alice Lange; no matter how flat and inanimate that one seemed, when we looked at it, all we could think of was her walking to school, delivering us loaves of bread, running behind the wobbling bicycle as the boy on it careered forward and laughed.

We thought of our husbands looking in the woods for a clump of hair, a shard of bone, a finger, a whole girl, and we understood, of course, why the children go into the woods. We understood why Christine wanted to hear Earl Phelps tell her yes, the little mermaid didn't get to be a mermaid, didn't get to be a girl, lost her voice, lost her tail, lost her legs, lost a corporeal form altogether and became something we didn't understand. And now with Alice Lange, we think we might understand, too, why she went and why she stayed away.

CHAPTER TWENTY-TWO

WESLEY MADE THE sun shine. Wesley made it rain. Wesley steered the winds. He never told Alice he was responsible for these things, but she began to see patterns emerge—the sunlight was yellow and warm on days when he woke up happy; if he was sick, it might still be sunny, but the light would be weak, as if it were fighting to make itself shine. On moody days, the weather turned, leaves drifted down, brown and curled. Wesley would grind them with his boot heel.

"I'll always call to you if we're apart," he told Alice once. They were lying in two sleeping bags zipped together out in the backyard. She had slipped her underwear back on and was wearing a T-shirt, but Wesley's hand was under her shirt, tracing the outline of her shoulder blades. It made her shiver.

"Why would we be apart now that we're finally together?" she asked, looking up at the stars. It hadn't been long, she hadn't meant to add the "finally," but time was moving differently here, the days and years leading up to this moment had been moving slowly, and only now that she was here did she see that time moved as we always said it did: fast.

"I don't know," said Wesley. "But there's always a chance people will try to tear us all away from each other." Finger down her shoulder. "This is where your wings would be," he said.

"If we're apart," Alice said.

"I'd move the earth to call to you," he said. "I'd tell the ocean to give you a message. If you're listening, it whispers to you." He leaned closer, made a quiet shushing noise in her ear, tickling her and making her laugh.

The sun, the wind, the flowers, the leaves. Water listened to Wesley too. It rarely rained, so when it did, they welcomed it. The dry ground drank up the moisture, and the girls slept late because no light streamed through their windows in the morning. "It's raining!" Alice said.

"I know," said Wesley, grinning, and there was something about his catlike, knowing expression that made Alice think he'd ordered it up for them.

This, Wesley told them, was why they didn't need to worry about where they would go or what they would do when everything ended. He didn't come right out and say it, but Alice knew—they all seemed to know—that Wesley was intrinsically connected to the events of the end, that his hand might be the one to shake the ground, his mouth to drain the sea, his gaze to start the fire that would never stop burning until everything was consumed by it.

On the day it rained, he said, "Come on, let's go outside." And they all went, huddled together under the cover of the porch, but Wesley leapt down the steps and out into the rain and tilted his head back, spread his arms out wide. No one else on the street was outside, though the dog next door was barking, and then a car passed by, but the driver didn't slow down, didn't seem to care about the man standing outside in the rain.

"It's not going to rain forever," Wesley said. "Come on." Alice went out first. Wesley pulled her to him and laughed until Alice laughed, too, and the rest of the girls came down, trailing him around the yard as the rain soaked the grass. "Enjoy this," he kept telling them. "It's a gift, enjoy it."

Wesley, giver of gifts, destroyer of worlds.

CHAPTER TWENTY-THREE

ONE AFTERNOON, WHEN Wesley was out and Kathryn was at work, the others sat in the backyard, smoking. They would pass the joint around—everyone except Hannah Fay, who would stay inside until this part was over—until it was too small to pinch between two fingers, and then typically they would switch to the cigarettes Apple kept on hand for when Wesley was gone.

Today, though, Hannah Fay had come out to join them, holding a tiny, shimmery bottle of nail polish, and said, "Who can I con into painting my toenails? I promise my feet are clean." So Apple closed up the pack of cigarettes, and Alice said she would paint them because she had very steady hands and got second place in her school's art show last year. "Say no more," Hannah Fay said and carefully lowered herself onto the grass beside her.

Alice, edges softened by the joint, untwisted the cap of the nail polish and thought about all the nice things that came with Wesley's absence: cigarettes, yes, which she had never smoked with any kind of consistency until now, but also less pressure all around. Apple was kinder, Janie sillier. It had the feeling of summer camp or any time she spent without the supervision of grown-ups, and perhaps the nicest part was that there was still something more to look forward to, the moment when Wesley returned home.

It was that sleepy window of time right after lunch, and the sun was warm but not too hot, bathing everything in light but not too bright. The nub of the joint sat in an ashtray in the middle of their circle, and the conversation meandered, stopping and then starting again. It was funny to Alice, because when Wesley was there, they always stayed close to the little patio, so that Wesley, who was very sensitive to grass, could sit in the one chair out there that wasn't broken, and they could sit cross-legged on the ground and listen to him speak.

But when he was gone and the girls came outside, they always went to the back of the lawn, where the overgrown garden began. They would sprawl out on the grass, arranged like a giant hand had scooped them up and scattered them across the lawn. Today Apple was picking the leaves off one of the overflowing bushes, tearing each one neatly down its middle seam and then shredding each half. Sometimes she would throw a piece of a leaf in Janie's hair, and if Janie felt it, she would stop talking and pose, like someone was taking her picture, and then she'd leave it there.

Hannah Fay sat with her knees up and her arms behind her, palms flat on the grass, her dress bunching up around her belly, while Alice hunched over her toenails, blowing on each foot after she finished a coat. "Happy birthday, Hannah

Fay," Alice said. "Don't say I never did anything for you." She looked up at Hannah Fay and grinned, squinting like Hannah Fay's belly was the blinding sun.

"Wait," Janie said. "It's not really your birthday, right?"

"Nope, not for another six months," Hannah Fay said. "My birthday's in May."

"I was teasing," Alice said. "But happy early birthday."

"How old will you be?" Janie asked, her hair dotted with the green leaves.

"Eighteen," said Hannah Fay. "Teen mom." She rubbed her stomach and laughed. Alice sat up and kissed her right on the crest of her stomach, and Hannah Fay rubbed Alice's head and laughed again. "Your hair is so soft, Alice," she said. "Like a little bunny's."

"Wait," Janie said again. "So you're seventeen now?"

"That's the way numbers work, Jay," Apple said. She leaned over and started picking the leaves out, and Janie instinctively leaned back toward Apple. Watching, Alice thought of monkeys she'd seen in the zoo as a little girl, how tenderly and unself-consciously they picked at each other, like there was no boundary between their bodies at all. She tried to remember if she felt like that with anyone before Wesley. Susannah, she thought, sometimes, and when she was a little girl, her mother.

"But you've been here a year," Janie said, shaking her hair out as Apple plucked the last tiny leaf. She held up a hand and ticked off each finger as she counted. "First it was Kathryn, then it was you, then Apple, then me right after Apple, then Alice."

"Right," said Hannah Fay. "I was sixteen when I came."

"Oh my God," said Janie. "Does Wesley know that?"

"Of course," Hannah Fay said, rolling her eyes.

"Do your parents know you're here?" Alice asked.

"Yes," said Hannah Fay. "Who do you think writes me all the letters?"

"Kathryn usually gets the mail," said Alice, surprised. "I didn't know you got letters from anyone. I never see you reading anything but Wesley's magazines."

"Well," said Hannah Fay, crossing her legs so that the toes Alice had just painted were hidden under her freckled thighs. "Wesley and I read them together."

"Wow," said Alice. She started thinking about Hannah Fay and Wesley sitting together in the study on Hannah Fay's mattress and reading letters from Hannah Fay's mom, and then that thought turned into a memory of her own mother, who had been lurking formlessly in her mind all morning, of her handwriting, how she always wrote—writes, Alice thought, she was still there in the old house—in a slanted script made of skinny loops and lines. And then she thought of her mother's hands, the nails and knuckles and the whorl of her fingerprints, and then the picture in her head expanded and kept expanding: the handwriting, the hands, the kitchen table and the same chair she always sat in, facing the direction of Alice's room so she could see Alice approaching, the kitchen, the living room next to it, the house that held the living room and the bedrooms and the bathrooms, and the swimming pool and the porch swing and the big trees, and Alice felt alone, separate from the other girls and separate from Wesley, who was gone somewhere she didn't know. Next door the awful dog barked, and Alice heard the other girls again.

"I haven't seen my mom in five years," Janie was saying. "I can't even remember my dad."

"This is what my parents wanted for me," Hannah Fay said. "They've always hated the establishment, too, and they'd pulled me out of school when I was fourteen. We'd moved in with two other families in this big old house on a bunch of acres of land. My parents wanted me to have an extraordinary and unconventional life." Her voice deepened on the last few words, a false baritone, and Alice took it to be an impression of her father. "Then they met Wesley," she said in her normal voice, "and fell in love with him a little. Then I met Wesley, and now here we are."

"Bearing his child," said Apple.

"Right," said Hannah Fay, rubbing her stomach again. "But hopefully not right this second."

"How did your parents meet Wesley, anyway?" Janie asked. They each had an origin story, how they met Wesley, how they arrived at this house. Janie had been plucked like Alice had, but from a street filled with people just like her, young and down on their luck and crowding the streets and alleys of the district. "He hung out with us for a few days," Janie had told her. "I watched him start to see me, like I stood out more than anyone else, even though all the other girls were all over him; he had his camera, of course, and they were all trying to get in his photos. Finally, he took me to this motel and washed my hair and my clothes and then brought me back here." Alice listened, waiting for Janie to articulate what she herself had felt when Wesley found her, the inevitability of good things happening simply because the girls were special. But if Janie felt that same way, she didn't say so.

Wesley and Apple struck up a conversation at a party a few hours away, and there was never a formal invitation but there was also never a question that she belonged with Wesley and the other girls and the house. The only one, to Alice's knowledge, who made her way to Wesley on her own was Kathryn, the first of all the girls.

"Oh, Wesley was just passing through, and we sometimes took in travelers and gave them a room," Hannah Fay said. "My parents and Wesley stayed up all night talking. I was sleeping at a friend's house, and when I came home in the morning, my dad said, 'Clara, this is someone very special, and I want you to listen to what he has to say.' And I didn't want to listen to a word my dad said because what does he know, right? But then I walked out onto the back porch—it over-looked a peach orchard we took care of—and there was Wesley, and everything smelled like peaches, and I stood with him and talked with him until I couldn't stand any longer, and then I pulled him down next to me right on the ground, and when we stood up, the backs of our pants were all dusty." Hannah Fay laughed. "Isn't it funny the things you remember?"

"Clara," said Apple. "I didn't know."

"That's a sweet name," Janie said. "If the baby's a girl, you should name her Clara."

"Wesley doesn't like that name," said Hannah Fay.

"Is that why he renames everyone?" Alice asked. "Is some-one's name not a true name if he just doesn't like it?" She hoped she sounded jokey and silly, but it was a sincere question: she hadn't been renamed, and it worried her, but maybe it was only because Wesley liked her name.

"No, it's about the essence of a person," Hannah Fay said. "He said I had a pure essence, and I needed a name that was more innocent than Clara."

"Clara seems very innocent," said Alice. "I'm dying to know why Apple got her name."

"If you have to ask, you'll never know," Apple said.

"Apple is very secretive about her name story," Janie said, "but I can tell you mine."

"Yes, please," said Alice. "I wasn't sure if it was a faux pas to ask. It feels kind of like, I don't know, like asking about someone's dead sister."

"I don't mind at all! Wesley called me Jane Blue, Jane like Jane Doe because he found me on the streets and I didn't have anyone claiming me or anything, and Blue for water because water gives life. He said he could tell I gave everyone around me purpose."

"That's so nice," Alice said. "I wish I gave someone purpose." (You did, Alice, and you could again. We see her. She's waiting for you, still.)

"So he started calling me Jane B., and it always sounded like Janebee, and eventually it became Janie," she said, "which I like much better."

"What were you before?" Hannah Fay asked. Her face was bright with curiosity, and Alice could see Hannah Fay really didn't know that the only version of Janie that Hannah Fay had ever known was this one. It had been a quick transformation for Janie, then, to go from a nameless girl on the street to something as precious and refreshing as clean water. If another girl joined them here someday, the way Alice had joined them, it was possible that girl would only ever know whoever the person was that Alice would become, whoever Wesley chose for her to be. No one she met from now on would ever know Alice again.

"Florence," said Janie.

"Wow," said Hannah Fay. "I really can't see that at all. Florence sounds so prissy. You're definitely a Janie."

"Thanks," Janie said brightly. "It's kind of nice talking like this, isn't it? About where we came from?"

"Only because of where we are now," Hannah Fay said. "Imagine if none of us ever made it out." They all looked around the yard where they sat, overgrown and wild. Alice breathed it in: there was a flowering tree in the corner with delicate white blossoms and there was a honeysuckle vine growing along the fence and there was the pungent smell of smoke in the air and in her hair, but she couldn't help but think of us too. (Imagine sleeping in an alley and begging for food, imagine being sixteen in a creaking old house you shared with adult men and women you weren't related to but also didn't choose for yourself. Here, at home, we have private rooms and beds and hot meals; we have flowering trees and honeysuckle too. We do not play games. We think for ourselves, we let you keep the names you were born with. "Last names," we could imagine someone arguing. Bev, perhaps. "We take the last names of our husbands." Yes, we would say, but that's an honor, a privilege. A different thing altogether.)

"Hannah Fay, did Wesley know you were"—Alice fumbled for the right word. A child? Underage?—"young?" she said.

"Yes, Alice," Hannah Fay said. "He's not blind. And he was very respectful, always. He didn't even touch me for a long time, even though I told him I wanted him to. He kept saying no, it wasn't right, I didn't know what I wanted, et cetera, et cetera." A breeze ruffled the bushes and blew a strand of her hair across her face, and she pulled it from where it stuck to her lips. "Finally, he went to my parents and asked them, and came back with a note from them saying it was okay by them if I did whatever I wanted with Wesley," she said. "They said they assumed it had already happened, but they appreciated having the chance to give permission."

"Oh my God," said Apple, her dark eyes round. "Okay, Hannah Fay, that's crossing some kind of line with your parents."

"So it was like a permission slip," Alice said. "Like you were going to the history museum with your fifth-grade class."

"Yes," said Hannah Fay stiffly. "If you want to reduce it to that, then sure. But it was really very meaningful."

"I think it's sweet, Han," said Janie. "And if you think about it, it really isn't that different from a wedding where your dad walks you down the aisle and gives you away."

Hannah Fay sat up straighter and began nodding even before Janie finished speaking. "Yes!" she said, clapping her hands together and looking up at the sky, like she was relieved someone understood. "Right! That's exactly right." She rearranged herself again, loosening the cross of her legs so that her pink toenails peeked out again. "No matter how I sit, things keep falling asleep," she said. "But I loved that, Janie. I know it's traditional and kind of lame, but my family is so weird—seriously, if you met them or saw the homestead where we lived, you'd understand—it was so nice to feel like I was a normal girl with a normal dad giving me away to a normal guy, and now I'm going to have a normal baby and a normal life." Abruptly, Hannah Fay stopped. "What, Apple?" she said. "Why are you looking at me like that?" Alice looked over at Apple, who had been quiet while Hannah Fay spoke, but now the quiet seemed less attentive and more like a sad, thoughtful kind of quiet.

"Nothing," said Apple. "It's all very sweet, but look around, Han. This isn't a normal life. It's a house filled with five girls and one man. None of us has a real job, except Kathryn. I know you know what some of us have done for money since we've been here."

None of them said anything right away. Alice hadn't ever been asked to contribute any more financially than she had in the beginning, but she knew that Apple and Janie sometimes left together at night and came home after she was already asleep. The next day there would be plenty of groceries for the next few days or the lights would be back on or, once, Hannah Fay got the antibiotic she needed for a UTI. Alice had considered this, what she would do if Wesley asked her, or if Apple did. She had decided she didn't really think she could. But maybe. If she had to.

Hannah Fay cocked her head to the side. "Well, yeah," she said. "This part isn't normal, but my relationship with Wesley is. When it's the two of us, we're just like any other couple getting ready to have a baby."

"That sounds nice," said Alice. "You're a team together in a way the rest of us aren't."

"Yes," said Hannah Fay, smiling at Alice. "But you'll all be like the baby's mothers too."

"Aunts," said Alice. Because she loved Hannah Fay, she already loved this baby, but she wouldn't be anything like its mother. She would be the mother of her own baby.

"Aunt Alice," said Hannah Fay.

"Aunt whatever Wesley will name me," Alice said.

"We'll have a party when he renames you," Janie said. "Combination early birthday party for Hannah Fay."

"I'll rename you," Apple said. "Phallus Alice. No, wait, Alice the Phallus is better."

"Apple!" said Hannah Fay, but Alice laughed.

"Linda," said Janie. "Because you're pretty. Tiny. Magnolia. Tree. Flower."

"Now you're just naming things you see," said Apple. "Mine was better."

"Don't worry, Alice," said Hannah Fay. "Think about it like this: you've always had a true name, and Wesley identifying it doesn't change the fact that it's always been there. You've just never known what it was."

"Thanks, *Clara*," said Alice, and the girls laughed, and a few minutes later, they heard a rumbling close by.

"Is that thunder?" asked Janie.

"I think it's the truck," said Hannah Fay.

"Wesley," said Alice.

"What's the difference," said Apple, and they all sat there, waiting for Wesley to come out and find them again.

CHAPTER TWENTY-FOUR

THE NIGHT BEFORE Wesley was scheduled to meet with the owner of a very prestigious gallery, a man known for selling art to celebrities and socialites, he spread photographs over every surface in the house, like a gallery show, and the girls wandered through the rooms looking at the pictures, murmuring to each other and to Wesley about his genius, his craft, pointing out the ones they liked the best, though Alice knew that in the end, Wesley would choose his own favorites. "Hey," Alice said, picking up one of the prints, which had another picture stuck to its back, one of Hannah Fay's sharp facial profile contrasting with the soft roundness of her belly. "How do I know this girl?" Alice asked, showing him the top image, a girl with her hair piled high on her head, looking past the photographer. In her hands, she held an animal skull, grayish bone, something with a long snout. "Is that a skull?" Alice asked stupidly.

Wesley looked at it. "It represents death," he said, but didn't answer her other question.

But Apple peered over Alice's shoulder at the picture when Wesley walked away. "That's Sadie," Apple said. "She lived here for a while."

"I met her," said Alice. "At the party Wesley took me to. What happened to her?"

"Oh, you know," said Apple. "She just couldn't hang."

"Well, it's a good picture," Alice said. "Kind of creepy. He should bring it to show the guy."

"He won't," said Apple.

In the morning, the girls watched him sidle up to the old truck, his portfolio in his hand. It was early, the sun watery and new in the sky, and he looked beautiful in the morning glow. "This is it," he said. "This is when our lives change." The girls waved as he drove off.

That night, they made dinner. They sat at the table with plates and silverware in front of them. The food—a stew made with everything that was about to go bad in the refrigerator and whatever Kathryn had pulled out from the garden behind the house, small green leafy things she barely washed, just ran under cold water from the faucet until the obvious dirt was gone—bubbled in a pot with a lid over it. Then it cooled, but the lid stayed on. "Wesley doesn't like it too hot," Kathryn said. "With the lid on, it'll cool down a little, but still be warm when he gets here."

The girls drained their glasses of red wine; Hannah Fay drank her glass of lemonade but wouldn't have any more. "I'm afraid it's going to give me heartburn," she said, rubbing at her chest already. "Just water for now, please."

Alice got up to fill Hannah Fay's glass, rinsing it out before she held it under the tap, so that there wouldn't be any lemony taste still clinging to its sides. She imagined herself pregnant, round belly tight with a baby pressing its hands and feet against her. She liked how she could see elbows and the curve of head bulging out of Hannah Fay. "It's like an alien," Alice had said when Hannah Fay showed her the other night.

Hannah Fay had laughed and said it was an alien, really, a parasite. Wesley had told her that was a rude thing to say about her baby, and Hannah Fay excused herself not much later. When she got up, Apple had taken her spot. She had lifted her shirt and showed off her tan, flat stomach. She had a tiny mole near her belly button, like a pinprick. "No babies in here," she said. "Thank God." Wesley had placed his hand against the plank of her stomach. "Not yet," he'd said, and raised an eyebrow. "After all, we're only as good as what we make," he said. "And what's better than making a baby?" Apple had laughed, and Alice had felt jealous.

Now, rogue water droplets dripped down the side of Hannah Fay's water glass, wetting Alice's hand, and she turned the faucet off. Then she lifted the lid of the pot and peered inside. The broth was reddish and thin. Potatoes and carrots bobbed in it like dinghies. Before they made it into the stew, the carrots had been whitish and dry, and the potatoes had begun to sprout little buds all over, like tiny, blind eyes. But the girls couldn't afford to be picky about their food; they'd been growing even thinner, so if it was edible, they would eat it. Recently, they had even stopped going to the grocery store, and instead went behind the restaurants and bakeries and the cafeterias at the university when it was dark and late and found the dumpsters where every night food would get tossed out.

Alice was small and strong, and with Apple's or Janie's arms around her waist, she could rummage through the boxes and bottles and cans for any food in bags or containers, anything that didn't look too unappetizing. It wasn't as gross as she thought it would be, mostly broken-down cardboard boxes and swollen black trash bags, and as long as those hadn't split open, the task was fine. They would take the food home, and Kathryn would hold it up and examine it under the buzzing yellow lights in the kitchen. When they saw it next, it had been transformed, chopped up into a soup or covered in sauce or garnished with curling shreds of the few vegetables she grew in their backyard. Like this.

Alice replaced the lid. "Shouldn't we eat?" she called out as she walked back into the dining room. "He must be stuck doing something. Maybe finalizing everything with the gallery?"

"No," said Kathryn, when Alice came back to the table and set the glass in front of Hannah Fay. "He likes us to eat together, like a family. Besides, he'll want to celebrate when he gets back."

"He could've called," said Apple.

But Kathryn shook her head. "We didn't pay the phone bill this month," she said.

"Hannah Fay should at least get to eat," Alice said. "She's growing a human!"

"At least we think it's a human," said Apple, wrinkling her nose. But she winked at Hannah Fay.

"No eating the stew," said Kathryn. She straightened the silverware in front of her and put her hands in her lap. "Not till Wesley gets here. Hannah Fay, if you're hungry, there's a jar of peanut butter in the pantry."

It wasn't a bad evening, really. Alice was reminded of one night she'd spent in the library with Susannah. They had a giant test looming over their heads, but they couldn't stop giggling, whispering stories about themselves to each other, or stories about people they knew or stories about people they never knew, only heard about, the tales that constituted the mythology of their neighborhood. (We understand this kind of closeness, remembering nights after most of the party guests have gone home, and it's just a few of us, sitting at the kitchen table, a bottle of wine or gin in the middle. We would tell those same kinds of stories: about ourselves, about our friends, about the people who had faded away or left, leaving only legends in their places.)

Finally, when the wine was gone and the girls' teeth and lips were stained crimson, when Hannah Fay had risked a second glass of lemonade, when the front door stayed closed and the rest of the house was silent and Wesley still hadn't come home, the girls decided to go to bed. It was nearly midnight. They ate spoonfuls of peanut butter and washed and dried the spoons, put them back in the drawer, before saying good night to each other. In the kitchen, on the cool stove, the stew sat in the pot with the lid still on it. Kathryn had sighed, said she was sorry she couldn't let the pot soak in the sink overnight.

"I dare you to tell that to Wesley," Apple had said.

"I'm not sure what you're implying," Kathryn said. "But we have a relationship of mutual respect, and I certainly wouldn't be scared to tell him he should have been home when he told us he would be."

"Yeah, okay," Apple had said.

"He can't call, Kathryn," Hannah Fay said.

Later, Alice woke to a hand on her shoulder, a face near her own. "What is it?" she asked.

"He's back," said Apple. "And we're going out."

The living room was dark, the soft glow of a lamp providing the only light, and Wesley stood next to it, so that half his face was warmed to gold and the other half was obscured. In the living room, he instructed "dark colors" to no one in particular. Janie and Kathryn went around the rooms and gathered up navy-blue shirts, black dresses, and jeans and dumped them at Wesley's feet in a pile that he then rummaged through, picking out outfits for each of the girls.

"Come here," Wesley said to Apple. She wore a big T-shirt and nothing on the bottom, besides, Alice guessed, underwear. She had athletic legs with slim thighs and pretty calves, and Alice pictured her before Wesley, before this bungalow of women. She pictured Apple—no, back then, she was Betsy—gripping a field hockey stick and charging down a lawn of trampled grass, her dark hair whipping behind her in a braid, like the flag of a standard bearer marching into battle.

"Arms up," Wesley said, and when she raised them, he pulled Apple's T-shirt over her head and off, flinging it to the side. Her breasts looked, like the rest of her, firm and somehow athletic, making Alice think of tennis balls. Wesley looked at them, but did not touch, and dressed her himself in a black sweater and jeans that used to belong to Alice.

Apple kept one hand on Wesley's shoulder as she stepped into the pants. They were too loose in the rear to be flattering, though when Alice had worn them back at home, they fit her tightly. She waited for Wesley to call to her, to peel off the shirt and shorts she slept in, to examine her body, to remember the feel of it under his hands, and to dress her, too, like he did Apple. Appreciatively, knowingly. But all he did was hand her a dark gray T-shirt and black pants.

"Okay," he said when most of the girls were dressed. "Hannah Fay, stay here. You can wait up if you want, but you don't have to." She was sitting on the brown armchair, her sleep shirt bunching at the top of her belly, a thin border of skin showing above the top of her pants. Wesley bent down, put a hand on her roundness. Hannah Fay placed her hand on top of his and looked up at him.

"Be safe," she said.

"We'll be back soon," he told her, leaning in until his forehead touched hers and her eyes closed. Janie stood beside him, and as he straightened up, he took her hand. The pair led the three girls out, and Alice, who was last, shut the door gently behind her. The street was quiet and still. Only a few blocks away, at the university and in the surrounding houses and apartment buildings, people would be awake and talking and partying, but here, their neighbors were asleep. (It goes without saying that we were asleep too. Not much good happens past midnight, this much we know.)

"So that's what you were doing tonight," said Kathryn, and Alice followed her line of vision. In the driveway, instead of the truck, sat a blue van.

"Are you taking us to soccer practice?" Apple asked.

"Yes," Wesley said. "To Kathryn's question. Apple, I'm ignoring you." He clapped his hands together and nodded toward the van. "Everyone in," he said. "Kathryn, you're driving." He tossed her the keys, which she caught in the little cup her hands made.

Alice, again, was the last, crawling into the farthest-back seat. It would have made more sense for Apple and Janie to sit back there since they got in first, but they sat just behind Wesley and Kathryn, whose heads were bent together in conversation. She was too far away to hear what they were saying, plus Janie and Apple were talking, too, about nothing, about stupid things. She wished they would shut up.

They sat in the driveway. Alice buckled her seat belt, then unbuckled it.

Finally, Wesley spoke up, raising his voice so that it filled the van. He twisted around in the front seat so that he was looking at the girls in the back.

"It's time for us to take action," he said. "No more hanging around. So we're going to do it, and you need to trust me. Okay?"

"What kind of action?" Janie asked. "What about the guy with the art gallery?"

"And the photos?" asked Kathryn, who had turned her body toward his.

"I changed my mind," Wesley said. "He wasn't the right person."

"What happened?" asked Alice.

"The world is asleep," Wesley said. "Practically comatose. Everyone wants the same old things. They don't want to be challenged; they just want to be comfortable." He sneered this last word, then sighed. "Things need to change," he went on, "and it's never going to happen unless someone makes them change. This place is shit. It's not any good."

"But we're good," said Kathryn. "You're good."

"Right," said Wesley. "We are, I am. And someday we're going to be very, very powerful. But for now, we need to shake things up a bit." Alice worried about how they might do that, about what Wesley had in mind. She couldn't see the faces of the other girls, but one or two of them must have looked concerned, too, because Wesley held up his hands and laughed. "Relax," he said, grinning. "This is going to be fun, I promise."

"Let's go, then," said Kathryn, and he clapped her on the leg.

"Let's go," he said.

CHAPTER TWENTY-FIVE

KATHRYN DROVE UNTIL the neighborhood changed, then the city, but they couldn't go too far, as the sun would be up in a few hours. Next time, Wesley said, they would go farther. They would go to a better neighborhood, where the houses were nicer and bigger, where the people had more money but they were less awake, less alive, where they had more to learn than others. But for now, he said, this one would do.

(This neighborhood didn't look exactly like ours. This is a comfort, if a small one. Ours is comfortable but modest. We like to think that when people drive by, they imagine themselves there, their children playing, their husbands coming home from work, their friends complimenting their gardens. Maybe, they think, they could put a pool in. When they drive through our streets, they are not lusting after our homes; it isn't that kind of neighborhood. There are some neighborhoods that are flashy, their houses voluptuous, almost indecent. These are the houses of the sleeping people,

Wesley would say, the mausoleums of the blind. What would he say about ours? What would he say about us?)

They stopped, finally, at a two-story house with big windows, wide and long as film screens. It was the home of wealthy people but not the wealthiest people. This, Wesley insisted, was practice.

When they got up to the front door, Alice tried to peek inside one of the windows, but squinted as if the room were filled with too much light instead of darkness and more darkness. She thought she saw a piano, a big one like they had in the lobbies of fancy hotels.

It was Kathryn, surprisingly, who picked the lock, before stepping back, letting Wesley take her place. Alice thought of Andrew on his knees in front of the glass doors of the high school, his uncoordinated fingers fumbling around, telling Alice to stand back. Kathryn could have done it. Alice could have too.

"Don't take anything," Wesley said in a low voice, his hand on the knob. "Be very quiet," he said. "If you see anyone, don't touch them, don't speak to them. Just get out."

Wesley sent Kathryn in first, and they waited for her to return with a thumbs-up. "All clear," she said. "Only one bedroom occupied, and it's upstairs." That seemed right to Alice, when she thought about it: they were sequestered away like royalty in a tower, as far away from the outside world, as far from the earth, as they could be. No one was safe, Alice thought. Wesley could get to them anywhere, and now she could too. All they had to do was want it.

She thought of that walk to the school, the dark houses they had passed. She remembered thinking those houses would be lifeless to her until she was in them herself, and now look, that had come true.

In the van, Wesley had given them instructions for what to do once inside. "All we want to do is make them pay attention, wake up," he'd said. "Do only what I've told you." They started with the living room, with the couch and chairs. Wesley took one end of the couch, Janie and Apple the other, and they picked it up and moved it to the other side of the room. Alice and Kathryn put the chairs where the couch used to be. Alice rearranged some pictures. She picked one up and looked at it: a man and woman, attractive, not old, not young. Blond and smiling, an ocean behind them, but not their own. The Caribbean, Alice guessed. In another picture, the man stood in profile, shaking hands with a long-haired man. Alice was surprised to recognize the second man, and for a moment she couldn't place him until an image of him on the TV screen at her mother's house popped into her head—he was an actor.

Apple walked by, and Alice tried to get her attention. "Whose house is this?" she whispered, thinking of what Wesley had said about the gallery owner's celebrity connections, but Apple either didn't hear her or ignored her. She looked around. The walls held paintings, photographs; on the table right next to the picture of the long-haired man rested a series of small, ornate sculptures that looked to Alice like mutated creatures.

Apple and Alice picked up the coffee table, oval shaped and light, made from some kind of cheap manufactured wood, trendy and no doubt overpriced, and carried it carefully into the kitchen. They set it down, lifted the kitchen table up and out of the way, and put the coffee table in its place. The kitchen table took the spot of the coffee table. Alice went into the kitchen and opened each of the cabinets until she found a stack of plates. She pulled out all the drawers until she found one full of silverware. In a china cabinet, she found cloth napkins, neatly pressed. Then water cups, wineglasses. On her way out, she noticed a knife block next to the stovetop, the black handles sticking out, and she thought of how much danger was sitting right there.

In the living room, she set the table, slow and careful with the plates so she didn't make a sound. She set a lovely table. (We are saddened to think of this eye, this attention to detail, gone to waste.) After putting the last fork in place, she studied the table for a minute; she still felt something was missing. So she went back into the kitchen, grabbed a knife from the block, and carried it back to the dining-room table. It was a short kitchen knife, the kind her mother used for peeling potatoes. She pressed the tip of its blade into the wooden surface, carving sharp letters into it. Then she walked out. The table, she knew, was perfect.

Janie and Apple swapped the bedding in the two first-floor guest rooms, the bedside tables, the lamps. Kathryn smoothed out a wrinkle in the rug. She arranged the pillows on the couch, just like she did at home. Wesley watched from where he stood, barely two steps into the house. "One last thing," he said. "The pièce de résistance." From behind his back he produced a rectangle, and Alice squinted at it in the dark.

"Is that one of your photos?" she asked.

"Leave it on the dining-room table, would you?" he said. Alice took it from him—it showed a slithering snake, in what looked to be the desert, cracked brown earth under its long dark body, and the brown toe of a boot, unmistakably Wesley's, she thought—and placed it faceup on the table, right next to her own message.

Alice went back to him, standing close enough so that their arms were touching. "Very nice," Wesley murmured. "Good work. I wish I could see their faces when they come downstairs in the morning."

"Me, too," said Alice. He pulled her to him so that he was facing her, and he kissed her, put his hands under her shirt. She hoped the other girls were watching, but knew already they were.

When he let her go, he gave a low whistle, and the other girls straightened up. He waved a finger in the air, a circular motion, and jerked his head to the door behind him. As they quickly followed him out, Alice thought she heard movement upstairs.

This time Alice cut to the front of the pack of girls, sliding open the door of the van. Behind her, Janie gasped. "Alice," she said, and Alice turned around to face her. "Why do you have a knife?"

It was in her back pocket, flush against her backside, the point of the blade sticking out. She felt someone pinch it gingerly out of her pocket.

"It's fine," said Wesley. "We'll get rid of it eventually."

"But why do you have it?" Apple asked.

Because she needed to leave a message, just like Wesley had told them to do. She needed them to read it, open their eyes. Touch each letter she'd engraved: *Wake up.*

CHAPTER TWENTY-SIX

THE NEXT TIME, at a different, even nicer house, ran even more smoothly, and Janie was the one to hold the paring knife and stab it into the throw pillows on the couch. One of the pillows was furry and sat like a scared, square animal beside the others, and when Janie thrust the knife into it, Alice felt an abrupt sadness at seeing the fur and the feathers fly up and float back down. And then she remembered the pillow wasn't alive, and besides that, its owners weren't really alive either, not in the way they were intended to be. "They need some fear to wake them up," Wesley would say.

It always made Alice shiver when Wesley talked about it, their mission, the desert: how eager he was and how confident. Though she knew it would be bittersweet to leave the bungalow, Alice found herself longing for the day they would venture out and start life anew. It wasn't the bungalow that was important anyway; it was Wesley, the girls. Alice was a better, more authentic version of herself now, and her transformation had nothing to do with the house, the yard, the beds where they slept. (We have to disagree: a place is important too. A place shapes you. It protects you. Even that sad little bungalow they lived in was better than the desert—all that wide-open space, the blazing sun, and beneath it, dry earth, creatures that bite and sting. Where is the protection in that place? And what kind of person comes out of it?)

Alice and the others were a family now. And there were others out there like them, Wesley promised, but he hadn't found them yet, though when he did, they would go and start building a new civilization, one in which they could make the rules, run the world.

In the second house, they left another photo, one Wesley had taken especially for the purpose. He had posed the girls in a row with their backs facing the camera and brown paper grocery sacks over their heads, hiding their beauty, he told them, from a world that didn't deserve to see it.

After the third house and two weeks later, a fourth, Wesley came home one afternoon with a TV. Kathryn helped him carry it in, though it was small, and he could have managed it himself. They watched the news that night, hoping to see a story about the rash of break-ins around the city, but there was nothing. The only crime reported was the robbery of a gas station off the freeway. Wesley and the girls never took anything, only the knife from the first house, and that, Alice was always quick to explain, was an accident.

When the news report was over, Wesley stood up from the armchair and turned off the TV set. He rubbed at his eyes. "Let's go outside," he said. "Clear our heads."

In the backyard, Wesley lowered himself into the green lawn chair, and the girls arranged themselves around him, with Alice at his right. Apple had cut the grass so that the blades were even and short, and it felt like the bristles of a rug. Alice kept running her hands over the grass.

"Maybe we *should* start taking things," Kathryn suggested. "That might make them take us more seriously. Besides, we could sell them for cash."

"No," Wesley said. His voice was calm and thoughtful, as though he had already considered this himself and decided against it. "The last thing we need in this world is more stuff," he said. "If we take anything, we might let it ensnare our minds and hearts the way it did for its owners."

"But we need to up the stakes," Kathryn said.

Across from them, Apple reclined next to Hannah Fay, whose belly rose up like a hill. She might have already been asleep, Alice wasn't sure.

"I don't know," said Janie. "It doesn't seem like a good idea. I like it the way it is."

"It doesn't matter what you like," Kathryn said.

"Down, girl," Apple said, holding up a hand. "Wesley, control your bitch, please."

"Hey," said Alice brightly, sitting up straighter and placing her hand on Wesley's arm, hoping to change the subject. "When do you think I'll get a new name?"

"When I can see who you truly are," Wesley said. "I think I've almost got it." He didn't look at her but put his hand on her head, laced his fingers in her hair, rubbed her scalp.

"You'd probably better fuck her again," Apple said. "I bet that will help." She arranged herself so that she was sitting up now, chin lifted, and looking up at Wesley on his chair. She looked, to Alice, like a queen.

"I hope you aren't jealous, Apple," Wesley said without looking at her, his face tilted up to the night sky. It was like he was talking to the stars, the moon, the creeping vines. Apple had left those alone. "As you know," Wesley said, "I fuck you as well, but I don't have to. Don't try to start shit, Apple, or there will be consequences."

"Is that a threat?" Apple asked. "How can you threaten me if you chose me? Does that mean you were wrong about me? Wrong about something? About someone? Again?" Alice thought of Sadie.

He looked at Apple, and Alice saw in the set of his face, the flash of his eyes: Wesley, who didn't experience the same mundane emotions other people did but instead felt things burn brightly inside him all the time, was suffering. He felt he had been wrong about something, hadn't been able to wake up the sleeping people. But Alice knew he wasn't wrong, and she'd convince him. She'd eat his suffering, drink it up until all that was left was the new world he'd promised them. Apple just stared back at Wesley, still defiant.

Hannah Fay sat up now too. So she hadn't been asleep. "Apple," she said, her voice soft and sweet, "no one's threatening you. No one's mad at you. We love you."

"Kathryn, you know what I feel like right now?" Wesley said. "Go get the good shit. We'll all take some and calm down."

Kathryn stood up, and Apple did too. "Not me," said Apple. "You never take as much as the rest of us, and then you get to say and do whatever you want."

"It's fun," Janie said to her. "We always get to do whatever we want too."

"We can dance," said Alice. "You like to dance. And Wesley will play for us. Maybe Hannah Fay can bake us a cake for after." It was nearly ten, a little late for baking, but Hannah Fay nodded. "See?"

"I'll go get it," said Kathryn.

Apple threw her arms up. "I already said no," she said. "God! Are any of you paying attention? Go get it, Kathryn, because I know you will. But I'm going to bed." She went inside the house without closing the screen door behind her, but it gently floated closed anyway.

"Go on, please, Kathryn," Wesley said.

That night, even though they took Wesley's little pills, there was no cake and no dancing. Each of them existed in their own strange world, and Wesley only played his guitar for a little while. He talked and talked without stopping, and Alice thought it was brilliant, everything he said, but when he finished, she couldn't remember what the words had been, the thoughts they created when they came out of his mouth. The words themselves were too loose, like eels in a river.

Later, he sent the other girls inside and he did fuck Alice after all. He pinned her underneath him by her wrists, his hands like tight cuffs or claws squeezing her bones, and she lay still in the grass and tried to project peace from her body, and finally he stopped, calm and spent, and Alice thought it had worked, impressed by what her body could give him. She imagined him calling her by her new name, whispering it into her ear, but all he said was, "Go inside." His tone wasn't kind or unkind, and truthfully Alice wanted to sleep in the house anyway, not in the yard with the vines like snakes hanging in the trees. As she crawled in bed next to Apple, she put her arms around the other girl and held her the rest of the night.

The next day, no one discussed Apple's outburst, and when Wesley suggested another trip a few days later, Apple joined in and they all danced. She kept her eyes closed the whole time.

CHAPTER TWENTY-SEVEN

ALICE DID NOT know her neighbors at the bungalow. She only knew that the house across the street was occupied by two men she saw walking their dachshunds in the morning and the evening, and that Wesley said they were lovers. He always said it in a lisping way and with a little shi-shi shake of his shoulders. "Oh please," Apple said once to Alice in a low voice. "Like Wesley hasn't fucked some guys in his life." This shocked Alice at first, but the more she thought about it, the more she could see it. Wesley was passionate, and he liked a bit of a fight sometimes, some muscle behind their lovemaking, telling Alice to push or pinch or pull at him, how she imagined he might be with another man.

Sometimes Alice ended up bruised herself. When she did, she tried to wear clothes that revealed the purple and blue marks, so that the others would see how game she was, how willing to do what was desired. The marks reminded her of her mother's eyeshadow, which she used to smudge on her body when she was a little girl. (Her mother remembers the makeup, too, how Alice would ask if she was a beautiful woman now and her mother would tell her that beautiful women only put that on their eyes and not their arms, their legs, their hands.)

So the men with the dachshunds. Then to the left of the bungalow was a single dad and his little boy; Alice assumed the mother had died. There was an older woman—a grandmother, she thought—who came to stay with the boy after school. Wesley did not like the single dad either. "He needs to find a wife," he said once. "Plus he looks at me funny every time I see him."

"Maybe that's just his face," Alice had joked.

"He should get a new one, then," Wesley said.

Then on the other side of their bungalow was an older couple with the horrible dog. They drove a van even though it was only the two of them who lived there, and Alice liked them because they were both tiny people, almost elven, and the woman gardened in the afternoons and the man tinkered with his car on the weekends, flat on his back underneath it with only his legs sticking out, just like you saw on TV. She enjoyed seeing them outside together, each in their own private world within the world they had created together. Otherwise, she had no real basis for an opinion of them. She had never spoken to them other than the occasional hello.

Wesley didn't seem to have feelings about the couple, but he hated the dog. They all hated the dog, even Hannah Fay. She claimed the pregnancy had given her superhuman hearing powers, so that the dog's bark sounded even louder to her. It was an average-size dog, and it looked like any old mutt you'd see in any yard in the world—sort of orange and sort of brown, a tail that permanently curved up like a scythe, two alert, triangular ears, a white spot on his chest shaped like a crest. His name was Charlie, which they only knew because they heard it shouted so often: "Charlie! Stop! Charlie! Be quiet!" In fact, it had become a joke around the house that whenever one of the girls was being too loud or obnoxious, someone would say "Charlie! Stop!"

One evening they were all out in the backyard, and Wesley had just finished photographing the girls, this time in the kind of animal masks they sold at the zoo. Now he had pulled an old easel out of the garage and was flinging scarlet paint at a canvas from a foot away, which meant that barely any color made it onto the canvas, instead freckling the grass with red. Not long after they had crept into that first house, he had revealed he had a new plan to get his message out to the world, fuck that asshole who turned him down because he had found someone better, bigger—an art dealer this time, not just some stupid gallerist—and this time Wesley wouldn't take no for an answer. He'd been weak with the last one; the last one could smell it on him, the weakness, but this time things would be different. Alice wondered who this new guy was, this bigger, better man, and though she would never admit it to any of the others, she felt herself wondering if there even was another person at all. But why would Wesley lie? She told herself he wouldn't. "Big things are coming," Wesley said, inhaling deeply. "It's in the air."

So that night everyone, even Wesley, was a little stoned, and it had been so, so pleasant, and they had been dancing in bare feet, and then they'd found two badminton racquets and a dirty old birdie in the garage, and Alice and Janie were batting the birdie back and forth, laughing each time they swung. It was the easy kind of night when Wesley just wanted to paint and talk, and Apple was in a good mood, and Kathryn too.

Kathryn wasn't wearing her glasses, and when they were off, it was a little like she was drunk; Alice thought it might be that the world was just a bit unfamiliar to Kathryn, enough that she wasn't quite herself either. They had hung a string of lights across the backyard, and Kathryn said they looked like tiny, fuzzy suns burning only for them. Alice crossed her eyes and looked at them and saw that Kathryn was right.

Then the elven couple to the right opened their back door, and Charlie was out. He barked. Wesley stopped painting. The dog kept barking, and he seemed to be right up against the fence. He snuffled and barked. "Motherfucker," said Wesley, fingers tightening around the paintbrush.

"It's not even that he's so loud," said Apple.

"But he is," said Hannah Fay. "He's so loud."

"It's the pitch, though." Apple rubbed at her temples. "It's like it's some frequency that God designed to punish us."

"Too bad Wesley burned his cassock," said Alice, "or else he could forgive us for whatever sins we committed to deserve Charlie."

"I'm so sick of this fucking dog," Wesley said. He dropped his paintbrush into the grass, walked over to the fence, and pounded against the wood with his fist. "Shut up," he yelled. He kicked the fence and yelled again. On the other side, Charlie yelped and then continued to bark. The girls watched, Alice and Janie standing side by side holding the delicate racquets, Kathryn waiting for direction, Apple sitting in the chair Wesley had just vacated.

"Whoa, whoa, we'll get it figured out," said Hannah Fay, putting her hands on his shoulders. "We can talk to them. They're sweet people. They won't want you to be upset."

At Hannah Fay's touch, or perhaps the gentle nudge of her

stomach against his back, Wesley's shoulders relaxed and he took a step away from the fence. Charlie barked, as if he could sense the retreat. "Fine," said Wesley, turning to face her. "Get rid of it."

"Me?" asked Hannah Fay, looking around and lowering her voice. "Get rid of the dog?"

"Anyone," said Wesley. He looked past her to Alice and the others. "I don't care who, but someone needs to take one for the team."

In Wesley's chair, Apple straightened up. "Just so we're clear, you don't mean killing it, right?" she asked. She said *killing it* in a dramatic stage whisper. "You mean opening the door and letting it out."

"That's one way to do it," Wesley said, already walking back toward the house. Apple hopped up from the chair in case he wanted to sit, but Wesley didn't stop until he got to the back door. Then, his hand on the knob, he turned around and said, "Get it done. I can't get involved. I can't take a scandal at this stage." And he went inside, shutting the door behind him. Charlie barked.

Apple sat back down in the chair. "This might come as a shock to you," she said, "but I'm an animal lover, and I don't think I can get behind letting this dog out."

"For Wesley, though," said Janie. "Well, all of us really. The whole street!"

"All of mankind!" said Alice. Janie tossed the shuttlecock in the air and swatted it toward Alice, who caught it in one hand. For a second she imagined it as an actual bird, and she closed her fingers around it and squeezed before uncurling them and picturing it flying away.

"I can't do it either," said Hannah Fay. "I'm conspicuous."

Kathryn stepped forward. She was wearing her glasses again, and the reflection of the string lights twinkled in the lenses. "I'll do it," she said. "It's no big deal."

"He's man's best friend, Kathryn," said Apple.

Kathryn shrugged. "Our family dog bit me when I was four. I have a scar on my calf." Alice had noticed it. It looked like a zipper.

"You can't do it by yourself," Alice said. She tossed the birdie at Janie, who swung and missed, and it sailed deep into the bushes. "I'll help."

"Did Kathryn's family dog bite you too?" Apple asked.

Alice ignored her. She couldn't think too much about the elven couple, but maybe they didn't like the dog either. Maybe he belonged to a deceased family member, and they'd had to take him in. Maybe they would be relieved. They could get a new dog who was nicer, quieter. Besides, like Janie said, it was for Wesley. "When should we do it?" she asked. As she spoke, she felt overcome by the thought that she was the one meant to join Kathryn in this mission. It couldn't be anyone else.

Kathryn walked over to the easel, picking up the brush Wesley had dropped in the grass, and looked thoughtfully toward the fence. "We need to do some recon on their schedules," she said. "I imagine they do the same things every week. Maybe even every day. And we shouldn't talk about it out here." Charlie barked.

"Like anyone could hear you over this fucking dog," Apple said loudly.

"Alice," Kathryn said, "tomorrow I need you to monitor. Maybe even make contact with the owners but only if you can play it cool."

Alice nodded. "I'm very cool."

"Is everyone laughing at me?" Kathryn asked, looking around. "What's so funny?"

"I'll do the monitoring," Alice said. "I promise. But can't we just open the front door at some point and let him run out?"

"That won't work," Kathryn said. "He'll just come back when he's hungry."

"What if," Apple suggested thoughtfully, "Janie and I had the van out in front of the house? You and Alice herd the dog out the door and into the van. I'll drive it away. How hard can it be?"

"We should do more than that," said Kathryn. "I just don't know what. We need to wake the people up."

"No, no, no, no," said Apple. "Wesley wants you to be discreet. This is not like the other stuff."

"Fine," said Kathryn. "Whatever. I'm going to bed. Someone move the easel back in the garage, please."

"She is a certified lunatic," Janie said admiringly, once Kathryn was inside. "I love it."

"She doesn't have any outlet," said Hannah Fay. "She's at work all day. Let her play army commander if that will make her happy."

"She's going to end up smearing a message in blood on the walls," Apple said. "'We killed your dog.'"

"No one's killing anything!" Alice protested. "And no one is smearing blood on any walls."

"Just make sure Kathryn's on the same page," Apple said.

"Imagine her coming home with blood all over her hands," said Alice. She spread her fingers wide and turned them over and over again, looking at them in mock horror like Lady Macbeth. "Out, damned spot," she said.

"His name isn't Spot," said Janie. "It's Charlie."

Alice and Apple looked at each other and laughed, and Alice refigured the evolving picture of Apple before that she kept in her head: a girl with field hockey legs and a bad attitude, sitting in an advanced English 4 class just like any other girl Alice would have known back home, and Alice felt herself soften toward her friend, who was, in the end, like her after all.

Next door, Charlie continued to bark.

"I'm off to bed," said Alice. "I need to rest up for my long day of espionage tomorrow."

The girls told her good night, and Alice slipped back inside. She wanted to find Wesley, but when she called for him, he didn't answer. She poked her head in Hannah Fay's study, stepped outside onto the front porch, and finally paused in front of Kathryn's closed door, where she heard an unmistakable, familiar sound: Wesley's harried breathing, small and hungry noises coming from a girl, Alice knew, beneath him. She stood there for a full minute, palm flat against the door like she might push it open, and listened. She had never understood the appeal of Kathryn to Wesley, who was so handsome, so dynamic and smart, but listening at the door, it occurred to her Kathryn brought an intensity with her to everything. Alice imagined that in bed, the physicality of it. She thought of how far removed Kathryn could seem from her feelings and how that might appeal to Wesley too. Kathryn didn't care about being typical, comfortable, safe, all the things Wesley disdained.

How different than Alice, who felt everything, everything in both places, her body and her heart. She wondered what it would be like to cut one out. The heart, she thought. She imagined herself, strangely, uncomfortably, as Kathryn right now in bed with Wesley and closed her eyes and leaned against the door. She would try it, next time Wesley chose her. Or better: she could take the best from each of the girls, their very finest quality, and make it her own. The no-nonsense physicality of Kathryn, the challenge of Apple, Hannah Fay's gentleness, Janie's optimism. Maybe, Alice thought, this was why Wesley had to keep them all. Together, they made someone perfect, the only kind of person Wesley deserved, but if anyone could embody all the attributes of Wesley's perfect girl, it was Alice Lange.

She heard voices in the house, and she leapt away from Kathryn's door and darted onto the couch in the living room, where she closed her eyes and pretended to sleep. The girls shushed each other as they walked around her, and Alice listened to the familiar sounds of their bedtime routines: Hannah Fay washing her face, Janie eating a handful of cereal in the kitchen before brushing her teeth, Apple locking the back door, then the front door. Alice kept her eyes shut.

Outside, Charlie barked until his owners called him back inside, and the street went quiet again.

For three days, Kathryn went to work and Alice sat outside on the front porch and monitored the comings and goings of the couple next door. When Wesley was home, he would sit outside with her, his legs spread wide, strong and sturdy as tree trunks. He kept up a constant run of conversation the whole time, only occasionally turning his head toward Alice as he spoke. Otherwise he mostly kept his eyes on the street ahead, and she thought he must only be seeing whatever passed directly in front of him: the two men walking their dogs, a man on a bicycle who dinged his bell at them as he passed, the blue trash truck rumbling past, which made Charlie bark; they could hear him even though he was inside.

Keeping his voice low, Wesley talked a little about the dog, the neighbors, the other girls. What interested Alice most (and what interested us most, too, because who doesn't like to hear about themselves, how other people see them—isn't this very thing Wesley's trick with the camera?) was what Wesley had to say about the day he met Alice. About what he saw in her before he really knew her, about the neighborhood, about us. "Sometimes I know where I'm going and why," he said. "Like with Janie. I knew exactly what would happen and who she was, so I took my time. I didn't want to startle her. Like a deer in the woods. You know I thought about naming her Bambi? It was almost right, but it wasn't. It wasn't right enough.

"But with you, I ended up in your neighborhood because someone needed a man to do a job, a friend of a friend, and I didn't want to go because it was so far from here, and the truck was acting up, but we were low on money, and I knew I had to. I wasn't even going to bring my camera, but a voice inside told me I needed to, and I grabbed it on my way out the door.

"Did you go to church when you were a little girl? My aunt took me a few times, but every time I didn't want to do something, she would tell me the story about Jonah and the big fish. She never said whale. She always said fish. God wanted Jonah to go somewhere, and he didn't want to, and he ran away, and God sent the big fish to eat him, and he ended up right back where he didn't want to go. So my aunt would say, if it's right, you're going to have to do it one way or another. Or else a big fish is going to eat me? I asked. And she said yes, or something like that, but even then I knew eventually I'd be so big, nothing could eat me. But I don't know, I thought about that fish that day, and I ended up in your neighborhood. It's nice. I pictured myself there. Not me, not who I am right now, but another version of me. Me if my life were different." (Alice nodded. This was how she had begun to feel in the last days before she left. Another Alice, a different Alice—different only to her; to us, this would have been the Alice we always saw, the one we thought we knew. We try to hold both versions of Alice, but it was hard then, and knowing what we now know, it is harder still, and we must admit that only one Alice existed, and the one we saw was only a fabrication, a story we told ourselves.)

"So I finished the job," Wesley went on. Alice was surprised to hear him share so much about his life, his past, even without that cassock, outside of the protection afforded by the rules of the made-up game. She had done this, somehow, cracked him open like a nut, and a warmth spread through her. "It was a stupid, short job," he was saying, "but I got paid, and I decided to walk around the neighborhood. It's much nicer than where I grew up. Everyone was outside. There were kids playing in the street, and I watched a car approaching, and the kids just parted. Like a miracle. And the grass was so fucking green. What's that about? It looked like carpet. Every single yard. I just kept walking, and I was starting to feel kind of down because I thought about what it would be like to raise my baby there, if it was me and Hannah Fay in one of those stupid fucking houses with a pool in the backyard. Anyway, I started looking at the houses, and I realized the windows were like eyes, you know? They were all shut. No real life there. I remembered what I knew was true. These people are blind. They're asleep. They aren't like us. And someday things are going to come crashing down around them, and we'll be the last ones standing. Then I started feeling sad again, and I couldn't tell why, because it's the natural order of things. But you know the feeling you have when you're positive you're forgetting something? It felt like I couldn't leave yet, so I kept walking, and that, Alice, is when I saw you, and I knew what I was forgetting."

"But you didn't ask me to come with you," Alice said.

Wesley nodded. "It wasn't time. You weren't ready."

"You were just going to let me stay there?" she asked. "What if everything came crashing down while I was still there?"

"Don't you trust me more than that? I know when these things are going to happen. And look." He waved his hand at what was before them: a street intact, houses with people and dogs and children, and then just out of sight, around the corner and down another street, people teaching classes and writing papers and sprawling out on the university quad. And then farther still, in another world, her own neighborhood still stood. Her friends, her mother. Nothing had fallen apart yet.

"Today's the day," Wesley said abruptly. "Now's the time. They're leaving." She looked over to see the elven couple easing their van out of the driveway. They backed out into the street and then the van lurched forward, taking a right at the stop sign. "Go," said Wesley. He stood up.

"Hang on," said Alice. "By myself? What about Kathryn?"

"Look," he said, and he took her hand and pulled her up too. There was Kathryn coming swiftly down the sidewalk. She was in her work clothes, a black skirt and a dowdy, cream-colored blouse that Hannah Fay said used to be hers, but it was hard to imagine her ever having worn. Her purse was slung over her shoulder, and bounced against her hip as she walked.

"How did she know?" Alice asked. She watched as Kathryn

slowed down in front of the house next door and looked down the driveway and then continued on toward Alice and Wesley.

"I called her at work," Wesley said. "I told her to come home."

"When?" Alice looked at Kathryn, who waved at her solemnly from the bottom step of the porch.

"Ready?" Kathryn asked. "I'm going to change clothes so I don't get these dirty."

"It doesn't matter when," Wesley said. "It just matters I knew enough to call."

"Dirty?" asked Alice. "Aren't we just letting him out?"

"We're going to hop the fence," said Kathryn. "Okay, I'm going to change." She walked up the steps and squeezed herself between Wesley and Alice and through the door. Alice heard Apple saying, "Oh no, look what the cat dragged in," before Kathryn shut the door behind her.

"Did you two plan this already?" Alice asked. "What have I even been doing for the last few days?"

"Come on, Alice," Wesley said. "How else were you going to get over there? If you went in the front door, people would see you."

"Well," she said, "I guess I'm not destined for a life of crime."

"This isn't crime," Wesley said, putting his hands on her shoulders. "You're doing everyone a favor. I guarantee everyone hates that fucking dog." He leaned in and kissed her, quick and light. "You're definitely doing me a favor, at least."

She sighed. "Okay." She gestured down at her clothes. "Are these fine?"

"Yes," said Wesley.

"Does it even matter what I wear?" she asked.

"No," said Wesley. "You know how Kathryn is."

"I'll go wait in the backyard," she said, turning away, but Wesley caught her before she could open the door.

"Listen," he said, and his voice was gentle. "Someday soon, your old home is going to be destroyed. Like everything, everywhere. It's going to crumble, and then it's going to burn." He reached toward her and touched her cheek, then pushed a lock of her hair behind her ear. "I'm sorry," he said. "That night, when I came back here after I met you, I couldn't sleep because I worried I was wrong, and that it would happen before I could get you out." She looked up at him. Once in a while, Wesley could be soft and tender; Alice loved his roughness because it was a part of him, the way his dark hair was, his blue eyes, but she treasured the gentleness when she saw it.

"You rescued me," she said. She believed it, that he had saved her from a life she didn't want, but she also said it to soothe him. She moved closer and leaned against him, and he wrapped her up in his arms. (We picture her in this same embrace, but with someone different, somewhere different. A boy like Ben Austin, sturdy, stable. But wishing for a different Alice is like Alice wishing for a different Wesley—this is the one we got, the one we always had.)

"Okay," he said into her ear. "Kathryn will be waiting for you. Go serve your fellow man."

Alice pulled back and laughed, saluting him, and went inside to find Apple and Hannah Fay on the couch with her swollen feet on the coffee table. Janie was gone, hired by a friend of Wesley's to babysit her children. "Kathryn's ready to rumble," Apple said. Kathryn came out of the kitchen with her hair pulled back in a ponytail, wearing a stretchy pair of knit pants and a long-sleeved shirt that said SKI NEW MEXICO on it. Alice had never seen the shirt before, and wondered who had gone skiing. "Let's go," Kathryn said.

Alice looked at the other girls and rolled her eyes. "You volunteered," Apple said.

"Okay," Alice said. "Come on." A baseball bat, something else she had never seen at the house, leaned against the wall by the door, and Kathryn swiped it in a single fluid motion and opened the back door. "Seriously?" Alice asked.

"Protection," said Kathryn.

"There's no one home!" said Alice.

"Alice, maybe you need something too," Apple said, and Alice didn't react—it was better to ignore Apple sometimes—but she heard her hurry into the kitchen and open a drawer.

"Here," Apple said breathlessly, and Alice turned around to see the little knife she had stolen on their first midnight run.

"Fine," she said, unsure if the knife was Apple's idea of a joke. "Let's just go."

Outside, the girls dragged the patio chairs across the grass and positioned them next to the fence. Kathryn pulled out two sets of gloves she had kept tucked into the waistband of her pants—the large wool pair was clearly Wesley's, and the other was a pair of stained gardening gloves, which she tossed to Alice. She dropped the baseball bat over the fence, where it landed with a muffled thud in the grass, and reached up to the top of the fence, gripping it. Kathryn hesitated for only a minute, and then suddenly she was up, toes against the fence board, then one leg over and then the other, and then she was gone. "Just like that, Alice," she said from the other side.

"I'm impressed," Apple said. "And a little surprised."

"Honestly," said Hannah Fay, "I'm not."

"Off I go," Alice said and climbed up on the chair.

"Drop your knife over first," Kathryn instructed her. "I'm up on the back steps." The volume of Charlie's barking had increased, and the sound was urgent and excited. He sensed visitors. Alice stood on her tiptoes and gingerly tossed the knife.

"All clear," said Kathryn.

Kathryn was taller than she was, so Alice had to jump a little to get her hands on the top of the fence, but then she was up, too, and it felt good to be doing something physical, and she thought again of Kathryn, how she lived in a physical world of movement and action. A buzz of adrenaline zipped through her as soon as she landed, like she was absorbing energy from the ground itself. Inside the house, Charlie was still barking. She looked around until she found her knife, winking like a hidden diamond, and she picked it up. Kathryn's baseball bat was still lying where it had fallen, near the base of the fence.

"I'm guessing their back door is unlocked," Kathryn said in a low voice. "I climbed over a few nights ago and checked it."

"Oh my God," Alice said. "Kathryn! Didn't Charlie bark?"

Kathryn smiled. When she smiled, it was always because she was genuinely happy or pleased. When she had to smile for pictures but didn't feel like it, it always came out wrong somehow, her lips too loose. Alice could see this being attractive to Wesley, too, the purity of being unable to fake happiness.

"If your dog barks all the time, you wouldn't be able to check on half the things he was barking about!" Kathryn said. "At least that's what I was banking on, anyway." She went up the back steps to the house and twisted the doorknob and cracked open the door. Immediately, Charlie's black nose poked through the open sliver. He sniffed, his nostrils flaring, then disappeared behind the door again to bark, and Kathryn pulled it shut. "Ready?" she asked.

"Not really," Alice told her.

Kathryn's gloved hand was still on the doorknob, and Alice watched, hanging back, as she began to turn the knob. "Come on," Kathryn said. "We've been inside strangers' houses before."

"But Wesley is always with us," Alice said. "And it's night-time."

"Which is arguably creepier," said Kathryn.

"It's different," said Alice. Darkness made everything feel exciting and fantastic, like she was dreaming. And though she knew Apple would make fun of her if she could hear this, having Wesley there made her feel like she was invincible.

"Wesley told me eventually we're going to be doing all nighttime activities outside the house on our own," Kathryn said. Alice opened her mouth to protest—it wasn't even safe for them to go out without him, was it? But Kathryn held up her hand. "People are watching him, and it's getting too risky for him to be out and about. So think of it as practice."

"Okay," Alice said. "Open it."

Kathryn opened the door and grabbed ahold of Charlie's collar as he bounded toward them, lifting him up a little as she did. His bark sounded raspier as the collar pressed against his throat, and his nails scuttled on the wooden floor as Alice slipped inside and shut the door behind her. Kathryn dragged Charlie through the laundry room and into the kitchen and down the hall and into the living room. His feet were scrabbling fast against the floor, and he was, of course, barking, but he didn't seem upset, just kind of eager, like they were playing a game. Alice walked toward the front window and peeked through the blinds. There was the van, ready and waiting. "Apple's in the van outside," Alice said. "Ready?"

But then as Kathryn adjusted her grip on Charlie, she stepped on a purple rubber ball, and the toy let out a frightened squeak, and Charlie's ears perked up, and he pulled away from Kathryn, who instinctively stepped out of the way, and Charlie pounced on the ball, grasping it between his jaws and biting so the toy cried again and again. "Fuck," said Kathryn. She went to grab the dog, but he darted away again, still holding the ball. She took another step toward him. His tail wagged. He dropped the toy to the floor and waited for Kathryn to do her part.

"He wants you to throw it, Kathryn," Alice said.

"I know that," Kathryn snapped. "Shit. What can we do? Wesley is not going to be happy if we don't get rid of this dog."

"We could just leave and come up with another plan," Alice suggested, but even as she said it, she knew they couldn't go back to the bungalow without taking care of the problem.

Kathryn shook her head. "We need a new plan *now*."

"All right," Alice said, thinking. They couldn't get him to go outside on his own. They couldn't pick him up and carry him out. She looked around the room. "Okay," she said. She walked over to the doily-covered end table, where she had left the knife next to a pewter dish filled with potpourri. Blood will be spilled, Wesley had promised them once. Violence. Alice held up the knife.

(In the weeks following Alice's disappearance, when we all struggled to reconcile the Alice we knew with the one who left us, Susannah found herself returning to the memory of Alice punching Randy Neely. She'd tapped him on the shoulder, and when he turned around, she punched him right in the gut, knocked the wind out of him. Everyone laughed, and Alice felt a swell of pleasure.

But it was what came next that Susannah thought about: how they had walked home together, and it was spring, and her eyes were itchy from the pollen in the air, and Alice had laughed so hard about Randy Neely. Head thrown back so her long hair nearly reached her bottom. "Susie," Alice was saying, "it felt so good to do it! It was like punching a pillow. Or like a big tub of melty butter! My hand went right into it."

"You didn't need to," Susannah said. "I could've handled it myself."

"You couldn't have," Alice said. "Do you want a tissue for your eyes?"

"No," Susannah said, simultaneously hurt and touched her friend had noticed the swollen skin around her eyes, the pink blooming in the corners.

"When I punched him," she said, her eyes wide, "I loved it. I felt good doing it, and then everyone loved me for it."

"Not Randy," said Susannah.

Alice waved her hand dismissively. "Someday he'll tell people Alice Lange punched him," she said. "And it will be a good story."

In fact, he told no one, not even his mother, until Alice disappeared, and Randy said, "Did you know that once Alice Lange socked me in the stomach?"

It was such a strange conversation that Susannah thought about it for days after and found it troubling in a way she couldn't articulate, but eventually it crossed her mind only occasionally, until after Alice left. "You didn't know her the way I knew her," Susannah said to anyone who would listen. One summer night, at a party before everyone left for college, she found Randy Neely, and they talked about Alice. Then they disappeared into the bathroom in the master bedroom, and she let Randy put his hands up her shirt and then inside her pants, and they both thought of Alice Lange.)

"Okay," said Kathryn, nodding at Alice and the knife. "That's good. You're right, that's what we'll do." Charlie took a step closer to Kathryn, as if he wanted to remind her they were playing, and she suddenly lunged toward him, grabbing him by the collar.

"What about the body?" Alice asked, watching the dog strain to get away. "It's going to make a big mess."

"Well, we can't clean it," Kathryn said. "We'll leave it. We'll take some things, anything small and valuable we see. It will look like a robbery, and that we had to kill Charlie to stop him from attacking us." Charlie, hearing his name, looked up at Kathryn, who was still holding him by his collar. The collar was red leather, slim as a ribbon around his neck.

"Okay, yes, right," said Alice, wishing Kathryn wouldn't call the dog by its name anymore. "He's just an animal. We eat animals."

"I'll hold him," said Kathryn. "And you just stick him, I guess. I think you'll have to push really hard."

"Me?" said Alice. Kathryn nodded. "Oh no," said Alice. "I don't think I can."

"Quit wasting time," said Kathryn. She crouched down next to the dog, one hand still grasping the collar, but now she had one arm around his body, too, like she was hugging him, posing for a picture with a beloved pet. "He's nice and calm," she said, looking at Alice with serious eyes. "This will be easy. One day, one day soon, we'll be asked to do things a lot harder than this."

Alice thought of what Wesley said about the shaking and

cracking of the earth, the blazes to follow it, but she couldn't conjure up the image of her own home splitting wide open; all she could picture was Pompeii, that video they watched in class, with Vesuvius spewing in the background, angry or maybe not angry—maybe just careless, heartless, unfeeling.

And so Alice walked over to the dog. Kathryn's fingers clenched tighter around the collar and her other hand pressed harder against his body to keep him still. He started to bark. He wanted to go, he wanted to run, he wanted to play. A warm-up. This was a warm-up. Wesley would love her. Wesley would thank her. Wesley would know he could count on her. She was a girl who was constantly distinguishing herself. She was meant to be here. She was meant to do this.

She put the tip of the blade up to the dog's skin, near his chest, through the coat of coarse hair, and she pressed. She thought she might throw up. He barked, then cried, and she pulled the knife out. For a moment the blood didn't come, and then it did. The knife was so little, the slice so neat, like a surgical incision. *Again*, said Kathryn, *just to be safe.*

This time, she moved her hand to another spot and pushed the knife in harder. This, she thought, would be like piercing Randy Neely with a knife, Randy who had turned out well, whom she'd seen shirtless at the beach last summer, his stomach all muscle, no softness. This time, instead of pulling the knife right out, she dragged it down, like she was pulling a lever, and then took it out. *Alice!* came Kathryn's voice. *That's enough, I think.*

"Oh my God," Alice said. She dropped the knife. Kathryn released the dog onto the floor, but he didn't move, and blood was beginning to pool around him.

"Don't look," said Kathryn. "Go into the bedroom and grab some things. Be careful not to touch anything you won't take with you. I'll get stuff from out here."

Alice, stunned, floated into the bedroom the couple shared. There was a necklace on the nightstand. A pair of earrings. She put them all in her pocket. She found herself in the bathroom and then wandered back into the living room.

Kathryn came in with the man's wallet, and she held it up, waving it. "A bonus," she said. "Let's go. I have the knife."

"Is he dead?" asked Alice.

"He will be soon," Kathryn said. "His breathing is very shallow."

Alice took a step forward, but her view of the dog was blocked by the couch. "Don't look," Kathryn said.

"It's cruel to leave him there suffering," said Alice. "We can slit his throat."

"He's fine, Alice," Kathryn said. Alice watched Kathryn look down to the ground and step carefully around something. "He's almost dead."

"I'll slit his throat," said Alice. She was meant to, she knew. Now Kathryn was walking around the couch toward Alice, moving quickly, the knife in her hand. She passed Alice and headed for the back door. Now that Kathryn was gone, Alice moved so that she could see the dog. There was so much more blood than she had thought. His eyes were closed, but he was breathing, his abdomen rising and falling and covered in puncture wounds.

"Did you—do it more?" Alice called after Kathryn. "To the dog."

"No," came Kathryn's voice from the back of the house.

Alice followed the sound to find that she already had the back door wide open.

Outside, the air seemed cooler than it was when they went in, and only then did Alice realize she was damp with sweat. Kathryn jogged down the two steps and toward the fence, where she picked up the baseball bat that had never made it inside the house. She stood on the plank of wood running perpendicular to the fence slats and dropped the bat, then the knife, back into the girls' yard. "Take your gloves off," she said to Alice. "You've got blood on them, and we don't want blood on the fence." She held her hand out to Alice, who, as she peeled them off, was shocked to see how red they were. How, when she only cut the dog twice? Kathryn dropped the gloves over next and then propelled herself up and over the fence.

Alice followed behind her, and when she landed back in her own yard, Kathryn was on the back patio, wearing only her bra and stepping out of her pants. "Strip," she said. "These are all going straight into the washing machine." Alice didn't move. "For goodness' sake, Alice," Kathryn said, "do I have to do everything?" She took a step closer to Alice. "Arms, please," she said. Alice lifted her arms, and Kathryn peeled the shirt off of her. "Shoes," she said, and Alice removed those herself. Then Kathryn reached over and pulled down Alice's pants so that she could step out of them. "Okay," said Kathryn. "You're fine. You did it. You did a great job."

"There's a necklace in the pocket," Alice said, pointing to the pants on the ground. "And earrings, I think."

"I'll take care of it," said Kathryn.

The back door opened, and Hannah Fay and Apple stuck out their heads. "What happened? You never came out," Apple said. "So I just pulled the van back into the driveway. I didn't want anyone to see me loitering out there."

"Hang on," Hannah Fay said, pushing past Apple and coming to Kathryn and Alice. "Why are you in your underwear?"

"Change of plans," said Kathryn. "Where's Wesley?"

"Out for a walk," said Hannah Fay. "He said he couldn't be here for what was about to happen." (Cowardice disguising itself as importance. What kind of man gets girls to do his dirty work?)

"We can talk about it inside," Kathryn said. "We have some laundry to do."

"Alice," said Hannah Fay carefully, "is that blood on your clothes?"

"Kathryn wouldn't let me slit his throat."

"Inside," Kathryn said, and she put a hand on Alice's bare back to guide her. Kathryn's hand was warm, and Alice wanted to be wrapped up inside it, like a tiny creature held securely in the palm of a giant.

"Go take a shower, Alice," Kathryn said once they were inside. "Do you want me to run the water for you?"

"I'll do it," said Apple, taking Alice's hand. "Come on."

"What happened?" she heard Hannah Fay ask as they left the room.

"Alice went nuts in there," said Kathryn.

Had she?

"We couldn't get ahold of the dog, so we killed it," Kathryn went on. "She stabbed it a bunch of times."

Alice looked at Apple to see if she had heard. "I thought Kathryn did it," said Alice. "All those other times."

"I don't think so," said Apple.

"We'll never get the stains out," Alice said.

"Probably not," Apple said. "But it's okay."

They were in front of the shower now, and Apple pulled back the curtain and turned the knob, stuck her hand under the streaming water to test the temperature. When Alice was little, she would wake up and hear the water running in her mother's bathroom. She'd go in and sit on the toilet, the lid closed, as her mother showered, letting the steam envelop her. Her mother would say "Alice?" when Alice first came in and closed the door, and Alice would say yes, but beyond that, they didn't speak. When her mother turned the water off, Alice would slide off the toilet and leave the bathroom, shutting the door behind her. Then Alice would wait for her in the bedroom or the kitchen or the living room, and her mother would come in and greet her as if this were the first encounter they'd had all morning. Alice thought it was funny her mother always made sure it was her—who else would it be? But now she knew how permeable the imaginary borders around someone's home were, how easily they could be crossed, and she shivered when she imagined her mother in the shower, hearing the opening and closing of a door, the light sound of feet. She could have told herself it was only Alice, the way it was every morning, but what if, one day, she'd been wrong?

"Warm," said Apple. "Go on."

Obediently, Alice took off her bra, which fit a little more loosely these days, and panties, and stepped in. She closed her eyes and let the water run over her body, and a minute later she heard Apple shut the door, and she knew she was alone.

CHAPTER TWENTY-EIGHT

KATHRYN TOOK THE rest of the day off, calling the library to say that she'd become ill, and the girls all took turns waiting on the front porch or peeking through the windows to see what would happen when the elven couple arrived home. They were jittery and restless, and when Hannah Fay began making paper cranes out of magazine pages, soon they all joined her. The coffee table began to disappear beneath the small glossy birds. "We could make a mobile from these," Alice suggested, "for the baby."

"Alice," said Hannah Fay, "what a sweet idea."

After the shower, Alice had felt better—she had done what needed to be done. The other girls were tender with her, treating her as if she were a sore or maimed part of themselves that needed care. This, to Alice, almost made it worth it.

Wesley still wasn't home when they heard the neighbors' van pull into their driveway. Kathryn was on the front porch with Janie; later, Alice felt grateful it was Kathryn, unflappable and cold, and Janie, who wasn't anywhere near either house when it all happened, who were outside. Alice watched through the window as the neighbors walked into their house, screamed, and ran out. She couldn't stop herself.

The girls inside could hear him approach the porch and ask Kathryn and Janie if they had seen anything. There had been a break-in, he said, and later Janie told them his face had been pale, sick looking. If they hadn't seen anything, had they heard anything? The dog barking?

Nothing, said Kathryn. Oh God, how frightening. Should I call the police?

I can, said Janie, getting up.

No, the man said. We've already called them. Whoever did it, he killed our dog. My wallet is missing, but that's it.

I'm so sorry, said Janie. I wasn't even here.

The other girls? the man said. I know there are—lots of you who live here. Or are visiting? And—your husband?

Family, said Kathryn. She did not elaborate, and she said later the man nodded, in a dazed kind of way, thoughts elsewhere.

We'll ask them, said Janie. But if any of them heard anything, we would have called the cops. We all have to look out for each other.

The world is a terrible place, said Kathryn.

Yes, said the man. Alice couldn't see him, but she imagined him in front of the girls, small-boned hand on balding head, looking in the distance for any kind of information, anything to fill the gaps of the horror story that had taken place.

We're happy to talk to the police, Kathryn said. If you need us to.

I'll tell them, the man said. My wife won't go back inside. I'm going to take her to a friend's house.

I'm so sorry, said Janie. We can send over a meal.

Cookies, said Kathryn. I think we have ingredients for cookies.

Thank you, the man said. I need to tend to my wife. And to the house. It's very—messy.

Do you need some help? Kathryn asked.

The man must have shaken his head. But thank you, he said.

Good luck, said Kathryn. Let us know if you need anything.

He seemed like a good dog, said Janie.

He was, said the man. Good-bye. And Alice went to the window again, watched him cross over to his own yard, and then he turned out of sight.

Kathryn and Janie came inside after a beat. "I think we're in the clear," Kathryn said. "They won't suspect us."

When Wesley finally came home, he said the same thing. "Brilliant," he said, slapping his knee as he listened to Kathryn and Alice recount what happened. "Really. This is the best outcome I could have imagined. We'll finally have a good night's sleep."

They sat in the living room, all of them but Hannah Fay, who was making dinner in the kitchen; it was nearly dark when Wesley strolled in, chipper and hungry, wondering what there was to eat. Now the last shards of light cut in through the window, sharp and cool as a blade.

"No one ever thinks girls could do something like that," Wesley said.

"That seems vaguely sexist," said Apple.

"No, no, no," said Wesley. "The rest of the world is sexist. Not me. I know you're just as capable as a man in certain regards. Or that Kathryn and Alice are."

"I could have done it. You know that," Apple said.

"I don't," said Wesley. "You haven't proved it."

Apple rolled her eyes. "Whatever." She looked at Alice. "Have fun sucking his dick as your reward for slaughtering a defenseless animal," she said and walked into the kitchen.

"Apple," said Wesley, her name a sigh.

Janie laughed. "She's fine," she said. But she got up too. "I'll go set the table."

"Alice, Kathryn," said Wesley. He shifted from where he sat on the loveseat so that he could see them both: Alice sitting cross-legged on the floor, Kathryn in the chair above her. His voice was tender, eyes solemn and dark. Feet planted on the floor and knees far apart, hands clasped together, elbows on his thighs. "I knew it would happen eventually, that the first blood would be spilled. I didn't know the circumstances, but I knew it was coming." He closed his eyes and leaned back a little and rubbed the corners of his eyes. "I guess I don't mind telling you," he said, opening his eyes again, "that things haven't been moving as quickly as I had thought they would. I thought that our night missions would wake everyone up the way I wanted, but it isn't happening. It just keeps"—he opened his hand like he was scattering ashes—"not happening."

"I know," said Kathryn. "I'm sorry."

"It isn't because of you," Alice said.

"I know," said Wesley. "It's them." The three of them all looked toward the front window; night had finally fallen, and Alice could see nothing, but she thought of the world outside the way Wesley saw it: not only in darkness that would lift in twelve hours but in a darkness that would never lighten, a blackness that only they could penetrate. Out there were her mother, her friends, all of us whom she had known and (we thought) loved. But she had seen for herself that our lives weren't what she wanted, that there was a darkness there, thick and choking. She didn't feel that way here, with Wesley, with the girls, where a brightness had begun to appear around the edges of her life and seemed to spread until all around her there was light. In the desert, she knew, it would be even brighter.

"This man who came over," Wesley said. "He was frightened?"

"Yes," said Kathryn. "He was very upset."

Wesley nodded. "He was awake," he said. "He was in the now. He could see that the world was a different place than he thought it would be."

"The world is a terrible place," Alice said, echoing Kathryn's words to the man from next door.

"Not for us," said Wesley. "Not if we're together. That's why it's important we stay with each other." He shifted so that he was once again facing the front window, and pointed. "Out there is where all the bad things are," he continued. "People who want the world to stay asleep, stay blind. People who want to hurt us. That's why we have to go to the desert. We'll be safe there when everyone wakes up and everything comes crashing down."

"But when?" asked Alice. "Do you know now? Now that we've—done what we did?"

"Soon," Wesley told her, nodding. "I have ideas. Things we can do to kickstart it. You've inspired me." He grinned, his white teeth like a wolf's. "There's one thing left to do over there, though. At the house next door. Something is missing."

"What is it?" asked Kathryn. "We were very careful."

"A picture. Like we've left at the other houses," Alice said.

Wesley pointed at her. "Bingo. We want them to know it's

all connected. When they figure it out and piece it all together, we need them to know this is something big happening to the world. And this is only the beginning."

"All right," said Kathryn. "Do you know which picture? I can slide it under the front door."

"One of Alice," he said, and Alice flushed with pleasure. This was the prize he was giving her. She wanted to tell Apple. "I know the exact one. It's in my portfolio on your bedside table, Kathryn. She's at a party by the pool, but you can't see her face, of course. You'll know it when you see it."

"Got it," said Kathryn.

"There's more to do," Wesley said. "But we won't discuss it now. Tonight we'll eat, and we'll sleep. Tomorrow is a new day. I'm going to cancel my meeting with the art dealer. I'll admit that I was wrong. It isn't art that's the way."

"Oh no," said Alice. "But you've worked so hard. You're so gifted."

"Don't do it, Wesley," said Kathryn sternly. Alice tilted her head so she could see Kathryn's face. She was frowning. "Whatever you're thinking, it's important to carry on with business as usual. Don't give anything away."

"Maybe," he said. "I'll consider it."

"Have you mentioned this to the others?" Kathryn asked. "To Hannah Fay?"

"No," said Wesley. "Only you two for now."

Hannah Fay's voice came from the kitchen, calling them for dinner.

"I'm not sure I can stand," Alice said, leaning her head back against Kathryn's chair. "I'm exhausted."

"Then I'll help you," Wesley said. He stood up from the couch and walked over to her, then bent down, placed one arm around her back and one under her legs. He stood and lifted. She felt her body glow.

"You feel like my bride," he said.

"I do," she said and laughed.

He carried her into the kitchen, where everyone, even Apple, clapped for her, for them, for strength, for beauty, for the warmth of their little sanctuary, for a savior, a leader, for a street that was, finally, quiet.

CHAPTER TWENTY-NINE

WESLEY DID CANCEL his appointment with the art dealer. "I was beginning to wonder if he even had a meeting at all," Hannah Fay confided in Alice, and Alice didn't tell her she had wondered the same thing herself. "I bet those people all talk to each other." That was all she said, but Alice could fill in the rest: the gallery owner might have said to the dealer, If Wesley calls you, don't answer. I feel positive he broke into my house once. She cringed imagining the conversation. "He'll get it figured out," she told Hannah Fay.

Wesley began spending more time alone, going for walks and then runs, from which he would return shirtless and sweaty, dark hair shiny and limp, the hair on his legs dark, too, curled in places, slick in others from where sweat had flattened it. Sometimes he didn't shower after, just stood in front of the open refrigerator until he had cooled off and then left his damp running shorts draped over the railing on the front porch to dry. At night, he told them frightening stories about all the terrible things happening in the world: the wars being fought overseas, the hatred men held in their hearts for one another, what it could do to them, to Wesley and his girls. Often he talked late into the night but then woke up early and disappeared before anyone else was up.

Alice and the other girls monitored his behavior like scientists in a lab, analyzing his moods and hypothesizing in quiet voices about why now, what now:

Hannah Fay's expanding stomach, fatherhood approaching. Encroaching? He always had seemed excited about the baby, though.

Creatively stalled. After the girls moved the easel back into the garage, Wesley hadn't taken it out again. His brushes sat next to the kitchen sink, their bristles growing crusty and stiff. Then one morning he left on a photography excursion, but when he got home, he ripped the film out of the camera, overexposing it. "There weren't going to be any good ones," he told the girls.

The house itself. Too dusty? Too dark? Too small? Too full? When Wesley was home, Alice tried to make herself small, imagining herself as physically shrinking, just in case he was feeling cramped with so many girls around him. One night, after Wesley distributed the tablets to the girls, Alice felt herself begin to shrink, and though by that point she had taken many trips with Wesley and knew that no matter what she felt, no matter what she saw, it was only an illusion, she began to panic that what she'd been imagining was really happening. Limbs thin as toothpicks, eyes like pinheads, brain and heart and stomach still thinking and pumping and pulsing but so small they would have to stop, wouldn't they? Alice began to cry, but the tears felt normal size, the tears of a normal-size girl, and she was so tiny, and she knew she was going to drown in an ocean she created herself. "I want to be bigger," she kept saying. "Wesley, please, let me be bigger. I'm going to die. The water is rising." That was all she remembered.

"So dramatic," Apple said to Alice the next morning. "You cried so much."

"I was worried," Alice said defensively. "It seemed so real. What did Wesley say?"

"He said he likes small things," Apple said. "Easier to hold." She opened up her hand wide, palm as open as the desert, and then closed her fingers into a tight fist until it wasn't a desert but a stone.

(We know that outside our neighborhood, the world is different. We have traveled. We have been young. We have seen it. Streets of other cities and towns so dirty, cramped, smelly—the men there aggressive, the women desperate and sad. Things we want no part of. Children abducted, women killed, men with guns in their hands, knives, ropes. Those things they use to stop you, hurt you, tie you up, tie you down. Even their hands, empty, are dangerous. Sometimes they are the most dangerous because they are empty.

Our neighborhood is different from the world outside. We work to keep it that way. Look what happened to Rachel Granger, even though she wasn't, technically, one of us. Look what happened to Alice, when she left. Blood on her hands now. That's what waits for us outside.)

A couple of days after Charlie's death, the single dad from next door knocked on the door. He was just checking in, he said, because he noticed Wesley was gone a lot, and it had to be scary to be a group of girls on their own. "It's so crazy," he said. "That kind of thing never happens here."

"That kind of thing can happen anywhere," said Apple.

"Well, if you need anything, just come knock on my door," he said.

"Anything?" Apple asked, a wink in her voice, and the man smiled.

After that, he made a point to wave at the girls when he saw them, but somehow it always seemed to Alice that the greeting was really meant only for Apple.

Once they happened to be outside at the same time—the man closing his car door as Apple and Alice sat together in a sunny patch of the front yard, the last place the light touched before it was gone. Already the shadow was covering Alice, leaving Apple alone in the golden light, and Alice could see how lovely it made her friend look, like a girl from a painting, highlighting her sharp cheekbones, painting the lids of her closed eyes so they glowed, and Alice even thought, briefly, of putting her mouth on Apple's throat, the way Wesley always did, like he wanted to take a bite out of her. (She also thought, just in passing, of the night of the fire, when the boys had caught the love between Susannah and Alice, had egged them on, how she thought about kissing Susannah if only to make the boys happy, to give them something to talk about, to think about later that night as they went to bed. But that was just foolishness. The stakes were so low.) So when the man's car door closed and the girls looked up, and Alice saw him see them, two pretty girls in the dying sun, she knew how he must have felt.

"Hey there," he called.

"Hey," said Apple. "How was work?" Like she knew him. Apple had her legs straight out, one crossed over the other, the palms of her hands flat on the grass.

He shrugged. "Another day, another dollar," he said. Like he knew her.

"I feel that," Apple said, grinning. Like Alice wasn't even there.

"Do you even go to work?" he asked. But he was grinning too.

"I do all kinds of things," Apple said.

The man began walking toward them, like Apple had conjured some kind of spell.

"I'm about to go inside," Apple said. "The light is almost gone."

"Are you a vampire?" he asked.

"That would be the opposite," Alice said, and two sets of eyes looked over to her.

"Oh," he said. "You're right."

"Good night for now," Apple said, standing up. She brushed off the bottom of her shorts—cutoff, denim, the fraying fringe of white bright against her tanned skin—and Alice stood up too. Now they were all in the shadow.

"See you around," the man said.

On the porch, Alice hissed, "Wesley would be so mad at you, flirting with that man like that. You know Wesley hates him."

"Aren't you ever bored?" Apple asked.

Alice thought of Carl Miller. She thought of Ben. She thought, again, of Susannah, the desire to do something memorable, if not for herself, then for others. The walk to the school in the dark, slipping inside, the dark hallways, the dark room, and finally a bright, burning light. "Not really," she said.

That night, Alice woke up when it was still dark outside and realized that Apple wasn't next to her. She went out into the living room, where Janie was sleeping on the couch, the crocheted blanket over her body, one foot peeking out, then peered into the study where Hannah Fay slept. Only Hannah Fay, no Apple. Alice put a hand on Kathryn's door, as if she could somehow sense through the wood if Apple was in there, but Alice knew she wasn't—Wesley had gone in there with Kathryn hours ago. She opened the front door and the screen door and stepped onto the porch, the wood cool under her bare feet.

From somewhere down the street, Alice could hear laughter, loud snatches of conversation she couldn't quite make out, and Alice remembered it was Friday night; other people, people her age, were still awake, and they might not sleep for hours more, might not sleep at all. To think that sounded exhilarating once. Now it only seemed exhausting. And meaningless. All those people seeing nothing, doing nothing important, trying to create meaning out of nothing. Alice felt angry at Apple, who was taking for granted that Wesley had chosen her, had taken her out of the darkness and invited her into the real world. Into the now, and soon into the future.

She went back inside and into the bedroom, where eventually she slept. In the morning, Apple was beside her. "Where did you go last night?" Alice asked her.

Apple frowned, rubbed at the corner of her eye. Smudges of makeup that Alice was certain she hadn't gone to sleep wearing blackened the outline of her eyes, softened them. "Nowhere," she said.

"I guess I must have dreamed it," Alice said.

"I guess so," said Apple.

"Weird," said Alice. "I just don't remember any other parts of the dream."

Apple leaned in closer to her, so their foreheads were

nearly touching. Apple smelled like smoke, like silvery night air. Alice reached up and rubbed at the black makeup under Apple's left eye. "Maybe you're still dreaming," Apple said.

Alice pulled away. "Stop," she said. She turned away and slid off the bed, searched for a bra in the pile of clothes at its foot.

"Are you mad," asked Apple, "because you dreamed I was gone but I wasn't?"

"That would be dumb," said Alice, standing up and clasping the bra. "No, I'm hungry. I'm going to eat breakfast."

"Fine," said Apple, flopping back onto the pillow. "But don't be mad at me for something you made up."

Alice left the room without responding, and she shut the door behind her. In the kitchen, she found Wesley eating cereal. He was, miraculously, alone. "Morning," he said. "Was that you I heard creeping around last night?"

"Where is everyone?" Alice asked.

"Kathryn and Janie went to the grocery store," he said. "Hannah Fay walked to the post office. Apple, I'm sure, is still asleep."

"She's awake," Alice said. Wesley's hair stuck up a little in the back, mussed from sleep, and a few drops of milk dotted his beard like tiny snowflakes, and something about the messy hair and beard—the innocence of it, like Wesley was a clueless little boy—made Alice's anger with Apple sharpen. On the one hand, she couldn't prove Apple had done anything wrong, but on the other hand, she would hate for Wesley to be the last to know if she *had*.

Wesley, the spoon paused before his lips, looked at Alice. "What?" he asked.

"I need to talk to you," she said, and she took the seat across from him, and words rushed out of her, as hot and angry as lava.

CHAPTER THIRTY

THAT NIGHT, WHEN it was dark and they had eaten dinner and cleaned the kitchen, Wesley suggested they sit outside on the porch. On one side, the house was dark—the elven couple was gone for good—and on the other side, the single father with the face Wesley hated had a light on in the living room, so that the window that faced their house glowed yellow. Wesley walked down the steps. His hands were in his pockets, and his hair had gotten longer, almost to his shoulders, and now it had a curl that bounced as he descended. When he got to the bottom, he turned around to face the girls. Alice didn't know what was going to happen, but she felt certain that this would be how Wesley handled Apple. The girls were standing together in a loose line on the porch, and Alice leaned forward to see Apple's face, but it was still. Her hair was in a ponytail, baby hairs around her ears curling a little in the night air. As if she felt Alice noticing, she smoothed them down against her head, but they sprang back out. Something about those hairs made Alice soften toward Apple. But it was too late.

"Tell me what you see," Wesley said to them.

"Where?" asked Janie. "Outside?"

"Just look around," Wesley said. "This is the world."

This, Alice knew, was Wesley giving them a clue about what he wanted them to see. If you were listening, people almost always told you what answer they were looking for. What was the world? "Darkness," said Alice.

"No shit," said Apple. "It's night."

"You know what I mean. Physical darkness, yes, but also evil. Moral darkness. People who want to hurt us," Alice said.

Wesley nodded. "It's everyone," he said, "who isn't us."

They could name anyone in the world—their mothers, fathers, sisters, brothers, their old teachers, the cashier at the grocery store, the man who delivered the mail. "Be polite," Wesley had warned them. "Don't get on anyone's radar. They'll be able to sense it on you anyway, how different you are from them, and we don't want to give them any more reason to hate you."

"The driving man," said Janie. Alice often thought about the driving man, the one who picked up hitchhiking girls, but she hadn't known if any of the others did. Until recently, she had always thought of the world as an essentially good place: if not flawless, then like an imperfect diamond, still brilliant and lovely despite its shortcomings. And sometimes still she looked out at the world around her and could barely believe what Wesley had taught them. That there were people who would present themselves as one thing, but in their heart of hearts, be something else entirely. That the world was so full of badness that it eventually would crack under the weight of it and shake off all the people who lived there.

Other times Alice saw for herself the darkness Wesley described. The old magazines Wesley kept around were full of it—stories of wars and deaths and disease, all of it years ago, and now things were only getting worse. If she didn't see it for herself, she heard about it from Wesley, and then she would start to notice it. It made her want to weep, these pictures of the world she saw in her head, but it also made her heart beat faster because everything Wesley said was going to happen was happening, right now.

"If anyone out there had a chance to get at you," Wesley said now from the bottom of the steps, "they would. They'd hurt you because you scare them. People are always scared of what they don't know and especially what they don't understand. Evil can't understand goodness. Darkness can't understand light. They'd kill you." He paused, and Alice watched him swallow, as if he didn't want to say what he needed to. It was like there was a voice speaking through him, a voice older than the light, older than the darkness, and he wanted to stall that voice, to put off what it was telling him to do: *Tell them how the world will hurt them.* "Slit your throat," said Wesley. "Rip your clothes off, rape you. Tie you up, keep you alive for days to torture you. Then strangle you. Poison you. Stab you. Shoot you. I don't know. How many ways are there to kill a person?" Beside her, Hannah Fay swayed a little, and Alice put her hand on her friend's back to steady her. "Don't lock your knees, Hannah Fay," Wesley instructed.

"Wesley, I don't want to be rude," said Hannah Fay. "But I need to lay down. Everything is hurting."

Below them, Wesley nodded. "I'm sorry," he said. "Go inside. This doesn't concern you, anyway." And then Alice knew she was right, that the person this concerned was Apple.

"I'm sorry," Hannah Fay said softly to the others. "Nights are so bad for me."

"We know, Han," said Janie, who opened the door for Hannah Fay. When she was inside, Apple didn't close the gap her absence left, and Alice felt cold.

"The driving man, though, might pick you up for the opposite reason. Because you seem lifeless, asleep. Because you don't seem special," he said and shrugged. "He might pick you up because you aren't really special."

Alice felt a panicky wave building up inside her, beginning to crest, and she worried she would drown in it, and it would wash her away.

That morning, when Alice had told Wesley about the man next door, he'd listened carefully, had one hand on Alice's on the table as they spoke, his face creased in various places: forehead, the space between his eyebrows, around his mouth. "Okay," he said when she finished. "I'll handle it."

"Okay," Alice replied. "I feel kind of bad."

"Here's the thing," Wesley said, picking up the spoon again and pointing it at Alice. "We don't all have to like each other here. We don't even really have to get along. We just have to agree that we all have the same vision, we're all on the same page, and that our issues won't jeopardize that vision." He sighed. "Apple isn't the easiest. But I'll take care of this."

"I love Apple," Alice said. "I love all of you."

"I know," Wesley said, then leaned across the table to kiss her. He tasted like milk and honey.

"Am I interrupting?"

Wesley and Alice pulled apart then to see Apple standing

in the doorway. She had washed her face and was wearing Alice's yellow dress.

"Not at all," he said. "Alice was just telling me how much she loves you."

Apple looked at Alice, and Alice felt her face burning. Apple cocked her head to the side, her ponytail listing, the tips of it brushing her shoulder. "Is that right?"

"You know I love you, Apple," Alice said.

"Of course," Apple said. "I love you too."

"Kiss and make up," Wesley told them.

"We weren't fighting," Alice said.

"Weren't we?" Apple asked.

"I wasn't," Alice said.

"Weren't you?"

"Girls," Wesley said, and Apple walked over, put her hands on Alice's shoulders, and Alice thought of a bird perched on each side, talons sharp. She felt Apple's lips on the top of her head, a quick brush. "There," said Wesley, and then her hands were gone from Alice's shoulders and picking up Wesley's bowl and spoon from the table, and she walked over to the sink.

"Apple," said Wesley now, from the bottom of the steps. "Come here."

Without looking at the others, Apple slipped past them and walked down to join Wesley. She turned to face him so Alice could only see her profile, the pretty sweep of her nose, the point of her chin. "You need to remember the rules," he said. "You're lucky you weren't killed last night. We'll see if your luck continues."

"God, Alice," said Apple, whipping around to look at her. In the night, her eyes looked even darker than normal.

Alice said nothing, heart thumping. She put her hand to

her chest to feel it, but from the outside she was still, and this calmed her.

"Wesley, we're broke," Apple said. "Did you know that? It's a problem. He thought I was a prostitute, that we all are. He hired me." She shook her head, and her ponytail swung from side to side, making Alice think of a noose. "You've never had a problem with it before," she said.

"You're lying," said Wesley.

Beside her, Alice felt Janie shift her weight forward. Don't say anything, Janie, she thought. You'll only get punished. Alice grabbed her wrist, and Janie went still.

"I'm not," Apple said. "You don't know."

"I do know," Wesley said. What he didn't say, but what Alice heard, was: *I know everything.*

"We're going," he said. He reached into his pocket and pulled out the keys to the van.

"I'm barefoot," said Apple, looking down. The game had changed. Alice felt it, and knew that Apple must have too. In the yard, no matter how black the night, no matter how angry Wesley had been, no matter Apple's attitude, they were in a neutral zone. Wesley ruled here, yes, but there was nothing he could do to her as long as she was here, as long as there were houses around them, windows, eyes.

"Janie will get you shoes," said Wesley. He looked at Janie, who went inside the house silently and emerged a moment later with a pair of sandals that she handed to Apple, who grabbed them and bent over to put them on. Wesley stood up straight and tall, nodded at Janie to return to the porch.

"I'm sorry," said Apple, standing back up. "I was only trying to help." She didn't sound like Apple anymore, not the one Alice had known. To see her this way, to watch this unfold, was awful and thrilling. Alice wondered if Janie and Kathryn felt the same way: both repulsed and enthralled.

"Say good night to the girls," said Wesley. He steered Apple around until she faced Alice and the others.

"Good night," she said, and then Wesley led her away, her yellow dress in the dark like a night-light in a child's bedroom. He opened the door for her on the passenger side and then walked around to the driver's side and climbed in. Alice watched them through the window as Wesley backed out onto the street, but Apple's head was turned, so all she could see was her ponytail.

The girls did not move until the van was out of sight. The night was quiet, except for a few sounds: the TV coming on at the single father's house, the footsteps of a woman walking a dog, small and white as a bunny, by the stop sign at the corner.

"Alice, do you know what happened?" Janie asked. "Why was Apple mad at you?"

"I don't know," Alice told her. "A misunderstanding."

"That can't be right," said Janie.

"She snuck out last night," Alice said carefully.

"So you tattled on her?"

"This isn't kindergarten, Janie," Alice said, but she felt her stomach tighten and something inside it twist and sink.

Janie sighed. "I'm going to go fill in Hannah Fay."

Then it was only Kathryn and Alice on the porch. "You were right to do what you did," Kathryn said.

"I didn't do anything," said Alice.

"Stop," said Kathryn. "Please." She took her glasses out of her pocket and put them on, then blinked. "I know what you are," Kathryn said. "You know what you are too."

"Fine," said Alice. "Whatever."

The woman with the little dog was closer now, the dog at the end of its leash, sniffing the border of the single father's yard. The woman waved at the girls and smiled, and the girls waved back.

"Do you think she'll be okay?" Alice asked.

"If she isn't, good riddance," said Kathryn. "She isn't like us."

"Like who?" said Alice.

"Us," said Kathryn. "All of us."

Headlights turned down the street. Wesley, thought Alice, and for a second, she was relieved that Apple was back so soon, that no damage could have been done, but then it turned out to be a small car, and it passed them by as they stood on the porch together, and Alice felt a smaller wave of relief rush at her, that Apple was not yet back, because truth be told, she wanted to sit with the pleasure that comes with not knowing for just a while longer.

(She isn't like us.)

Alice did not wait up, but in the morning Wesley was there, sitting shirtless and barefoot in the backyard. Hannah Fay was stretched out in the chair beside him, shirt tucked under her breasts to expose her pale pink seashell of a belly to the sunlight. Janie, who was lying on a beach towel on her stomach, lifted her head as Alice approached. "Hey," she said. "Are you going to join us?" But Janie didn't move at all, didn't sit up to make room for Alice to sit beside her. Alice felt stung. She tried to tell herself that Janie wasn't mad. Janie, who never held a grudge, who right now lay prostrate at the feet of a man who hit her.

"I'll stand," Alice said. "Where's Apple?"

Janie flipped over onto her side, elbow bent, hand supporting her head, as if she needed to get a good look at Alice. Alice looked at Wesley instead.

"I drove an hour north of here," he said. "Then I found a good spot and let her out."

"Is she coming back?" Alice asked.

"We'll see," said Wesley.

Alice glanced at Hannah Fay, who had both her hands on her stomach, pressing down, something she had started doing often, to make the baby move. "It's like a little game," she had said once. "I think it helps us both to know the other is here." Now she shrugged at Alice, still pressing her fingers into her belly. Then she widened her eyes suddenly, reached over and took Wesley's hand and put it on her stomach. "There he is," she said.

Wesley got out of the chair and knelt beside Hannah Fay, and he spread his hands over her belly, his hands big, tan, and hairy against the blush of her skin. "There he is," Wesley repeated. He put his face to her stomach, and Hannah Fay laughed. She put her hand on his head, ruffled her fingers through his hair. Alice watched and suddenly felt like crying.

"Apple has to hitchhike home," Janie said, and Alice turned toward her. Her voice was bright, but there was a coolness in her expression that wasn't usually there.

"Here home?" Alice asked. "Or home home?"

"This is home," Janie said.

"I made it clear to her that she can do what she wants," Wesley said. "She can join us if she's ready."

"She is," said Hannah Fay confidently. "It was a mistake, everyone makes them. She's sorry."

"I think she is," Wesley agreed. "She was scared in the van. It was actually kind of beautiful to see her like that. She was—I don't know, soft. Anyway, if she wasn't sorry then, she will be."

"If she doesn't get murdered," said Janie.

Alice didn't look at her. She took a step over to Hannah Fay, and when she let her hand hover over her friend's belly, Hannah Fay took it, pressed it to her warm skin.

"They still haven't caught the driving man," said Janie, "and the last girl wasn't far from here."

"He could be anywhere," said Hannah Fay.

"Exactly," said Wesley, standing up. "I'm going to shower." He left the girls, who sat without speaking.

But then under Alice's hand, the baby kicked. "There he is," she cried.

"The driving man?" asked Janie.

"No, silly," said Hannah Fay. "The baby."

And now Janie rose from the towel, moving to Hannah Fay, and the baby did seem to be everywhere at once, kicking and moving and living, and Janie looked up in delight, smiled at Alice. Alice smiled back. "I love you," said Hannah Fay, and Alice wasn't sure if she was talking to them or to the baby, but all of them murmured back *I love you too, I love you too.*

Apple showed up in the afternoon, when everyone's cheeks were flushed from the sun and they had eaten a poor and lazy lunch of peanut butter sandwiches. She didn't come inside, though, so they only discovered she was there when Alice went out to get the mail and found her sitting on the top step of the front porch. Ponytail, yellow dress, bare feet. She looked up when Alice opened the door. If it had been Alice out there, she knew, she would have cried. But Apple seemed harder than ever.

"What happened to your shoes?" Alice asked.

Apple stood up, flexed her toes. "They broke."

"From walking?"

"I wasn't allowed to walk," Apple said. "Wesley said I had to get in a car. He said I had to get in the fourth gray car I saw." She leaned against the column beside her and crossed one foot in front of the other. "Then I had to get out after ten minutes and get in another car. This time it had to be a red car. Then I had to get out again after ten minutes. Find a truck, like an eighteen-wheeler." She shrugged. "But I didn't get murdered."

"Of course not," Alice said.

"The driving man didn't get me," Apple said, wiggling her fingers like she was casting a spell, but her voice sounded a bit thinner when she said it, and Alice thought of the Apple of last night, saying good night, worrying about being cast out barefoot, being driven away and left.

"I'm glad," said Alice. "Wesley knew you would be okay."

"Did he?" asked Apple. "I guess we'll never know."

"Come on, let's go in," said Alice. "Everyone will be happy to see you." She held the door open for Apple, but Apple paused in the doorway. "What?" Alice asked.

"The mail," said Apple.

Alice looked out to the mailbox, the red flag on the side of the box flush against it. "I'll meet you inside," she said. Apple moved past her, and Alice lingered at the closed door for just a moment.

"Wesley?" she heard Apple say. "Janie?" Then there was squealing; Janie, she thought.

Alice stayed by the mailbox and put her hand on it, and it was warm to the touch, and she thought suddenly of her mother, standing and ironing in front of the TV. "If you touch this, it will burn your sweet little fingers," she heard her mother say. Alice closed her eyes and let herself think of us. (She was so far away now. When she thought of us, we always tried to call her name, as if our voices could bring her back.)

"Hey," said a man. Alice opened her eyes. It was the single father next door. He was holding his son's hand. The boy looked nothing like his father and was very solemn, the kind of boy, Alice thought, who would have a telescope, a rock collection. "Are you okay?" asked the father.

What could she say? Leave us alone. Go away. Look what you made me do. But Wesley wanted the girls to be soft and lovely for the world, he wanted the girls to fool everyone, never to let on what they knew, never to reveal their strength. "Yes," she said, smiling. "Of course. I'm sorry if I alarmed you."

"Your friend," the man began.

"Hello," said Alice to the little boy. "Shouldn't you be in school today?"

The boy looked up at his dad, who shrugged. Alice watched him squeeze his son's hand. "It's Saturday," the boy said. "We went to the zoo."

"Oh," said Alice. "I lost track of time. Who was your favorite animal?"

"The tiger," the boy said. "He yawned, and I saw all his teeth." He raised his hand, the one his father wasn't holding, and lifted it over his head as if showing how monstrous the mouth had been.

"Wow," Alice said. "Big teeth are very important. And claws. And very fast feet so you can run if someone is chasing you." She looked up at the father, at the face Wesley didn't like. She gave him a brilliant smile, the kind she used to give to boys when she caught them staring at her in the hall. A gift.

"Come on," the father said. "Let's see what cartoons are on."

"Bye," said Alice. When the man got to his front door, he looked back at Alice, who waved again. The door shut, and Alice nearly laughed out loud. She took the mail inside, and she didn't think of us again that evening.

CHAPTER THIRTY-ONE

APPLE CAME BACK changed, Alice thought, but only if you were looking closely. When she was around Wesley, she lit up, always touching him, but only teasingly, only with the tips of her fingers. She would slip them into his belt loops like hooks and pull him closer, or graze his shoulders while he sat on the couch playing his guitar, trace the back of his neck under his shirt collar until he shivered, and then she would be gone, and he would follow her only with his eyes.

One night, as she slept beside Apple, Alice awoke to the feeling of heat beside her, and turned her head—there was Apple, and Wesley, too, his shirt already off. "Oh God," said Alice. "I'm sorry." Though she knew she had done nothing wrong, she was still flustered, embarrassed to have unwittingly intruded on someone else's intimacy. Apple sat up, and Alice was grateful to see that she was wearing the same pajama shirt she had gone to bed in a few hours earlier. Wesley sat up, too, pushing his hair behind his ears. With Apple's dark head next to his, they looked like they belonged together, like she had been formed from him or he from her, and the burn of embarrassment spread from Alice's stomach up and out until even her fingertips began to sting. "I'll go," she said.

"Not yet," said Apple as Wesley moved farther down the bed, leaving the girls together. Then she was leaning forward and kissing Alice, her hair like a curtain secluding them, then she pushed it back so that they were exposed, and Alice could feel Wesley watching. She thought she could feel his pleasure even from where he sat a foot away.

Unless it was her own pleasure she felt because it did feel so good to be kissing Apple, and so different than kissing Wesley, and she didn't want to admit that it was nice to feel something foreign, to move against it. But it felt like a betrayal of Wesley, who she had sworn was enough for her, enough for all of them.

But then Apple was done with her. Wesley reached for Apple, and there went Apple's fingertips, resting lightly on the button of his jeans. Alice sat up and waited for a moment longer than she should have before scooting off the bed, just as Wesley was laying Apple down, and exiting into the cool darkness of the hallway and the open cave of the living room.

She slept on the couch and was already drinking a cup of coffee there when Wesley and Apple came out of the bedroom the next morning. "Morning," Wesley said, still shirtless, and walked straight into the kitchen, though Apple, also still in the pajama shirt and underwear, lingered at the mouth of the living room. She smirked.

"Apple," Alice started, but Apple held up a hand.

"For Wesley," she said. "Nothing more. That's why I didn't let you stay any longer than that."

"Well," said Alice. "Thanks?"

"You're welcome," said Apple magnanimously. She looked down at the pajama shirt, touched a loose thread unraveling near a button.

"Are you okay?" Alice asked. "I mean, are you feeling all right?"

"I'm fine," said Apple, looking up, and Alice saw something around her eyes tighten and then soften. "I have everything under control."

"What does that mean?" Alice asked. "What's under control?"

"Oh, Alice," said Apple. "Like I'd ever tell you anything ever again." Then she left, trailing after Wesley, leaving Alice alone.

"What do you think Apple's deal is?" Alice asked Kathryn. She had walked up to the school library to bring Kathryn her forgotten sack lunch after spotting it on the kitchen counter.

Alice hadn't felt right since Apple came home. Janie had warmed back up to her again, but Alice remembered the chill between them. Hannah Fay wasn't her normal self either; achy and swollen, she spent the days walking around the block, praying, she said, for the baby to come out, or lying on the mattress in her little room with the window open, and when she did leave her room and visit with the others, she was often moody. "This could be the last Saturday, just us," she might say mournfully. Then a minute later, she would turn dreamy and say, "I can't stop thinking about who the baby will look like."

The library at the university was quiet, almost sacred, with its deep colors and heavy wooden tables, and Alice felt herself imagining a different life, the same life as before, the one where she was a girl sitting at one of these tables, reading poetry, frowning at a research paper. A girl who was well fed, well taken care of, well loved. You are well loved, she told herself. And well cared for. This is a trap. All of this an illusion. "Let's eat outside," Alice suggested to Kathryn.

In the fresh air, she felt better, and they found a stone bench under a tree near the library. "Apple is up to something," Kathryn said between bites of her sandwich.

"She—" Alice started, thinking of Apple leaning toward her last night, Wesley watching. "She seems kind of— slippery." A bird landed near them and began to hop forward, head cocked. "I can't put my finger on it. Just when I think I know, the feeling sort of slips away."

"She's not really one of us," Kathryn said. "I know, I know, she and I have never gotten along. But Apple is only thinking about one thing, and that's herself." She tore off a piece of crust and tossed it at the bird.

"She loves Wesley," Alice said. "I really believe she does."

"Maybe, but she's not a good person," Kathryn said.

Alice was quiet. "We're good people," Kathryn said, angling her head so that she was looking into Alice's downturned face. "We look out for each other. We look out for Wesley."

A burst of voices cut through the quiet courtyard outside the library, and Alice looked up to see two girls exiting the library, laughing with their heads together, as though they couldn't wait to get out the door, into a world where they could be raucous. Alice felt a pang of something unpleasant, and she surprised herself when she identified the feeling as jealousy. You have that, she told herself, with Wesley, with the other girls. But when she imagined herself as the girl leaving the library, she pictured not Apple or Janie or Hannah

Fay or Kathryn as the friend by her side, but Susannah. (Susannah, who at that moment was in class, still famished after lunch because Alice Lange's departure had left an opening in the social hierarchy at school, and Susannah thought perhaps if she could lose a little weight, perhaps if she wore her hair differently, taught her voice to lift and lilt like a soprano, she could fill that void; she could be Alice Lange. Trevor, the boy who sat behind her, tapped her on the shoulder and passed her a note. When she unfolded it, it was a drawing of a penis. Susannah considered her options, and did not write back.)

"Earth to Alice," called Kathryn.

"You're right," Alice said finally.

"I know," said Kathryn, and they finished their meal in silence.

That evening, when everyone was home, Janie and Apple said they had something they needed to share. "Go on," Wesley said. They sat in the kitchen while Hannah Fay cracked eggs into a mixing bowl. In the middle of the day, Janie told them, there had been a knock on the door at the bungalow, and when she opened it, it was a police officer. "Hi, little lady," he said. "I'm Officer Francis. I'm here following up on the incident that occurred at the house next door."

"Goddamnit," said Wesley. "What did you tell him?"

"Oh, yes," Janie said to the officer. "We heard what happened, of course. I'm not sure they've even been back since, have they?"

"No," said the officer. He smiled at her in a friendly way and asked to come in, and she acquiesced. Hannah Fay was napping, but Apple came in from the kitchen.

"To what do we owe the pleasure of this visit, officer?" Apple asked.

"The man next door found a picture of a girl he said lived in this house, and he was concerned," the officer said. "He said there are lots of girls living here?" Without moving from the spot where he was standing, he looked around then, Apple told the others, as if all the girls were hiding somewhere out of sight, behind the door, in the kitchen pantry, in the crawl space below the house, like bodies buried under his own feet.

"Family," Janie said.

"What's this picture?" Apple asked, and the officer pulled out a photo of Alice. "This," Apple told them that evening, "was when I knew we were fucked."

"I told you to leave the one where you couldn't tell it was Alice!" Wesley said to Kathryn.

"I did," Kathryn said. "Her face was covered. All you could see was her hair."

"Oh," Apple said then. "There were two. Two pictures of Alice."

When the officer handed Apple the first picture, she saw that it was clearly of Alice, but part of her face was missing, torn or peeled off, leaving behind a little white mark. Apple asked to see the other picture, which featured Alice as well, though it could have been any bright-headed young woman dancing in a crowd of people. This was the photo Wesley had meant for Kathryn to leave. "It was a good photo, Wesley," Apple said. "Joyful."

"Yes," Wesley said wearily. "That's why I chose it. This was supposed to mark the beginning of an exciting time for us."

"It still can," Apple said.

She'd turned the picture over to see a thicker spot on the

back, and when she held the other picture of Alice behind this one, she realized that they had been stuck together. "So you must have grabbed two without knowing," she said to Kathryn.

"Fuck me," groaned Wesley.

Kathryn's face grew pink. "I'm sorry," she said.

"We took care of it, though," Janie said. "Honestly, he didn't really seem too concerned."

Apple said that the officer asked if Wesley had anything to do with the incident next door—"We didn't even have to lie," she told Wesley—and did she know how the pictures of Alice might have ended up in the house. Janie and Apple said they didn't, that it was very peculiar, and if anyone should be worried, it should be the girl in the photos, because she might have a stalker.

The officer had shrugged. "He told us the owner of the house said we were very nice girls, but the officer personally thought something seemed fishy, but also he was busy with real murderers, not petty thieves," Janie said.

"You did kill an animal. That's not nothing," Hannah Fay said over her shoulder. She was standing by the stove, a spatula in her hand.

"For Wesley," Alice said.

"I don't know. Maybe he's not a dog person either. Anyway, we paid him off," Apple said. "Subtly."

"What?" Wesley asked. He rubbed his eyes. "How do you subtly pay someone off?"

"I could tell he wasn't in this line of work because of any sense of justice," Apple said. "He seemed sleazy. Honestly, he reminded me of my dad."

Apple had walked closer to him, close enough that she could smell his lunchtime cigarette in his hair, on his clothes, close enough that he could see the freckles on her nose, the shape of her mouth, smell her shampoo, and said she was sorry he'd had to come out here. "I have something for your trouble," she said. "Stay right there." She went into the kitchen and found the Tupperware container where they kept their money from the odd jobs they sometimes took, including the bills from the man next door's wallet. "So it's kind of like we paid them back," she said.

"You gave him the money?" Wesley asked. "All of it? We needed that."

It was true. The girls had grown even thinner, their meals leaner. Beyond that, they were going to the desert soon, and they would need to pay for some kind of shelter. Wesley had told them about a crumbling old ranch that they could get for cheap because the owner was old and the land no longer offered him any income. But cheap didn't mean free, and now they didn't have anything.

"This is all my fault," said Alice.

"Kind of," Apple agreed.

The officer had taken the Tupperware from her with a dubious look, but then he nodded and thanked the girls for their time. "I'm sure it was just a random thing," he said. "Someone passing through town. And that it won't happen again."

"I hope not," Apple said. "It's very frightening. Who knows what kind of monster could have done it?"

"That part was unnecessary," Alice said, but Apple laughed.

"Crisis averted," Janie said. "See?"

"Only now there's a new crisis," Kathryn said. "We have no money."

"I'm going out," Wesley said, sliding his chair back from the table and standing up. "I've got to get out of here for a while."

Kathryn got up too. "What about tomorrow?" she asked.

Alice looked from Wesley to Kathryn and back to Wesley.

"What's happening tomorrow?" she asked. Kathryn glanced at her, then back to Wesley.

"We're going to the desert tomorrow," Wesley said. "Not all of us. Just Kathryn and me. To look at the ranch."

"But now we can't buy it," Apple said. "Can we?"

Wesley sighed. "Maybe we can cut some kind of deal. Or maybe we could sell this house."

Hannah Fay was walking over to the table with bowls of scrambled eggs in her hands. "You're taking Kathryn?" she asked, and Alice could hear the hurt in her voice that she wasn't getting a first look at the place her baby might call home, a sanctuary while the rest of the world fell apart.

"It's a long drive," he said. "On bumpy roads. You would be very uncomfortable."

"Do you want eggs before you go, Wesley?" Hannah Fay asked. Her voice was bright again, but she still seemed fragile, like the cracked porcelain plate in their kitchen cabinet, a fracture running across its face and threatening to break it for good.

"No," he said. "I'm not hungry."

"So are we going tomorrow?" Kathryn asked. "I can pack for both of us, if you'd like."

"Yes," he said. "I'll see you in the morning."

The girls ate their eggs in silence. Alice's mind felt too full—the desert, the dog, the officer, the money, gone. Wesley, gone. Coming back but then leaving again. Suddenly, she felt like she wanted to cry, and she excused herself. "You can go to my room," Kathryn said kindly, and Alice nodded. Once inside, she curled up on the bed, her back to the door, and fell asleep.

Later Kathryn came in and lay beside her, whispering over her shoulder. "Apple didn't have to give that man our money." Her breath was hot in Alice's ear, waking her up. "She could have paid him in another way, if you know what I mean. Apple isn't stupid. She's sabotaging Wesley."

"She had to think on her feet," Alice said, though she wasn't sure if she was talking aloud or only in a dream. "She had to be quick. No one is sabotaging anyone."

"Wake up, Alice," Kathryn said.

"I am awake," Alice said. "You woke me up. Now I'm going back to sleep." She listened as Kathryn went into the bathroom. But even after Kathryn came back and got in bed beside her, Alice found she couldn't sleep. Her stomach ached, and she didn't know why.

(It's sadness, we would tell her. It doesn't feel good to be left behind, does it?)

CHAPTER THIRTY-TWO

THE NIGHT WESLEY and Kathryn were in the desert, the remaining girls made spaghetti without meat, just pouring in some cheap jarred sauce they bought that afternoon at the grocery store. Janie had wanted garlic bread, the kind in the warmer, but they hadn't had enough money. "We can make garlic toast," Hannah Fay suggested. So they put slices of stale white bread in the toaster and spread butter on them, and Janie used a can of peas to mash up some garlic, which they tried to spread on top of the butter, ripping little gashes in the bread.

"This is disgusting," Janie said around a mouthful of food, and they all laughed and once they started, they couldn't stop. For Alice, it was like a valve had been loosened, all the pressure releasing and turning into laughter. She tried the garlic toast and agreed it was terrible, and she put a piece in Apple's mouth, and Apple sputtered around it until finally she swallowed and howled, tiny bits of toast flecking her lips.

After dinner, they draped themselves around the living room, Janie and Apple on the couch, Alice on the chair with her legs over one of the cushioned arms, her head on the other, and Hannah Fay propped up on the twin mattress they'd dragged from her little room. They were quiet.

"You know what," said Apple, breaking the silence, "for some reason, Hannah Fay's mattress always makes me think of that night Wesley put on the priest robes."

"Why?" asked Alice. "It wasn't even out."

"It was. It was up against the wall," Janie said. Alice sat up so she could see Janie and Apple, who looked like mirror images of each other. If Alice squinted, it looked like there were four of the same girl. A little army.

Apple nodded. "I kept looking at it," she said. "I don't know why. What a weird night."

"I'm sort of sorry I missed it," Hannah Fay said, brushing her belly with her fingertips, back and forth, like a little broom sweeping across a surface.

"It was nothing, Han," said Alice. She'd noticed Apple watching her, and saw she had that sharpness she'd gotten lately around Wesley, the sizzle of electricity. Her expression was relaxed, casual, but her body seemed rigid, like she was a creature made of steel, trying to bend herself into the shape of a girl.

"That's not how you felt then, Alice," said Apple, frowning. Hannah Fay looked up from her stomach, head cocked.

"Well," said Alice, "it was helpful to learn some facts I didn't know. I understood Wesley more. But it's stuff I'm sure Hannah Fay already knows."

"It was about how Wesley was in jail," Apple said to Hannah Fay.

"Oh yeah," Hannah Fay said, nodding. "The prison system in this country is broken."

"My dad's in prison," Apple said.

"I didn't know that," Hannah Fay said. "Goodness. I'm sorry." Janie didn't say anything, and Alice wondered if that was because she already knew.

"I'm sorry, too, Apple," Alice said.

"Embezzlement," said Apple. "He got picked up at my field hockey game freshman year." She shook her head, as if clearing her brain of the memory. Her hair shone, and Alice thought of how the other night it had concealed them. "Anyway," she went on, "I'm just glad your baby won't have that. I'm glad that was in Wesley's past."

"Oh, me too," said Hannah Fay. She began rubbing her belly again, this time with her whole hand.

"It's sad," Apple said, looking at none of them in particular, "that I guess Wesley's first son didn't get that." Beside her, Janie shifted, pulling her toes away from Apple's, but Apple's face gave nothing away.

Hannah Fay's hand stopped moving, and she knit her pale eyebrows together, a little crease popping up between them. "What?" she asked.

"Oh my God," said Apple. "I thought you knew. That night—with the priest's robe—Wesley told each of us something different, a confession. That's what he told me."

Now Hannah Fay shook her head. She tucked hair behind her ears. "No," she said. "I don't know anything."

"Apple," Alice began.

"Tell me," Hannah Fay said.

"I don't know much. He was vague. But he has a son," said Apple. "A little boy. I think he said he'd be seven now."

"A son," repeated Hannah Fay. "Another son."

"But he must not love him, Han," said Janie desperately. "You know? He left him. He found you! He loves you."

"That doesn't help," said Hannah Fay. Her cheeks were flushed and clammy. "And Janie, you knew too?"

"I told her," Apple said before Janie could answer. "I'm sorry. I had to—unburden myself." Her right hand fluttered around her chest, as if Wesley's son was trapped inside it and she had to free him.

"The mother," Hannah Fay said. "Who was she?"

Apple looked at Janie, who looked down, away. "I'm sorry," Apple said. "I don't want to hurt you."

"Then stop!" said Alice.

"His wife," said Apple.

"He was married?" asked Hannah Fay quietly.

Alice watched Apple swallow. Alice thought of killing the dog, how she realized it was something she had to do. Telling Wesley about Apple and the man next door—she'd had to do that too. Apple felt the same about this, Alice could tell. Her face was placid and resolved; it reminded Alice of a movie she'd seen once, about spies in World War II, in which an executioner in a firing squad waited for a signal, finger on the trigger, watching the person before him look around wildly, eyes covered by a blindfold, trying to catch the last glimpse of their world.

"Is married," Apple said. "He never divorced her."

Hannah Fay shook her head again. "He told you all this?"

"He was confessing," Apple said.

"You're lying," said Hannah Fay. Her voice sounded, to Alice, hopeful and angry.

"She's not," said Janie. "I knew he had a wife. He told me that part too. Just not about the boy." She got up and went to sit by Hannah Fay on the mattress, then put her arm around Hannah Fay, but Hannah Fay did not move at all. "I really thought you knew, Han," Janie said in a soft voice.

"Well, I didn't," said Hannah Fay curtly. She put her hands down on either side of her and pushed herself up from the mattress. Janie looked up at her. Alice stood, too, but couldn't bring herself to go to Hannah Fay and embrace her.

"I need to go," Hannah Fay said. "I'm leaving. I just need to go."

"You don't have a car," Alice said, feeling stupid as she said it.

"I'll find a ride." Hannah Fay started walking back to her room.

"That's dangerous!" said Janie.

"She's right," said Apple. But Alice heard no urgency in her voice.

"I'll call someone to come get me," said Hannah Fay.

"We didn't pay the phone bill," said Janie.

"I'll figure it out," Hannah Fay snapped. And then she opened the door to her room and disappeared inside.

Alice turned to Apple. "You did this on purpose, I know you did," she said. "But why would you want to hurt Hannah Fay?"

"I don't want to hurt Hannah Fay," Apple said.

"But you did, and you knew you would! Look at her." Alice gestured toward the study. "She wants to leave!"

"She just needs some time to collect herself," Apple said.

"Why do you think Wesley told you that, Apple? About being married and having a kid?" Janie asked.

Apple sighed and pushed her hair out of her face. "I had a baby once too," she said. "Right after my dad went to prison. My mom sent me away to live with my aunt and uncle, and after I had the baby, someone adopted her and I went back home. I never even got to see her. Wesley told me he understood, that baby wasn't meant to be mine, and the baby he had wasn't meant to be his."

"You're lying," Alice said. "No way is any of this true." All of these things about Apple—her father, another father, some nameless child of Wesley's, a baby. Alice had told Kathryn that Apple was slippery, and she'd been right. Every time Alice held a version of Apple in her head, it slipped away, phantomlike, and Alice had to start reconstructing her again.

Apple shrugged. "Whatever," she said. "I'm not going to try to convince you. But it is."

"Oh, Apple," said Janie, crossing over to her and putting her hand on Apple's shoulder. "You never told me."

"I don't like to discuss it," she said. "I don't want to discuss it now. But that baby was lucky. I would've been a shitty mother."

"You would've been a great mother, I know it," Janie said. Alice thought of how gentle Apple was with Janie. She thought of one of her own early nights here, the first trip she took, and Apple taking her to bed, tucking her in. She thought of Apple running the shower for her to wash off all the blood, sticking her hand under the water to make sure it was warm enough before she got in.

"I don't care," said Apple. "And Wesley doesn't care about his other kid. He does, however, care about Hannah Fay and this baby."

That was when Alice put it together. She wasn't punishing Hannah Fay for anything. She was punishing Wesley, and Hannah Fay was a casualty. "She won't really leave," Alice said.

"God, I hope not," said Janie. "Wesley will kill us."

"I'm going in," Alice said. "I'll sleep with Hannah Fay." But when Alice tried the door handle, it was locked, and no sound came from inside. "I'll wait on the couch then," she said.

"Good idea," said Janie.

In the night, Alice heard Hannah Fay come out of her room, and Alice realized she herself had been sleeping. It happened so quickly—Hannah Fay opening the front door and slipping away—that for a second after she woke, Alice told herself it was too fast, she didn't have time to stop her.

But she knew this was wrong; of course she could have stopped her. She could have leapt up from the couch and followed her out onto the porch, pleaded with her to stay. She knew that's what Wesley would want her to do. She could close her eyes and feel Wesley directing her all the way from the desert, feel his voice in her throat, his bones under her skin, his muscles in her legs as she stood up to follow Hannah Fay. His hands in her hands to grab her, bring her back.

She loved Hannah Fay, but she could give Wesley a baby, too, and isn't that what Wesley loved most about Hannah Fay? (Yes! He loves Hannah Fay because when he looks at her, he sees himself reflected back, as if that stomach of hers was a mirror and not a real flesh-and-blood thing, housing a beating heart and growing limbs, but something cold, the only life there the image of himself he sees. Men like Wesley, this is what they want above all—to look into a woman's eyes and see only themselves reflected there.)

She could tell the others she fell asleep and that when she woke up, Hannah Fay's room was empty, and they wouldn't think anything but the best of her, that she had been vigilant but exhausted, and they wouldn't know that Alice had simply let her go.

CHAPTER THIRTY-THREE

WESLEY AND KATHRYN came home the following afternoon, as the day was winding down and the light was gold, to find the girls assembled in the living room. They came into the house like lovers arriving home from a honeymoon. They'd only been in the desert for a day, but already Wesley's skin was tanned even more deeply, and Kathryn sported freckles no one knew she was capable of conjuring.

"It's magical," Kathryn said as soon as they walked in. "You'll love it."

"The ranch itself leaves a little to be desired," Wesley said, sliding his bag off his shoulder to the floor. "But all things considered, when you think about what's going to happen everywhere else, it's pretty damn good." He scanned the room. "Is Hannah Fay napping?" he asked. "I want her to hear about this too. We'll still need more money, but we made a deal. It's good news."

"Wesley," Apple said, "she left."

"Where'd she go?" he asked, his face darkening.

"We don't know," Janie said.

There was a long silence that stretched like a bridge between them. "But why?"

Alice watched Apple and Janie look at each other. She glanced over at Kathryn, who she realized had been watching her with a questioning look.

"She found out about your son," Apple said. "And wife."

Wesley bit his lip and squinted up at the ceiling, where the domed light glowed weakly, like a small, sad sun. "Motherfucker," he said. "Apple. What the fuck? Why?" Kathryn put her hand on Wesley's shoulder, but he shrugged it off, and she took a step back. "You are ruining everything," he said. "Everything."

"I thought she knew!" Apple said. "I'm sorry, Wesley. You have to believe me." Janie took a step closer to Apple and slipped an arm around her waist as if to steady her.

"She is having my baby, Apple," Wesley said through clenched teeth. "She is having my baby any day now. And now she is gone, out wandering around a world full of people who want to kill her."

"They don't want to kill her," Apple said. "No one would kill a pregnant woman. Besides, the world isn't as dangerous as you say it is."

Wesley laughed. "That's certainly a change in attitude from the other night." He made his voice higher pitched, frightened. "'Please, Wesley, no. What if the man who picks me up kills me?'"

Apple's cheeks flushed. "I'm sorry."

Wesley put his hands on his hips and leaned his head back, exhaling. Kathryn tried to put her hand on his shoulder again, and this time he let her. "Okay," he said. "She'll come back. I know she will. I will bring her back."

"Are you—" Kathryn started. "Are you going to—do anything else?"

"Wouldn't you like that, Kathryn?" Apple said. "If he punished me?"

"No, actually, I would not. God, Apple."

"I'm not doing anything else yet," Wesley said. "Apple, I know you would never hurt Hannah Fay intentionally. I believe it was an accident but a very unfortunate one, and of course there will be consequences. I just don't have the capacity for dealing with them right now. My focus is on Hannah Fay and our baby."

"I understand," Apple said softly. Beside her, Janie squeezed her waist. Alice said nothing.

"I need to shower," Wesley said. He started down the hall, and Kathryn followed after him, but he stopped suddenly and turned around to face the others, nearly colliding with her. "Apple," he said, and she looked up. "I assume you've told the others about your own child you left."

"Yes," she said.

He nodded and went into Kathryn's room. Soon they heard the sound of running water.

"I told you," Apple said to Alice, and then Apple turned and left too. Janie went after her, and Alice was all alone.

(We have a guess as to why Wesley skipped Hannah Fay the night of the confessions, why he burned the cassock: the game had to end. It was an oversight, he said, though we think it's possible he realized that Hannah Fay, the gentlest of his girls, would receive none of his confessions well, and she would leave, and his child would be lost to him. This would be the worst thing to happen. Apple saw that too. It had been a good idea in theory, to share secrets with them, create the illusion that they were in a partnership that, yes, went five ways, but also existed between two imperfect people, flawed but good, and it was only when it came to Hannah Fay's turn that Wesley could see he had run a terrible risk. What if they left? What if he realized his grip on them wasn't as tight as he had thought? That last worry—we know how that feels, we who have lost Alice Lange.

But anyway, this is why he got rid of the cassock.

And why burn it? Wesley is the kind of man who loves a spectacle. We've seen it, Alice has too. We have a feeling that wherever he is now, it will only get worse.)

That night, Wesley asked Alice to sleep outside with him. They lay on a blanket, another blanket on top of them. When they had sex, Alice knew her primary role was the comforter, the pleaser, the secondary role to be pleased herself.

"Everything is so fucked," he said after.

"I know it feels that way," Alice began, but Wesley was already shaking his head.

"It is," he said. "Trust me. We need to get out of here soon."

"We will!" said Alice. "Tell me more about the ranch." She rolled over on her side to face him, but he stayed on his back, like he was looking at the stars, though the night sky was clouded over.

"It's primitive. I mean, we'll be able to cook and take showers, but they might not be hot."

"That's okay!" Alice said in what she hoped was a bright tone. "We don't mind roughing it."

"Like I said, considering that everything else will be essentially gone, this isn't a bad deal at all," he said.

"So we'll just go out there and wait?" Alice asked.

"Yeah," he said. "Can I be honest with you?"

"Of course. Always."

"I'm so discouraged. We still need money, even with the guy cutting us a break. More than what we have. It was a stretch even before Apple—" He shook his head. "And now Hannah Fay is gone." He closed his eyes. Alice sat up and moved even closer to him, began to stroke his hair with her hand.

"She'll be back," she said.

Wesley said nothing but rearranged himself, putting his head in her lap. Neither of them said anything else, and when he drifted off, Alice gently lifted his head and lay beside him, like they were two spoons, and she fell asleep like that too. When she woke up, though, they were apart. Either he had rolled away from her, or she from him—she wasn't sure.

Wesley was gone most of the day, looking for Hannah Fay, he said. But when he returned for dinner alone, he didn't say anything. No one asked him any questions.

After dinner, Janie went to take a shower, and the others all moved instinctively to the front porch. Alice wondered if it was so they could watch for Hannah Fay, see her as soon as she arrived home. Tonight, the stars were bright, but everything on earth felt somber to Alice. She wanted to fix it. "I have an announcement," she said. The girls looked at her, then to Wesley.

"Go ahead," Wesley said.

"I can get money," Alice said. "Probably not all we need, but some."

"Finally," Apple said. "You're going to start stripping."

"My mom keeps cash in the house," Alice said, ignoring

her. "I took some when I left but not all. I could go home, and I bet I could get it."

Wesley leaned toward her.

"How much?" he asked. "I don't think we should steal it. I want us to be honest in our dealings."

"I'll ask for it," she said. She sat against the wall of the house closest to the door. Behind her, she could feel the thrum of the water running through the pipes for Janie's shower. "I can pull it off. Wesley, can you drive me tomorrow?"

"No can do," said Wesley. "You'll have to take the bus. I have business here in the morning."

"That's fine," said Alice, though she had been hoping for another road trip, had even pictured herself introducing Wesley to her mother. But the bus would be fine too. She could stay for a few days, could get some more clothes for the girls, and the money, and then she would come back here. Then they would leave for the desert.

"One thing, though. Don't mention me," Wesley said now to Alice. "To your mother, to anyone. Don't tell them my name."

"Why?" asked Alice.

"They don't deserve to know it," he said. "You know names are a gift."

Across from him, Apple coughed. "What now, Apple," Wesley said.

"Nothing," she said. "Sorry. I just need some water."

Wesley turned back to Alice. "All right. Get the money, say good-bye. You won't see your mother again when we go to the desert. So do what you need to do."

"Okay," said Alice. "But the only thing I need to do there is get the money."

"One condition, though, if you do," he said. "Come back. You have to come back."

"Of course I will," Alice said. "Don't worry."

"Remember where the love is," Wesley said. "It's only here. Nowhere else. I'll know if you're thinking of staying."

"I won't be," said Alice. "But it's nice to know I'll be missed."

"I'll take you to the bus in the morning," he said. "I'm sleeping alone tonight. Kathryn, you can sleep in Hannah Fay's room since it's empty."

Then he stood up and went inside, leaving the girls alone on the front porch. They sat there silently and then Kathryn got up and went inside, too, without saying good night.

Apple sat with her heels together and knees up, her legs open like the waiting mouth of a bear trap.

"Are you okay?" Alice asked her.

She tipped her head forward. "Yeah. I'm just tired of him being a fucking jerk, not saying what he means."

"I don't think that's true," Alice said. "Besides, you're hardly one to talk."

"When he said he doesn't want you to say his name to your mom—that's not about his true name stuff. He just doesn't want to get busted for anything if you get caught."

"So what?" asked Alice. "We have to protect him."

"Everything's a game to him," Apple said. "How can you not see that?"

"How can you say that? Look how he's been searching for Hannah Fay. He's serious. And he still cares about you," she said. "Even after what you've done. He cares about all of us. That's why we're here."

"After what I've done?" Apple laughed. "Oh please. Now look who's talking."

"I apologized," Alice said stiffly. But suddenly she wasn't sure if she had. Or if she should.

"For which thing?" Apple asked. Alice didn't respond.

"That first night," Apple said. She rearranged herself so her legs were folded underneath her. "I bet he took you to that library. He had Kathryn's keys, and he took you to the library and pointed out the window to all the lights and said some romantic bullshit and then fucked you standing up, and it was all passionate and intense, and you probably didn't come, but you got off on it in other ways, so you told yourself you didn't care." She pointed at Alice, thrusting a finger toward her chest, stopping just short of touching her. "Tell me I'm wrong," she said. "But I bet you can't."

They hadn't looked out the window. The curtains had been pulled back, there had been lights in the distance—Alice could remember thinking they looked like candles burning— but he had showed her the books. She had touched their spines. Those were the last books she'd touched. It was strange not to have any books for months, just those magazines, old and crumbling. "No," said Alice. "You're wrong. Sorry."

"I bet I'm close," Apple said. She tucked her hair behind her ears, which made her face look sharper, her cheekbones higher. "You don't have to tell me if you don't want to," she said. "I'm just saying I know more than you do."

"You are so mean," Alice said. "I mean, God. Why don't you leave if he's so awful?"

"Like I said," Apple said. "I know more than you do. And besides, not all of us have fancy houses to go back to."

"Tell me what I don't know, then," said Alice. "If it's so important."

"He isn't who you think," Apple said. "And you know

what? His photographs aren't that good. Anyone could take them. And his paintings are worse. Have you ever noticed he doesn't paint actual people?" She leaned closer and lowered her voice, like she was revealing a secret. "It's because he doesn't know how."

"They're abstract," said Alice.

"He left his own child," Apple said.

"So did you!"

"That was a very different circumstance, and you know it," Apple said.

Alice did know it. "Okay," she said gently. "I know. I'll see you when I get back."

"You know I'll be here," Apple said. "I bet you'll cry when you see your mom." She held her hand over her heart. "Mother and daughter reunited. A Christmas miracle."

Alice pushed herself up, brushing off the seat of her pants. When she got to the door, she paused and turned back to Apple. "What does your name mean?" she asked.

"That's something I only share with Wesley," Apple said. "Sorry. Some things are private."

The next morning, Kathryn drove Alice to the bus stop and waved her off with little sentimentality, though Alice felt a sting in her heart as she said good-bye, even though it was only Kathryn in the car, even though she would be gone only briefly. On the bus, she watched the sun come up through the little square of window over her seat. At the bus station near home, she called her mother. She answered on the first ring, and she sounded the same to Alice. She said hello and heard her mother breathe in. "Angel," her mother said, and Alice began to cry.

CHAPTER THIRTY-FOUR

H ERE IS WHAT we saw: Mrs. Lange's sedan backing out of the driveway, a practical car, a car for a mother but the color of champagne, like the shade of paint was the one place where she could afford to be frivolous. It was a Saturday, and she wore a simple dress with a big cardigan flapping open over it. When she rushed out of the house, her legs were bare, and though Mrs. McEntyre noted that Mrs. Lange's flats were either navy blue or black, she couldn't say exactly.

Here is what else we saw: when Mrs. Lange returned, she didn't pull her car back into her garage but stopped outside of it. We could see she wasn't alone, but the two figures we spotted in the car were so still that we would have thought it was empty, because who would just sit in there for that long? Then we saw the driver's-side door open, Mrs. Lange stepping out. Another open door. Alice Lange, even slimmer than she was when she left. We could have held her in our hands, slipped her into our pockets. Hair long and unbrushed but still as bright as a gold coin. Wearing unfamiliar clothes.

Her shoes, Mrs. McEntyre would tell us later in a hopeful, breathless report, were the same: slender white tennis shoes. Her feet always looked so tiny in them. They still did.

Mrs. Lange must have wanted us to see her prodigal daughter, our girl now returned. This is the only explanation for why she parked her car outside the garage. We knew that she would have given anything to keep Alice there in her car, in her house, under the joyful hand she used to hold Alice's fragile one. Her child was so thin now, with no mother to care for her. She held that bird-boned hand and let her imagination take her through Alice's time away.

That's how she hoped they would refer to this part of Alice's life, her time away, like her quick stint at a summer camp, or a tour of Paris, Munich, London, a barefooted pilgrimage through the mountains of Spain. Alice's time away was over and now her real life, her life here, could continue.

Alice did not plan to stay long, and she did intend to inform her mother of this fact, perhaps saying, "I'm only staying a night, maybe two, and then I'm going back, and we're going to the desert, and I love you, and I hope you will stay safe. Maybe someday I'll see you again."

She wouldn't tell her what she hoped she would stay safe from because she didn't know herself. She knew there would be destruction—the earth shaking, seas rising, war breaking out—and then rebirth, but besides that, nothing. She would have liked to explain the little she knew, but her mother, for as much as Alice loved her, was still blind. How strange, Alice thought, to spend your whole life believing your mother knew best, knew more, and then suddenly the roles were reversed:

you were the wise one, you were the one who understood the ways of the world.

"I tell you what you need to know when you need to know it," Wesley always said. "To know anything more would hurt you." The girls understood. Fear was one thing. Physiologically, it wasn't that different from excitement, Wesley had explained.

But pain was different. Wesley avoided flowers that bees might hover around, he didn't like to hold a razor to his face to shave it; once when he had a nick on his arm and covered it with a Band-Aid, he got good and drunk before he let Alice rip it off. He said *motherfucker* when she did, a slow hiss like the air escaping from a punctured tire.

And now, confronted with her mother's face, so open and radiant, she wanted to spare her that pain too. Couldn't tell her she was leaving again, couldn't bear to see that hope crack open and spill to the floor. So she let herself be scooped up and taken care of, her mother's hands brushing hair out of Alice's face, touching her on the arm, on the back, on the shoulder.

Here was her mother cooking her spaghetti and meatballs, baking her brownies from a dusty box in the back of the pantry. "I'm sorry," her mother said. "It's nothing special, but I didn't want to go out to the store. I just want to keep looking at you."

"This is perfect," Alice said.

"Tomorrow, though," her mother said, smiling, "I'll head over to the store early, maybe while you're still sleeping. That way I won't miss anything."

It was quiet while they ate, and Alice had seconds and four brownies. "I keep getting so hungry," she said.

"Bottomless pit," her mother said, pleased. When Alice tucked two more brownies into a napkin and carried them upstairs to her bedroom at the end of the night, her mother felt simultaneously worried and relieved—where had she been that she'd learned to squirrel away extra food? Somewhere with too many mouths.

Alice went to bed early, ate her brownies one after another while she looked out the window, and then crumpled up the napkin in her fist and let it drop to the floor. Here, the lights in each house went out around the same time every night, or they went out in stages: first the lights in the children's rooms, then the overhead in the kitchen, the lamps on the side tables in the living rooms, finally the light in the master bedroom.

While Alice sat in her windowsill, Billy Morris was trying to delay going to bed. April had already tucked him in, but there he was out of his room, standing in the doorway of the living room where his parents had been reading. "I have to find Orion's belt," he said. "For a homework assignment. I just remembered."

"Come on, buddy," Eric said. "Just pretend you saw it. It's some stars in a line, and they kind of look like a belt."

"Honey," April said to Billy, "I saw your homework list, and that wasn't on there. Go to bed."

"Please!" said Billy. "I need to go look for it. We're going to write a poem about it tomorrow."

"Fine," said April. "I'm going to time you. You have one minute."

Outside, Billy looked in the sky, but it was kind of cloudy. There was the moon, there were some stars. Weren't they all kind of in a line? Across the street was Alice Lange's house. And there she was. He could see her more clearly than the stars, framed by the window like a girl trapped in a painting. She was so pretty. He wondered where she had gone, and if now that she was back, his mother would let him ride his bike to the park again, instead of just up and down the street. He watched her until his mother stuck her head outside, told him his time was up a minute ago.

"Alice Lange came back," he told her, but when April went back outside just a few minutes later, the window was dark, and Alice was gone again.

CHAPTER THIRTY-FIVE

THE NEXT MORNING, while her mother was at the store, Alice checked all of the places where her mother liked to hide cash. She always said that this habit of hers had driven Alice's father crazy—he wanted it in a bank where it could make more money just by sitting there, but Alice's mother liked having it easily accessible in case of an emergency. "You just never know," she said.

Now Alice thumbed through the stack of bills, counting. There wasn't nearly as much as she had hoped, but it was better than nothing. It could help. It *would* help. It could get them closer to the desert. She imagined coming into the bungalow to find that the other girls were out somewhere, and only Wesley was home, the inverse of their regular world. In her vision, he would have been asleep, waking up when Alice crept in. She'd say guess what, and he'd smile in a lazy, sleepy way and would pull her on top of him, and she'd heap the bills onto his chest.

Then the other girls would come home—Hannah Fay

would be back too—and then they would all go to the desert. They'd wait until the rest of the world ate itself, like a hungry animal gnawing at its own leg. Then they would come back, and it would all be theirs.

"Allie?" her mother called. The front door closed behind her. "Sweetie?"

Alice put the money into her bag, shoved the bag in her closet. "Here!" she called, and her mother said something she couldn't totally understand, but it might have been "Thank you, God," and Alice thought she might stay just a little longer.

That night, Mrs. Lange made chicken pot pie, which Alice had loved as a girl and always craved when the weather began to cool in the slight way it does here. She rolled out the dough for the crust, lining a pie tin with it and then filling the pale bowl with potatoes, carrots, peas, gravy. Afterward, she baked an entire chocolate cake. Alice, who had been napping on the couch in the living room, laughed when she came into the kitchen and saw it. "This is amazing," Alice said. "And ridiculous."

"I'm just happy you're here," her mother said. "Let's eat. Do you want to eat the cake first? We can do that, if that's what you'd like."

Alice laughed again. "I can wait," she said, and she sat down at the table and let her mother serve her.

"We missed you," her mother began when they were both seated. "I didn't get the spices just right for the pumpkin bread in October. No one said anything, but I know it's true."

"You did it without me?" Alice asked, moved by her mother's generosity of spirit and sad that she hadn't been here months ago to be touched by it herself, to extend it to the rest of us.

"I had to do something," her mother said.

"Oh," said Alice. She imagined another version of her mother, standing in the kitchen in front of the stove, mixing and pouring batter into the tins, the spices lined up on the counter beside her. She also imagined another Alice standing with her, maybe waking up from another nap on the couch, in some other timeline, and saying, *Oh! I had almost forgotten!* Her mother turning to smile at her. *I would never have let you forget*, she might say. Alice would never trade her time with Wesley for anything, but if she could have let herself be in two places at once, she would have done it, just for a moment, to be next to her mother and measure out the spices just as she had done every year of her life.

"I thought it might bring you home," her mother said. "I know that sounds silly, but I thought it might be some kind of a—I don't know, a signal. That you would feel it and come home."

"Mama," Alice said, a name she hadn't called her mother in a very long time, the first word she had been able to say.

"I would do it again," her mother said.

They ate in silence for a few minutes when her mother put her fork down. Alice looked up. "I have to ask you where you went," she said. "I've been trying not to. I'm not even sure I need to know, but I know I have to ask."

"Nowhere," Alice said.

"That's impossible. Every place is somewhere."

"I don't know," said Alice. "I don't know how to explain it. I was in a house with some people."

"But what were you doing?" her mother asked. She pictured a house like the one they were in, a grown-up's house, but she couldn't envision any other people in it. All the people she imagined were more versions of Alice, more versions of herself, not different enough from the real her, the real Alice, to truly matter. But that couldn't be right. If it was her mother she wanted, she wouldn't have left. "Was there a boy?" she asked. She'd promised herself she would only ask Alice three questions.

"Sort of," said Alice. Funny to think of Wesley as a boy. "Yes."

Alice's mother hesitated. "Is there, still?" she asked. Alice didn't answer. "All right, darling," her mother said. She felt her face begin to crumple, before she shook the sadness back; she didn't want to make Alice feel bad or guilty. She only wanted her to stay. "Would you like cake now?"

"Yes," said Alice. "Please."

"Did anything bad happen to you?" she asked.

"No," said Alice. "Only good things."

Her mother nodded. "I'll get the cake," she said. Maybe she could ask three more tomorrow, three every day that Alice was home, until every minute Alice had been away was accounted for, but when she turned around and saw her daughter sitting at the table, safe and whole and lovely and here, she knew no other answers mattered.

It was like her mother had put a spell on her, binding Alice to the borders of the front yard. She would walk around on the grass barefoot, and we'd watch her curl up her toes and just stand there. Once Mrs. McEntyre walked the dog past her yard when Alice was outside. "Oh, that poor girl just lit up when she saw Sweetie, and Sweetie ran right over to her, nearly pulled my arm out of the socket," she told us. Alice, she said, got down on her hands and knees to play with Sweetie, who yipped at her and turned in spastic circles—by then, Mrs. McEntyre had let go of the leash and it trailed after the little dog—and when Alice sat and crossed her legs, Sweetie climbed into her lap and licked her face. "Then the blessed girl just started crying," she said. "Poor angel. So fragile. I told her if she needed a pick-me-up, she could visit Sweetie anytime."

"Oh," said Alice Lange. "Thank you, but I don't think I can."

And another time, when Earl Phelps, who walks up and down the street every morning for exercise, saw her standing in the yard, he stopped in front of her and asked her what the hell she was doing. "I just like the way it feels," she said. "I've never noticed what nice grass we have here."

"Your mama pays good money to keep your yard nice," Earl said. "Always gets that man to mow and fertilize it so it stays green. It's important for folks to keep a nice house and a nice yard." His own house was spartan, his yard as well, but especially for an older man living alone, we had to admit it was nice.

Alice looked at him, and later he said it was like she was listening to a voice only she could hear. "That's when I knew she wasn't quite right," he said later. "Those eyes. Too pale, like she wasn't all there."

"There are more important things than that," Alice said to him. "We just have to wake up and see it. All of us are blind until we open our eyes." She closed her eyes and opened them again, pushed herself up on her toes so she stood an inch taller, then sank back onto flat feet. "But the grass really is very nice," she said. "Like carpet. Ours isn't as nice."

"That is your grass," Earl said. Alice cocked her head to the side, looking confused, he said, like a deer right before you shoot it.

"Be sweet to your mother," Earl finally said to her and went on his way. "Never knew what a strange girl she was, but she was damned odd that day," he told us later. We tried to tell him she wasn't always. But it's very possible that we just never knew. That it was inside her all along, waiting for someone to stir it up, make it visible. But what do we know? We're just blind people. Ah, forgive us, we make ourselves laugh. What foolishness.

Alice couldn't bring herself to leave, but her stomach ached at the thought of Wesley and the girls waiting for her at the bungalow. She felt so tired, shocking herself by falling asleep after lunch and on the couch at night while her mother watched television. But at the same time a restless energy coursed through her when she was awake, every part of her humming. She kept her bag packed, kept the money in the back pocket of jeans she never wore; that way she was ready to go if she needed to, if Wesley came for her, if he sent a sign that her time was up, past up.

She somehow knew they hadn't left her, hadn't gone off to the rocks and the sweat and the dip of the desert already. Wesley needed her. But her mother needed her too. After a couple of days, they'd settled into a routine: waking up and having a slow breakfast of eggs or pancakes or, once, only bacon, one strip after another, so that their fingertips shone with grease and the kitchen smelled like a diner all day.

Her mother would read in the backyard, and Alice would lie on the grass and nap or eat strawberries from the same glass bowl. After dinner they watched movies on TV, reruns; then, the hour growing later, her mother would talk, telling her stories about the neighborhood, all the things she had quietly observed about us. We were surprised by how closely she was watching us; it was unnerving to be known, jarring to hear ourselves described like characters in a book. She spoke, too, about Alice's father, but truth be told, we didn't care so much about these stories—they didn't stick with us.

Later, her mother would think about this time as so special, when their days were so intertwined that she couldn't separate herself from her daughter, the way it had been when Alice was a baby and didn't understand she was a person herself apart from her mother. But the truth is it was only Mrs. Lange who really said anything. Alice listened and asked polite questions but didn't share. She kept a part of herself reserved for Wesley, a smaller part for the girls, a smaller part still for the men Wesley said were still coming, for the girls he hadn't yet found.

Only with them did love live, Wesley had told her, but couldn't it be somewhere else too? Here, her mother humming while she diced onions, and Alice listening, trying to decide if it was a song she knew from somewhere or one her mother made up, sprung from somewhere in her heart.

CHAPTER THIRTY-SIX

ABOUT A WEEK after Alice's return, she and her mother were just finishing lunch, their uneaten sandwich crusts still limp on their plates, when the doorbell rang. "Are you expecting anyone?" her mother asked.

Alice laughed. "Definitely not," she said. "Are you?"

Her mother shook her head, standing up to move toward the door. "It's a mystery guest," she said, and Alice's stomach clenched: Wesley. He had found her, had come to claim her and bring her home. Wesley in her house. Her mother's house.

But then she watched her mother open the door, saw her face register someone familiar. (It couldn't have been Wesley, of course. We would have seen him coming.) "Well, hi, honey," her mother said. "Can you come in? Alice, look who it is." Alice got up and walked over, and her mother opened the door wider, framing Susannah on her doorstep.

"Hi, Alice," said Susannah. Alice had missed that voice—she hadn't even realized how much until she heard it now, husky and shy, coming out of the girl she had missed too. Susannah looked the same, just as Alice had left her, and Alice wanted to hug her but instead just said, "Sit with me on the swing," and her mother smiled and shut the door so the two girls were alone.

On the swing, Alice sat near the edge so her toes skimmed the porch's concrete floor and propelled the two of them back and forth. "So," she said.

"Where have you been?" Susannah asked.

Alice didn't answer at first, fixated on the swing. No one had used it since she had left, and it was dusty, the slats covered in a fine layer of dirt. When she swiped her finger across its arm, her fingertip came back gray, each whorl of her print now visible, like she could press it against a piece of paper, leave behind proof of who she was.

"You just left," Susannah said, both amazed and angry. She wasn't a queen or a rebel. She wasn't our pride, wasn't our disappointment. Sitting here, she tried to imagine the kinds of stories people might tell about her if she were to disappear like Alice: Susannah, the nice girl with the deep voice, someone who belonged in a place like this. She was friends with Alice Lange, and, ah, there's the better story.

"I know," said Alice.

"So where did you go?"

"Well," said Alice, thinking how to explain the bungalow, Wesley, the other girls. How to tell Susannah how asleep she had been until Wesley woke her up. "Someone found me and gave me a place to live," she offered. "And a job to do. I'm doing something important now."

"This wasn't important?" Susannah asked. She waved her

hand at the street, at all of us working in our houses, pulling weeds in our gardens, driving our cars out into the world.

"No," said Alice. "It wasn't. It isn't." She wanted to sound firm and kind, to tell the truth. But Susannah looked down, picked up a tiny brown leaf that had floated onto the swing. She twirled it in her fingers and then bent it in half, rubbing a crease with her finger and thumb. When she opened it up, it had broken into two halves. She tossed them to the ground.

"It used to be," Susannah said. "You know it did."

Alice shook her head. Her hair was so much longer now, Susannah noticed. The brightness of it winked at her, and Susannah felt a coil of anger like a snake tightening in her belly.

"It was never important," Alice said. "I just didn't know then what I know now." She wanted to make Susannah understand. "Do you remember on our way to the school that night, those houses we passed? And everyone else was asleep, and it was like we were the only people in the whole world who were awake. It was like they didn't exist. Only we did. That's how the whole world is."

"Did you know Ben took the fall for you?" Susannah asked.

Alice closed her eyes. She was so tired. Susannah didn't understand, but she saw, too, that her old friend didn't want to understand, not really. She opened her eyes. "I didn't ask him to," she said.

"Of course you didn't," Susannah said. "But you had to know he would."

"I didn't," said Alice.

"It's a little selfish," Susannah said. "All of it. Letting Ben get in trouble, leaving without saying a word to anyone." She looked down, touched a silver screw in the swing with a gentle finger. "I didn't even get to go to homecoming," she said softly. "My last one ever." Her pink dress still hung in the closet, on the velvety hanger they'd given her at the store. The bare shoulders no one had touched. When she had left Alice's house the night the police came and she had told Mrs. Lange she needed to make a new plan for the dance, she'd gone home and watched TV with her mother and father instead, too angry and sad to see anyone or do anything else.

"I'm sorry," Alice said. "I had to do what was best for me."

Susannah looked up at her now, only her gaze rising, her chin still tilted down. "Okay," she said.

"You're going to grow up eventually too," Alice said, reaching a hand over and putting in on Susannah's knee. "I promise. It's just—I got there first."

"Is that what you think happened?" Susannah asked. "This is you growing up?"

Alice shrugged. "Yeah," she said.

Susannah slid off the swing, and Alice's hand slipped off her knee. "I should go," she said. "I just wanted to come say hi." She swallowed. "Tell you I missed you."

"I miss you too," Alice said, but that feeling she had when she saw her friend standing at her doorstep had dissipated. Or crystallized maybe, changed into something else. She missed Susannah the way she missed recess in elementary school, birthday parties with candles in cake, Santa Claus. Happy, sweet things that belonged in the past. "I won't leave without saying good-bye again," she said.

"Okay," said Susannah. "See you later, then." She left Alice on the swing but stopped halfway down the walk and turned around. "Can I come with you?" she asked. "When you leave?"

"No," said Alice.

"Okay," said Susannah again. But this time when she began to walk away, she didn't look back.

Inside the house, Alice found her mother washing the lunch dishes. "Mama," Alice said again, and her mother turned around, wiped her hands on a dish towel and pulled Alice to her chest. She thought she could feel her daughter's heart beating, and what a miracle, how this was the same heart that she had given a home to in her own body eighteen years ago. How that heart kept beating and beating. How lucky she was to feel it, hear it.

"It's hard to come home," her mother said.

"But good?" Alice asked.

"The best," she said.

"Am I good?"

Her mother let her go and took a step back, a hand on each of Alice's shoulders.

"The best," she said.

CHAPTER THIRTY-SEVEN

HER MOTHER CONVINCED her to attend the annual holiday block party. It isn't anything big or flashy, but it's special. There's homemade wassail and hot chocolate, caroling and gifts. Every year the Prices rent a machine that guzzles water and some kind of chemical and spits it back out as snow that falls over everyone who walks past their yard. Alice had been feeling slightly queasy all day and didn't want to go and have fake conversations with people who didn't understand anything about the world. "I'm too tired," she had told her mother. "You go, and I'll wait here."

"That's fine, honey," Mrs. Lange had said. "I'll stay here with you." But when Alice watched her mother removing the sweater she had just put on, she felt overcome with a tender sort of feeling, like a bruising, somehow, of her heart, and she said, never mind, of course she would go. Besides, her mother had begun talking, vaguely, gently, about Christmas, the things she and Alice would do together. Alice responded to these hints in her own vague and gentle way, giving the kind of noncommittal answers that could be interpreted however the listener chose. She knew she couldn't promise that she'd still be here, so accompanying her mother to the block party was, perhaps, the least she could do.

But as they went outside and she watched the children speed by on bikes, as she heard her mother's laugh and the white lights on the houses twinkled as the sun set, she had to admit it was lovely here. It was a beautiful neighborhood. In the distance she could see Susannah, and she decided she would find her and try to be kinder, more understanding.

Before she could make her way to Susannah, someone tapped her on the back. Startled, she jumped, turning so quickly that her golden hair flew around her, bright in the twilight. "Oh," she said, her hand over her heart.

There stood Ben Austin, whose mother, Audrey, watched him from a distance as he reached for a girl who did not deserve him. Audrey knew that though Alice seemed real before him, her shoulder firm and warm beneath his hand, the Alice he saw was only a mirage, a creation of his desperate mind and heart. Ben smiled at Alice, and his mother turned away.

"You're really here," he said. Now Alice smiled too; he seemed nervous. It was so different from the swagger and bravado of Wesley, but she found his uncertainty endearing, even attractive. What would it be like to be with Ben Austin? She imagined doing for him what Wesley had done for her— changing her, improving her. She could pull the strength and beauty from Ben, adorn him with it until he shone. How easy it would be to let him love her, to slip on her old life like a coat. There would be no other girls to compete with, none to argue

with, but also, she thought, no other girls who would understand that aching love in her heart, the passion they shared for
a common person. But still, it was tempting.

"I'm so happy to see you," she said, and she threw her
arms around him. He returned her embrace. We watched. We
wanted to cheer, but then she pulled away from him, and we
pretended we hadn't been watching. "I need to talk to Susannah," she told him. "But then maybe we could go for a walk
and catch up?"

"Of course," he said. He grinned, making a little dimple
appear in one cheek. Alice had to stop herself from reaching
for it, placing one gentle finger over it. A little breeze blew a
piece of her hair across her face, and now Ben, too, thought of
reaching toward her. "Aren't you cold?" he asked.

"I am a little," she said. "Okay. A walk later, you and me.
I'll find you." She touched him on his shoulder as she brushed
past him.

Susannah had disappeared from where she had been standing a few minutes ago, and Alice stopped in the middle of the
street, first looking for her friend and then simply taking it all
in. Down the street at the Prices', children frolicked like little
wild ponies under the spray of fake snow. Mags handed out
cups of wassail and hot chocolate from a table in her yard,
and in front of it, we stood together in small clusters, laughing and talking, toasting ourselves with the warm drinks in
our hands. Later, we would switch to liquor to warm us up,
when the children went to bed and the party became another
kind of creature, a wild and merry beast. Alice scanned the
street and sidewalk for Susannah, and her gaze landed upon
her mother, who must have felt Alice's eyes on her because she
looked up. She gave her daughter a tiny, quick wink, without

stopping her conversation with April. A breeze picked up once more, shaking the tree branches overhead, and Alice shivered.

As she stood there, we could see that she loved us again, how she loved this place. Here, she was a queen. We would let her be, we would let her play the role she was meant to have. She could be one of us again. She loved us, and we loved her in that moment too. It was the last time we truly, unequivocally, did.

Because she went inside her house. She needed a sweater, and it felt natural to walk through the door, like she'd never left. She wasn't thinking of Wesley. She was thinking of Ben and Susannah, who loved her. Of her mother, who loved her. As she climbed the stairs to her bedroom, the ground shifted under her feet. The picture frames climbing up the wall beside the stairs crashed down. She heard glass breaking, and she grabbed the banister. A rumble, a crash.

A reality of living here, what we exchange for an idyllic setting: sometimes the earth shakes, it splits open.

When the ground stopped shaking—it was so fast, over in seconds—Alice walked over to the window. She saw us outside, most of us laughing and playing as if nothing had happened. Trees were still standing, houses. No fires, no gaping holes in the street. If she had looked more closely, if she had gone outside and back into our circles of conversation, she would have seen our surprise, would have watched us checking our bones, our pulses, would have heard us marvel at that small winter quake. Outside, we hadn't felt it as keenly, though. It was a tremor, a spasm of the earth.

I'll know, Wesley had said. I'll know if you're thinking of staying.

He isn't who you think, Apple said.

A magician. A prophet. A god. The second coming of Christ.

Perhaps he was something else still, possessor of a darker, more terrible power. This rumble and growl that shook her was a message, a reminder there was more he could do; there was more to who he was. Shaker of earth, finder of lost things, seer in the dark.

She went upstairs to her room, yanked open her desk drawer, and pulled out a sheet of stationery that read ALICE LYNNE LANGE at the top. She left her mother a note. It said, "I love you. Be safe and open your eyes. I'll come find you, after." It had been months, she realized, since she'd put anything down on paper, and her handwriting didn't look the way she had remembered it, so different from the pretty looping "hello" she had written on Mr. Fielding's blackboard. Her mother, when she found the note later that evening, refused to believe Alice had written it herself, and that if she had, she had done it under duress, given that shaky, uneven script. "This is a stranger," she told us, holding it up, and we nodded but didn't believe her.

Alice grabbed her bag, the money she had found in the house. She went out the back door, hopped a series of fences; we were all together in the street, so we didn't see her scrambling over them, running across our backyards. When she got to the end of the street, the corner where she had met Carl months ago, in his little green car, she looked up and saw Bev. Bev saw her too. Bev, with her baby girl in her arms, who had wandered down the street away from the festivities to see if that would calm the baby, to see if perhaps she was overstimulated by the celebration. She had walked her with that slow bouncing gait that mothers develop when they hold their children, shushing in her ear, and the baby had fallen asleep. Now Bev didn't feel in a hurry to get back to us.

Alice waved at Bev, said nothing. There was something final about that gesture, and Bev knew it was a good-bye, not a hello. She wondered if she should go after her, remind her what—and whom—she was leaving behind, but her own child woke up then, beginning to cry, and Bev looked down to comfort her. When she looked up, Alice was gone.

When Alice's mother found the note an hour later, she wept and would not eat, would not sleep. Dr. Samuels had to come and give her a sedative. We took turns sitting with her until her sister arrived. She was like a paper doll, flimsy, no life in her limbs. We could fold her into anything we wanted, into whatever made us comfortable.

We would puzzle over that note for weeks. We still think of it. We wonder if her mother kept it. We would have burned it, buried it in the woods, thrown it into the ocean. After what? we wonder. If there's an after, there must be a before. There must be a now. We are already awake. Our eyes are already open.

We worry something is coming.

Alice has gone again, and something is coming. We tell ourselves we no longer love her, but it's possible that we do.

CHAPTER THIRTY-EIGHT

A T THE BUS station, Alice hid in a bathroom stall for
two hours before her bus was scheduled to leave, in
case any of us came looking for her, but because her mother
was too distraught to even think of checking the bus station,
no one did, and eventually she boarded the bus and slept. She
called the bungalow from a pay phone when she disembarked,
but the phone at the house was still disconnected. Everyone
would have been asleep anyway, and Alice, thinking of the
driving man for the first time in weeks, didn't want to hitch
a ride. Across from the bus station was a twenty-four-hour
diner, so Alice went there. She picked a booth by a window,
ordered a bottomless cup of coffee, and watched cars and
buses come and go in the gray parking lot until dawn began
to break. She dropped a couple of crumpled bills on the table
and left, a little bell above the door tinkling as she walked
out. Now that it was morning, a few taxis were waiting to
pick up passengers in front of the station, so Alice peeked in
a window, relieved to see a driver who looked safe, or at least

easy to escape from if need be, and climbed in. The new day-light was hazy through the car's smudged windows, and jazz played over the radio, the driver's wedding ring thumping on the steering wheel as he tried to keep time to the music.

When she finally got back to the bungalow, a stranger opened the door. "Hi," the girl said. She was older than Alice, and her light brown hair was pulled into a thick ponytail. She was wearing a dress Apple often chose, but she was bigger on top than Apple, and the fabric there was stretched taut. Alice thought of Wesley handling each of those heavy breasts. "This is Jennifer," Kathryn said, appearing behind her. "She got here a few days ago."

"Hi," the girl said, stepping out of the way and opening the door wider. She had deep dimples in her cheeks, like two small coins.

"My replacement?" Alice asked. She was still holding her bag, the strap digging into her shoulder. She had barely made it inside the house. The front door was still open behind her.

"We didn't know if you were coming back," Kathryn said. "But no, not a replacement."

"Definitely not!" said Jennifer. Her voice had a chirpy quality. "The more the merrier, right?"

"Right," said Alice. She looked around. "It's still early. Where is everyone?" The house was quiet and sun soaked. Alice thought of a picture she'd seen in her science textbook of bugs trapped in tree sap, silent and golden.

"Janie went to that farmer's market at the school to get a few snacks for the drive," Kathryn said. "Wesley is picking up some people, some other girl, and a guy, I think."

"Wait," said Alice. "Another girl and a guy? Where's every-one going to live? Here?" She took a few more steps into the house, passed into the living room. The other girls followed, and she let her bag slip from her shoulder.

When she turned around to face Kathryn, Kathryn looked surprised. "I thought you knew," she said. "I thought Wesley must have gotten in touch with you. We're leaving today."

"But I thought we needed money," Alice said. "I have it. Some."

"We do," Kathryn said. "But Wesley's been very antsy. I guess we were going to go, money or not."

Alice looked more closely at the living room. Everything was still there, the lamp on the side table by the couch, the little TV on the bookcase, the fat-leafed plants. She motioned toward all of it. "We don't need it," Kathryn said. "Bring some clothes and whatever shoes you have that will work well on the different terrain."

She looked down to see that Kathryn was wearing hiking boots, and Jennifer was in leather sandals. Her toenails were painted burgundy and looked like round little grapes at the end of her feet.

The door of the study opened, and everyone looked over. "Hi," said Hannah Fay, walking out. Her pale skin looked even whiter, pearly almost, and in her arms was a baby, small and pink and still. "She's asleep," Hannah Fay said. "But Alice, I heard your voice and had to come out right away."

Alice opened her arms, and instead of embracing her, Hannah Fay handed her the baby, who squeaked at the transfer. She was warm and smelled—Alice breathed her in—like Hannah Fay. "Did Wesley find you?" Alice asked.

"I came back on my own," Hannah Fay said. "I had the baby, and I looked down at her and saw Wesley and knew she needed to have a father and not just a mother."

Alice said nothing, thought briefly of her own mother, who, even alone, had been enough. She always had been. It was everything else in her life that wasn't. She wished then she could tell her mother that. Maybe she could still tell her someday, the way that Hannah Fay still wrote to her own parents.

"Besides, Wesley is me," Hannah Fay said. "I'm him. You know?"

"I do," said Alice.

"It's okay if she wakes up," Hannah Fay said.

Alice looked down at the baby. She had full lips, the bottom one plump and pouting in sleep, and lots of dark hair. "What's her name, Han?"

"Are you surprised to hear Wesley has an opinion about that? We aren't naming her yet. So far, she's just the baby, but I like to call her Sunshine, Bunny, Daffodil. I don't know. Do I sound crazy?"

"A little. In a sweet way," said Alice. "But I'll be offended if she gets a new name before me." When no one laughed, she said, "Kidding. She's so beautiful, Hannah Fay. I love her already."

"Isn't she cute?" Jennifer chirped, and Alice felt a flare of annoyance.

"This hair," Alice said.

"All Daddy," Hannah Fay said, reaching over to smooth a lock of hair that didn't lie flat. It was strange to imagine Wesley as a father. She thought suddenly of him wearing the cassock, Apple teasing him.

"Where's Apple?" Alice asked. "I brought a sweater from my mother's house that I thought she'd like."

"Oh," said Kathryn. "She's gone."

"Gone?" Alice repeated. "Where?"

"She left," said Kathryn, as though nothing could be more obvious.

"I'm just going to step outside," Jennifer said. "Excuse me." Before she did, she placed a hand on each of Kathryn's shoulders and squeezed.

"I'm going to change her diaper," Hannah Fay said, sliding the baby from Alice's arms and disappearing back into the study. Alice's skin felt cold in her absence, and she wanted, badly, inexplicably, to have her back.

"Why would she leave?" Alice asked. "She told me she'd be here when I got back."

Kathryn shrugged. "She and Wesley had a fight when Hannah Fay came back," she said.

"About what?"

"Apple painted a picture of Hannah Fay and the baby," Kathryn said. "And Wesley thought she was mocking him."

"How?" asked Alice, confused. "Apple can paint?" Even absent, here was Apple forcing Alice to alter the image she held of her in her head, changing herself again.

"Well, it was really good," Kathryn said. "I'd show you, but Wesley destroyed it. Anyway, you know Wesley doesn't ever paint people, and he thought Apple was showing off, trying to prove some point about what a bad painter he was."

Alice thought of what Apple said the night before Alice left for her mother's house. *He doesn't paint people because he doesn't know how.* "It's possible," she said.

"There's more," said Kathryn. "Wesley asked her why he wasn't in the picture with Hannah Fay and the baby, and Apple said it was because he might not stick around, he might leave again, just like he had left his son."

"Oh, Apple," said Alice.

"It was bad," said Kathryn, nodding. "But she was asking for it! She knew what she was doing. She wanted to get him all riled up. Anyway, they fought, and in the morning she was gone. No note, nothing. She just vanished."

Alice thought again of her mother, of the note she had written, and felt glad she had left her with that small gesture of kindness. "What did Wesley say?" she asked.

"He saw it coming," Kathryn said. "He said he'll miss her, but it's better without her."

"Wow," Alice said. "Are you sure she left? What if she didn't mean to leave forever, she just went out in the morning and then something happened to her?" A sudden image of a girl with a broken shoe entered her thoughts, but she couldn't get a hold on it. It must have been Apple she was thinking of, the time when Wesley punished her and she hitchhiked to different cars until the sole of her shoe peeled off.

"Wesley would know," Kathryn said. "He said she's gone for good and we shouldn't worry about her because she's fine. Now, go get whatever you want to bring," she said. "We're leaving as soon as he gets back." Kathryn began to walk into the kitchen and then paused, calling over her shoulder. "Don't forget tampons," she said. "We won't be able to go to the store as easily when we get there. And my period started a few days ago so yours probably did too."

The bedroom was messy, the bed unmade. Maybe Apple had left in the night, leaving Janie to wake up alone. Apple always made the bed in the morning, smoothing out the quilt and arranging the pillows so they sat proud at the headboard. Alice rifled through the community pile of clothes, picking out what she liked the best but also what seemed appropriate for their new home at the ranch—jeans, lightweight tops, a sweater. When they left, they wouldn't be coming back here. It wouldn't be safe. It would be a war zone, Wesley had told them. Think about that. Imagine that.

Pants and shirts and blouses, socks and bras and shoes missing mates, shoes with laces untied. Most of her own clothes were there in the stack, except the yellow dress Apple had adopted. She saw that Apple had left a heavier pair of sneakers in the closet, and Alice stepped out of her slim white tennis shoes and put them on instead. They felt bulky but powerful on her feet—she imagined stomping on scorpions, the heads of snakes.

In the bathroom, she rifled through the drawers until she had a handful of pads and tampons. It always bothered her that her cycle had synced up with Kathryn's, of all the girls, like nature was trying to tell her something about herself she didn't want to hear. But Kathryn was wrong—her period hadn't started a few days ago. It hadn't started at all. She put her hands on her stomach. She looked at herself in the mirror but she looked the same. Pretty and light, like an angel. A goddess.

It didn't feel right to leave the room untidy, so Alice straightened up. She pulled the quilt tight on the bed, and placed the pillows like Apple always did, and when everything looked as neat as it could, she went into the living room to wait.

They took turns riding shotgun beside Wesley at the front of the van on the drive to the desert. He drove meanderingly, pointing out what different places would look like after the war began. "Bombed out," he said about the university. "Empty," about the ocean. "Charred," about the trees. "When the war is over, that's when we'll come back, and we'll rebuild, just us, our own little family. We're the chosen ones, see? You are, I am. We'll remake the world into what it's supposed to be."

"When will it start?" asked Jennifer. She was sitting behind the passenger seat, leaning forward. The other two new people, a girl named Rosie and a guy who called himself Dallas, sat in the far back, bumping along as Wesley drove. Janie and Hannah Fay were there, too, of course, but they were quiet, even the baby in her mother's arms. Alice worried about Janie, how she was faring without Apple. She resolved to take better care of her; she could dance with her and laugh with her, the way Apple did. She could hold the ice to Janie's cheek when things went south with Wesley. She could do that for her.

"It's taking longer than I thought," Wesley said now. "Everyone is so asleep, like deep asleep. But we're going to kick things off, you know? I have a plan."

By the time Alice took her turn in the front seat, the land had turned tan and yellow and dusty. The sun was setting, a fiery orange, loose around the edges, a threat, like it might drop out of the sky and scorch the earth. Begin Wesley's war that way. She rolled her window down. The air was dry and sweet. "I wonder if we'll see coyotes," she said.

"Probably," said Wesley. He had one hand on the steering wheel, holding it steady under his thumb. He was relaxed, and Alice thought back to that first ride out to the bungalow, the energy thrumming under his skin.

"I'm excited," Alice said. "Are you?"

"I am," he said.

Alice stuck her arm out the window. Wiggled her fingers in the wind. There were so few cars out here, so few other travelers. Her mother and her aunt and uncle had taken her out to the desert once before, to a national park, they told her, but when they got there, it wasn't like any park Alice had seen before. The trees were spare and sparse and crooked, like skeletal fingers of underground giants punching upward, trying to break through the earth. They were going to go camping, but her mother wanted a proper bathroom, so they stayed at a motel and drove into the park first thing in the morning. Alice counted salamanders, jumped off rocks, ran away from her mother when she tried to put sunscreen on her bare arms, on her white cheeks. "I almost forgot," she said to Wesley. "But I came here once when I was little."

"Hey," said Wesley, glancing at her. "Want to hear something you're gonna like?"

"Yes," Alice said. "Actually, I have to tell you something too. Something I think *you're* going to like."

"What is it?" he asked, looking over at her again, eyebrows raised, one hand loosely on the top of the steering wheel.

Alice laughed. "You first," she said.

"I figured out your name," he said. "Your true name. Are you ready?"

Alice stuck her head out the window, gave it a shake in the wind like a dog, and closed her eyes. Dust, wind, light, all streaming in. New life growing. She pulled herself back into the van, leaned against the seat. "Ready," she said.

CHAPTER THIRTY-NINE

THE DESERT IS a wild thing. It could have eaten her, stretched open its jaws and swallowed her into its belly, a pit under the dirt and rock. We wonder about her. We tell her story. There is danger here, she taught us that. Things that will take our children, things that will change them. Things that threaten us. We won't let it happen again. We'll keep watch, we'll fight harder, we won't let the wrong ones in. If we have to, we'll lock ourselves up for good, for the good of everyone, for our neighbors.

Bev holds her daughter's hand as they walk down the street, Tim running in front of them. She'd just called April's house to see if she and Billy wanted to play, but it was Eric who answered the phone. He was home sick from work, his voice scratchy and tired. "I suppose you need April to take care of you," Bev said. "I was going to see if she and Billy wanted to meet outside, but if it would help, you can just send Billy over and everyone can get a break."

"Actually," Eric said. "She's over at Charlotte's."

"Ah," Bev said as if she understood and this was perfectly clear, but she did not, and it was not.

"You should go over there too," Eric said. "You know Charlotte likes everyone to know what a good hostess she is."

"I think maybe I will," Bev said. She wished him well and hung up. Bev called out to Tim, scooped up her girl, and when they made it outside, she let her walk on those chubby pigeon-toed feet, clutching her hand tightly.

Charlotte's house sits at the mouth of the neighborhood, and nearby there are construction workers busy laying brick and mortar. Billy and the Price twins huddle at a safe distance, hands in pockets. One of them holds a basketball. Without a word to his mother, Tim runs over to join them. "Bev," Charlotte says. "What a pleasant surprise!"

"Eric told me you were here," Bev says.

"I was going to call you," April says.

"It's okay," Bev says.

"The boys are obsessed with the construction," April says as Bev walks up. "They're hoping they can steal a drill or something." She grins at Bev, hopes she will forgive her, or better yet, that she hasn't noticed. But as Bev sits cross-legged on the lawn, the baby already pulling at the blades of grass, she gives April a polite smile, cordial but not warm. Bev's teeth are the same, the lips are the same, but it isn't her normal smile, and April feels her stomach clench, before she remembers that she has nothing to be ashamed of. It was Bev who's at fault, Bev who let Alice Lange go the second time. "You could have stopped her," April had said when Bev told her about seeing Alice leave.

"Do you really think so?" Bev asked. She was neither frowning nor smiling, and April couldn't tell if Bev was amused, skeptical, or if she genuinely wanted to know if April thought it was true.

"You could have tried."

"The baby was crying," Bev said. "I had to take care of her."

It's okay, April tells herself now. People change, drift apart, even here. We can't save everything. To tell the truth, we don't want to.

"Christine Pittman is very interested as well," Charlotte says disapprovingly as the child bikes up to the boys. The women watch Christine say something to them, point at the workers.

"Heavy machinery is very interesting," Bev says. "All those teeth."

"Enough to cut a limb off," says Charlotte. "Or a finger."

"Exactly," says Bev. "Isn't that the appeal?"

"Not for me," says Charlotte.

On the other side of the street, Mrs. McEntyre and Sweetie walk past. Sweetie pulls the leash, yanking her owner's arm straight as a board, barking at the workers or at the boys or at the women or at the trees, the sky, the squirrels. Mrs. McEntyre notes the women and their feet: Charlotte Price's crossed at the ankle, in slip-on shoes, April's jittery and nervy in white canvas sneakers, Bev's in espadrilles, despite the chill in the air. Those are shoes for summer days. A swell of power from Sweetie, and Mrs. McEntyre is pulled forward again. The women wave at her.

A burst of laughter comes from the square of boys watching the workers, and the women look over as their children break apart and scatter. Christine is laughing too. One of them passes the basketball to another.

It's been almost a year since Alice disappeared again,

before she escaped us once and for all. We have kept everyone safe, even installing the streetlights to fight the darkness, but it's not enough. Hence the small team of men here with saws and drills, measuring, cutting, building. Soon those materials will come together to be a gate and a little booth where a man in a uniform will sit and keep a lookout. He will be nice but not too nice. He will only let in those who we want let in. The man who took Alice away, with the boots and the beard and the pale eyes—he would never have made it past the guard, and she would still be here. In a way, this effort is done in Alice's memory, this booth and gate a monument to who she used to be.

There was a close call once, not long after Alice disappeared the second time. The body of a girl was found a couple of hours away, buried in a shallow grave. Police were working on identifying her, and out of either desperation or ineptitude, released some details to the public. She was wearing a yellow dress, the color of corn silk. Foul play, they said. Weapons: something blunt, then something sharp and small.

Alice's mother didn't watch the news, but her sister called. I could swear I've seen Alice in that dress, she said. The last Thanksgiving I came. Could that be right? Her voice was shaking. I'll call the police myself, she said, so you don't have to. When she called back, she said they told her it was best if Alice's mother came up there herself. I'll go with you, her sister said. But Mrs. Lange told her no. She couldn't put it into so many words, but if it was Alice, she wanted to have a final moment in which the world she occupied consisted only of the two of them and no one else.

She drove two hours to a somber building in another city, near the college she and Alice had visited once. A police officer guided her past the front desk, into a room where the light was blue and cold, and she couldn't bring herself to focus on anything, so she was left only with impressions: stillness, steel. A figure covered in a white sheet. She nearly threw up. The officer with her wouldn't even leave, though Mrs. Lange asked him to, tried to explain how she felt about seeing Alice alone. I'm going to pull the sheet back now, he said, if you're ready.

It wasn't Alice, just some other poor girl, Mrs. Lange said on the phone to her sister. They could have told you on the phone this girl had dark hair. It would have saved me a trip.

Thank God, her sister said.

Mrs. Lange wept anyway. On the drive home, she couldn't stop thinking about that girl beneath the sheet, who was missing, once, just like Alice, just like Rachel Granger. She felt bad for how callous she had sounded, telling her sister she had wasted her time driving to see this girl who, in the end, wasn't her daughter. But she was someone's daughter once, and Mrs. Lange felt suddenly thankful a mother had come to see her in that cold place, even if it wasn't her own.

Still, we do not trust Mrs. Lange. She only cared about her daughter, would have done anything to keep Alice with her, given anything, would have sacrificed any one of us. Knowing this, perhaps, is why we don't reach out to her now.

"Lots of neighborhoods are doing this," April says, nodding at the construction. "That's good, don't you think?"

"Better safe than sorry," Charlotte says. She looks at Bev, who realizes she is supposed to say something.

"Absolutely," she says.

"It'll be nice if we plant some flowers around the booth when it's done," April says. "Something that blooms year-round."

"Marigolds," says Charlotte.

The truth is Bev thinks Alice would have left anyway. Even if Bev had stopped her, grabbed her by the hand, and marched her back to her mother. She would have found someone else, somewhere else, and she would have gone. She hopes her daughter, who is right now pulling herself up as she holds on to the arm of Charlotte Price's chair, will leave someday too. Not with that man or any other man like him. No woman like him either. She doesn't want someone to lead her girl away; she wants the girl to take herself and make her own way. Bev will go with her if she has to. They can leave together. This, she thinks, could work. Light out for the territory, go somewhere new. They could start over, have new lives. They could escape. Her husband could come, and Timmy, of course. They could be pioneers somewhere else, could build their own small world together.

We cannot recommend this. We are working to make things safe and good here so that we don't have to leave, so that everyone who is here can stay. Out there is a wilderness we just cannot tame. We can't take care of the whole world, after all. We can only save ourselves.

ACKNOWLEDGMENTS

THANK YOU TO my agent, Stephanie Delman, for your warmth and encouragement, your guidance, and your insight. I am so lucky to have you on my team; you are truly the best!

To my editor, Emily Griffin—every phone call, email, and edit from you has been so generous and kind, and I am so grateful to have gotten to work on this book with you.

To the team at Harper Perennial: Jane Cavolina and Suzette Lam for their careful consideration during copyedits, and to Joanne O'Neill for the gorgeous cover.

To you, reading this book! What a miracle that you are here. I am so grateful.

Thank you to my teachers and friends at Vermont College of Fine Arts, where I learned how to take myself seriously as a writer. Thank you to Bret Lott for telling me I really should just *try* writing a novel, and to Wedgewood Circle for the financial support to do so.

To Britt Tisdale, my best writer friend, for fielding every

text message from me with good humor and love, for talking me down when I've needed it, and for always building me up. No matter what the problem is, I always feel better after talking to you.

To Cameron Dezen Hammon, who has believed in my work from the very beginning and has never let me get away with selling myself short.

To Brittni Austin for listening, for always being in my corner, and for making me laugh.

To Nsen Buo for loving me, for loving my children, for being the person I most like to sit on my couch with.

Thank you to Claire Wisdom, my sister and my best friend. Very few people get to have such a good sister or such a good best friend, and I'm very lucky to have both those things in the same person.

To the teachers at St. Andrew's Episcopal School, who cared daily for my daughter. On that same note, thank you to my in-laws, Don and Lannie Whatley, for babysitting both my kids almost every weekend so I could escape for a few hours to work on this novel.

Thank you to Jack and Diana Wisdom for being the best parents ever: for listening, loving, supporting, babysitting, encouraging, praying, and for so many things I can't even begin to list them all here. I love you!

Finally, thank you to my little family. To Margaux and Townes, I love you. To Josh, I love you. Without you, I'm not sure I would have ever written a thing. Thank you for believing in me, always.

ABOUT THE AUTHOR

B ORN, RAISED, AND based in Houston, Texas, Alison
Wisdom has an MFA from the Vermont College of Fine
Arts and was a finalist for the Rona Jaffe Foundation Writers'
Award. Her short stories have been published in *Ploughshares,*
Electric Literature, The Rumpus, Indiana Review, and other
publications.